Claypot Dreamstance

# Other books by Mario Milosevic

*Animal Life*
*The Coma Monologues*
*The Doctor and the Clown*
*Fantasy Life*
*Kyle's War*
*The Last Giant*
*Love Life*
*Terrastina and Mazolli: a Novel in 99-word Episodes*

# *Claypot Dreamstance*

## Mario Milosevic

To Mom,
with all
my love.
mario

*Ruby Rose's Fairy Tale Emporium • 2012*

Claypot Dreamstance
by Mario Milosevic

Copyright © 2012 by Mario Milosevic

mariowrites.com

ISBN-13: 978-1463577759
ISBN-10: 1463577753

All rights reserved.

Cover photo of flower by Kim Antieau
Cover photo of sidewalk by Mario Milosevic
Book design by Mario Milosevic
Special thanks to Nancy Milosevic

No part of this book may be reproduced
without written permission of the author.

Electronic editions of this book are
available at most ebook store.

A production of
Ruby Rose's Fairy Tale Emporium
Published by Green Snake Publishing
www.greensnakepublishing.com

# *Never Reach Out to Anyone Else*

CLAYPOT DREAMSTANCE.

Now there's a name. Not many people with a name like that. Not many people with a talent like his. Claypot is the best artist who ever lived. But you never heard of him, right? No, how could you? He created the most breathtaking pictures you have never seen, but not once did he try to sell any of them. Not once did he let anyone else try to sell them.

I'm cheating here a little bit. Claypot worked in chalk. On sidewalks. Sometimes on bridges and buildings, but mostly sidewalks. So no one could sell his pictures. Unless he did something crazy like lift up great slabs of concrete, which would only get him arrested. City authorities don't like that sort of thing.

Not that Claypot cared about authority. If he had the actual strength to lift concrete, he probably would have done it.

And gone to jail gladly. He relished punishment at times.

But I'm probably getting ahead of myself a little.

My name is Christopher Miller. Chris. Your humble narrator. Retired from the electricity business, now with way too much time on my hands, so I'm telling you about the greatest character I ever knew.

Here's how I first met Claypot.

No, back up. I knew about Claypot before I met him. It was about ten years ago. I was on my lunch hour from the power administration job I held in downtown Portland, Oregon. I had a hand in the allocation of electric power. I helped calculate projected domestic versus industrial consumption rates for the region, then correlated that to predicted weather conditions to determine how much electricity we had to push through the grid each day. The idea was to insure people got the electricity they wanted when they wanted it. It sounds boring only because it *was* boring. But you know, a lot of boring things have to happen everyday for life to work.

Anyhow. Late May. The winter rains were finally over, just a few lingering spring showers. A feel of summer in the air. I was on my way to the coffee place around the corner. A crowd of people clustered together halfway down the block. As I got closer I saw they were all looking down at the sidewalk in front of them. No one took a step forward because there was a hole in the sidewalk. It went about eight or ten feet down. It looked like a fresh hole, like someone had dug it and walked away.

First thing I thought: why isn't this roped off? It was

dangerous. Second thing: I hope if anyone falls in, I don't have to play good Samaritan and go down after them.

Then I saw no one was afraid to step into the hole. They were being careful not to step *onto* the hole. It wasn't a hole at all but a piece of trompe l'oeil so realistic that anyone would think they *could* fall into it. The people who stood on the edge of the picture recognized it was art. And such effective art that they did not want to mar it with their footprints.

I didn't know it then, but this was my first encounter with Claypot's work.

I admired the hole in the sidewalk for a few minutes, then tried to move on.

But the hole pulled me back. I wanted to take in all the details. I looked at the thing from several angles and it still looked like a hole in the concrete. It had crumbling edges. The bottom of the hole was far down, softened by darkness, shadowy. A curve of pipe hung out of the side half way to the bottom. A cut cable, with a frayed end, practically sparked in the folds of the ground. It looked so real I thought I could get a shock from touching it. I even saw a hint of water, way way down at the bottom.

I never did get to the coffee place. I stood and stared at that picture. Watched other people go by. Flipped open my cell phone and called my wife, Gayle. I took a picture of the hole for her to see. She thought it was as amazing as I did.

I got back to work late. The world felt different. I harbored the illusion that I could see through the surfaces of walls and doors. I had to shake my head to bring myself back to the present reality. My cubicle was exactly where I had left it, a fact that suddenly seemed amazing. I stared at the white wall and imagined a picture of a hole. A hole in the wall. I wanted a picture of a hole in my cubicle wall and I wanted the picture on my cubicle wall. Claypot's hole in the sidewalk turned my world inside out and ripped it open.

Flash forward a few hours.

It rained that night. The downpour drummed on the roof. I lay awake in bed and thought of the picture like it was a lost soul. Gayle slept beside me. I loved the warmth of her breath in the air. I knew I was nothing without her. I thought about a hole deep in my own heart. Strange, unsettling thought.

The next day I went by Claypot's hole in the sidewalk. I knew it couldn't be there anymore, not with all the rain, but I had this wild hope.

Of course it was gone.

Oh, a few streaks of chalk remained, all running together like some kid had taken watercolors and smeared them on a piece of paper. You could tell something had been there, but it wasn't much of anything anymore.

I'm not sure how to tell you exactly what I felt then. I had a tightness around my throat and my heart felt like lead in my chest. I had an incredible sense of loss.

All this over a picture?

Yes. Only it wasn't the picture. I knew it was temporary when I first saw it. You use chalk on a sidewalk, you know it will not last. What bothered me more was thinking about the person that did the picture. Whoever it was must have spent a lot of time on it, and now it was gone. That had to hurt. If something that beautiful and that real could disappear, then maybe nothing anyone ever did was important.

I know. A lot of baggage to put on some chalk marks on the sidewalk. I'm not saying it was a rational response; I'm telling you what was going on in my head.

I called the library. My wife Gayle picked up the phone. "Reference," she said in her librarian voice. "May I help you?"

"Hey," I said. "It's me."

"What's wrong?" she said. "Your voice is weird."

I told her how awful I felt about the picture getting washed away in the rain. I sounded nuts, even to me.

"You should find the artist," she said.

"What?"

"The artist that did this. It affected you so deeply, you should find and thank the artist. For some of them, this kind of deep response is the only satisfaction they get from their work."

She had a point. Only how do you find a more or less anonymous trompe l'oeil artist? "Thanks," I said. "You're right. I'll do it."

"Talk to you later," she said.

I flipped my phone closed and looked around. A sewing shop stood right next to the chalk marks. I went inside and said hi to the woman behind the counter.

"Hi," she said.

"Did you see who did that chalk picture?" I asked.

"Nope," she said. "It was just there a couple of mornings ago. Whoever did it must have done it at night. It was pretty cool. Someone told me she saw other things like it around town. Last week over on Alder, a big chalk picture of a hole in a building."

"Really? I don't remember that."

"Oh yeah. And here's a weird one. There's a public

toilet near the pastry place by the fountain on Broadway, right?"

I nodded.

"He did this thing on the floor there. He drew the sky. Or what you would see from a few thousand feet up. You open the door of the bathroom and you think you're going to fall cause he drew a picture of the ground from way way up. Nothing but the toilet floating up there. He even drew the pipe coming down from the toilet, like it really was way up there. Way up in the sky."

I thanked her and immediately walked the few blocks to Broadway. I found the public bathroom she talked about and opened the door.

The floor was nothing but plain old tile.

Obviously the city had cleaned up the picture.

Now I really wanted to find out more about the artist.

I went back to work. Late. The boss was nice. I'm never late, so he was concerned.

"Everything okay?" he asked.

"Sure," I said. "Sorry about the time. I got distracted."

"I'm not worried about it, Chris. Just making sure you're fine."

"Yup. No problem." My voice shook. I coughed to cover it and felt my face redden. Claypot did that to me. Something about him and his pictures put me off my game. And like I said, I hadn't even met him yet.

That was about to change in a big way.

# *Never Take Any Time Off Work*

I KNEW FROM the woman at the sewing shop that the guy worked at night. Then it was simple. I'd go into town at night and look for him. Hah. Gayle was not on board with that. At all.

"There's crazy people out at night," she said.

"Oh, not that crazy," I said. I had no idea what I was talking about.

"There's street people."

"Most of them will be asleep."

"The ones that aren't, you don't know how to deal with them if they approach you. Let's face it Chris, you don't have a lot of street smarts."

She had a point. I am about as nerdy as they come.

"It was your idea to find the guy," I said.

"So find him. But do it a different way. Call some galleries. Someone must know about him. The art world is small."

Now what did Gayle know about the art world? About as much as I did. But she had a point. So I found some art galleries in the yellow pages and started making calls.

Most everyone had heard of the chalk trompe l'oeil, but no one knew who did them. Some asked me to call back when I found out. They wanted to network with the artist, perhaps arrange a show.

Good for them. All I wanted was to talk to the guy.

A day after I started looking for the artist, with no luck, I was at my cubicle. My phone rang. The guard who worked the security desk in the lobby downstairs said there was a man there to see me.

No one ever came to my work to see me. "Um," I said. "Send him up."

"I don't think so," said the guard. "You need to come down here."

I told my boss I had to go downstairs. I got a look from him. "What's this about?" he said.

I shrugged. "Don't know. Something important." I felt like an idiot saying that. In the elevator going down I wondered what it would be like to have a trompe l'oeil on the floor. Maybe of a bundle of cables. Or on the roof. And the walls. It would feel like I was floating in mid air. Nothing to support me.

The elevator stopped, the doors opened, and I stepped into the lobby.

I saw a man pacing the floor in front of the security guard's desk.

This was my first encounter with Claypot Dreamstance, so I want to describe it to you as accurately as I can.

He had long reddish hair, that's the first thing I noticed about him. It was completely unkempt. And unwashed. It grew like a particularly obnoxious weed, every which way and with no grace whatsoever. His face carried a beard of epic proportions. The strands wove and curled and interlocked into a dense carpet on his chest. Why would anyone tolerate the inconvenience of such a beard? His coat: thin and grubby. His shoes: old, cracking leather. I put him at about age forty, maybe older. His teeth were yellow. Not simply plain old yellow, but a deep rich yellow, like some polished gemstone. A hat. He wore a hat. It sat on top of his hair like a rodent lost in a tangle of brush. Why have a hat under those circumstances? These were the thoughts that came to me. It never occurred to me, not for one instant, that this was the artist I had grown to admire in such a short time. Not until he held up his hand and pointed at me.

Chalk dust coated his fingertip.

"You the prick who's been asking about me?" he said. "You *Mis*ter Christopher *fucking* Miller?"

I wanted to fade back into the elevator, but the doors had already closed.

The guard looked at me. He smirked. "Friend of yours?" he said.

I looked from the guard and back to the man. I didn't know what to say.

"Not man enough to admit it, fuck face?" said the man in the red hair. With the yellow teeth. And the face turning red. His eyes were wide open, like he was mad enough to—something. I didn't know. I didn't want to know.

"Don't you even have the balls," he said, "to look me in the face and tell me you've been spying on me you cocksucking motherfucking asshole?"

"Enough of that," said the guard. "You two have business, take it outside. Either way," he pointed at Claypot, "I want you gone. Now."

"I'll go," said Claypot, "as soon as numb nuts over there mans up and treats me like a fucking human being."

A human being? I was supposed to treat him like a human being?

My heart banged against my ribs like a rattle. Adrenaline pumped through me like I'd disturbed a grizzly bear in the park and had nowhere to run.

"I like your work," I said.

He snorted.

The guard looked at me. "Outside," he said. "Or didn't I make myself clear?"

The wild man laughed. "Oh, oh," he said in a singsong voice, high pitched like a little girl's. "I *love* your work. It *moves* me. You're *such* a great artist. You *changed* my life." Then he spat on the floor and stared at me.

The guard looked at me.

I stepped forward.

Claypot looked right through me. Like I had a hole painted on my chest and he could see on the other side.

Everything in me wanted to back up, find the stairs, and fly up them to my cubicle.

But this man, this artist, came looking for me. I discovered I *did* want to give him the courtesy of a human response. I walked forward.

Past the guard.

To within breathing distance of one of the most repellant people I had ever met.

He stared at me.

I put out my hand. "Chris Miller," I said. My voice shook. I hated that. I wanted to sound like I was in control. "Pleased to meet you."

He didn't take my hand.

"You got any cigarettes?"

"Cigarettes?"

"Yeah. I haven't had a smoke in hours. You smoke?"

"Um. No."

"Figures. It's *bad* for you, right?"

"Something like that," I said.

"What have you got to live for? You an artist? No. You *stalk* artists, man. What kind of life is that?"

"I'm real sorry if I offended you," I said. "I wasn't trying to freak you out or anything."

"You a patron or something?" He looked me up and down. "No. Not if you work here. You're a wage slave. I can see it in your face. You're scared of me. I'm too out there for you. Too real."

He wasn't far wrong, but I didn't want to give him the satisfaction of admitting it.

"Buy me some cigarettes," he said.

"I have to go back to work."

"Fuck that. Buy me some cigarettes." He retreated to the front door and held it open. His hand left chalk marks on the door frame. Had he recently done a picture? Maybe last night? I wanted to ask him about it, but didn't want to rile him up.

He was right. I was afraid of him.

I put my hand in my pocket and pulled out a ten dollar bill. "This should get you some cigarettes," I said.

"God *damn* but you are a dense one," he said. "I want you to *walk* with me to the fucking store on the corner and buy me a goddam pack of fucking smokes. Now let's go." He grabbed my arm and pulled me through the door.

And we started walking together.

All I could think of at first was that I was going to be in big trouble with my boss.

That soon gave way to a feeling of invincibility. Everyone we passed gave us a wide berth. No one wanted to get close to either of us. I began to see the advantage of a repulsive look and personality.

We passed a conveniences store.

"Hey," I said. "They have cigarettes in there."

"I got a place I like."

So we kept going.

"Name's Claypot," he said.

"Hi Claypot." I thought it was an interesting name but I didn't want to tell him that.

"Your *sleuthing* uncover the teeny little fact of my name?"

"No," I said.

"Dreamstance," he said.

"What?"

"My name. Claypot Dreamstance. That's what you were trying to find out, right? Congratulations Sherlock. You put all the fucking clues together and deduced the truth."

"How did you know I was asking about you?" I said. At the same time I started to wonder how I was going to explain an extended unplanned mid morning absence to my boss.

"I know a guy at the gallery over on Foster and Eleventh. Told me you were poking around. Said you were kind of an asshole."

"Really?" I thought I had been completely polite and respectful in all my phone calls.

"Yeah, really." He laughed. "That bother you?"

"I don't like being thought of that way."

"What do you care what people think of you? He's just some guy you'll never talk to again in your life."

"I just prefer to be thought of as a nice person," I said, fully aware of how dweebish that sounded.

"The guy's pretty much a jerk himself," said Claypot. "That make you feel better?"

I felt my head spin around as I tried to come up with an answer. Would it be wise for me to agree that his acquaintance was a jerk? Would it be wise to disagree?

"Here we are," he said. We stopped at another convenience store. "You go inside. They don't let me come in anymore. I made some kind of scene once and they have long memories."

I'd known him for less than ten minutes, but it did not surprise me in the least that he could be barred from a convenience store.

"What brand you like?" I asked.

"Doesn't matter. As long as they're unfiltered."

"Okay," I said. "You want any food?"

He looked up at the sky and shook his head. I half thought he was going to start cursing me out again but instead he sighed. "Can anyone *be* so clueless?" he asked the clouds.

I went into the store. Bought a pack, then returned outside and handed it to Claypot. He tore open the wrapper and pulled out a cigarette, put it to his lips, and lit it with a lighter from his pocket. He inhaled so deeply I thought he was going to pass out. Then he exhaled, hooked a finger on his shirt pocket and tapped the ashes into it.

"Now," he said. "Let's go to the art supply place. I need some fucking chalk."

# *Do Not Volunteer*

I CAN'T EXPLAIN why I bought Claypot a pack of cigarettes. Or why I then walked with him to *Priorities*, the art supply store a few blocks away.

He didn't talk much.

Neither did I.

He smoked a couple of cigarettes, always depositing the ashes in his pocket, like he didn't want to litter.

"People are slobs," he said after a couple of blocks. "Ever notice that?"

I noticed he was one.

"Slobs?" I said.

"Yeah, slobs slobs. Jesus, you afraid of me or something? You scared to tell me what you fucking *think*? Look at these sidewalks. There's people that *piss* on them. Garbage everywhere. Gum stuck on the slabs. Took me half an hour to clean the sidewalk before it was ready for my chalk a few nights ago."

"Oh, yeah," I said. "The hole. That was great."

"The hole. That's what you call it?"

"I didn't mean that was the title of it or anything."

"A description, then, right?" he said.

"Yeah. A description."

"Listen, *Chris,* do you know anything about art? I mean anything at all? Do you know what art is? Ever took a drawing class? Ever study perspective? Ever hang around a gallery and try to, you know, absorb the fundamentals of the techniques? Anything?"

"I took an art appreciation course in college."

Claypot nodded, like I had told him something profound. "Survey course."

"Yeah."

"They throw up slides of famous pictures and you have to name the artist."

"Yeah."

"That it?"

"I go to the art museum sometimes."

"When they have some famous artist's pictures on tour."

"Yeah."

"You went to the traveling Monet exhibit, I bet."

"Sure. It was great."

"You liked Monet?"

"I *loved* Monet," I said, a little too enthusiastically. Claypot noticed. He smirked.

"So it's safe to say you're pretty ignorant about the nuances of artistic expression," he said. "You have no idea why anyone would *want* to do art. Why people would devote their lives to it. You have no idea about that."

He was feeling me out, trying to understand who I was. The same way I tried to uncover his identity a couple of days ago.

"To make beauty," I said.

"Uh huh." Another cigarette. More ashes. "You know we're all born naked into the world. You realize that, right?"

"Yeah," I said. "Obviously."

"And we die naked, too. You realize that? Nothing we make or buy in life goes with us. Nothing. All the shit we think is important, it disappears when we die. It doesn't stick to us."

"I see that," I said.

"So art, if you can wrap your brain around the fucking concept, is our way of not being naked. Get it?"

I didn't. "It's an expression," I said, a little too hesitantly. He caught the hesitation.

"You fucking sure about that?" he said.

I could have lied. Maybe I should have. But I didn't. "No," I said.

He sniffed the air, like he wanted to grab big gobs of the world through his nose. He had a large nose. He was large in all ways. I wanted to say something to impress him. Which surprised me. I had known him for less than an hour and I wanted to impress him. He seemed bigger than life and I didn't want to look puny to him.

We got to *Priorities*, a place it appeared he had not been barred from entering. We walked down an aisle lined with box after box of chalk. Claypot picked up several. Some of the chalk was the kind they use on blackboards in school. Others were at least two inches around.

"Doing a picture tonight?" I asked.

"Wouldn't you like to know?"

I wasn't sure anymore. Now that I had met the artist, I wondered if I had anything else to discover from him. I knew he wanted nothing from me.

Except maybe my money.

He grabbed up several boxes of chalk, handed me a few to carry, then grabbed up some more. We took the piles of chalk to the register. The bill came to a couple of hundred dollars. The checker stuffed the chalk into two shopping bags. "Welcome to the world of art," said Claypot, then he grabbed the shopping bags as I handed my plastic to the checker. "Be seeing you."

"You're going?" I said, surprising myself with the disappointment in my voice.

"Got to prepare for my next picture. Got to change people's lives, you know. It's a fucking calling is what it is."

"Wait," I said.

"Bye," he said and went out the door.

I wanted to run after him but I had to wait and sign the receipt. By the time I was finished and got outside he was gone.

I stood there like a kid who just lost his puppy.

FAMILY STUFF.

That's what I told my boss. He bought it, although I couldn't see how. My head felt so warm I was sure my face gave away the fact that I was lying, something I was definitely not used to.

He nodded. "Gayle okay?" he said.

"Oh sure. It's nothing to do with Gayle."

"Good."

"Yeah."

"Hope everything turns out."

"Oh sure. It already has. It's okay. It's good."

He looked at me a little peculiarly, then nodded and went back to his office.

The rest of the day dragged on. My fingers felt light. I couldn't concentrate on work at all. My brief moments with Claypot had turned me into a wreck.

At five o'clock, and not a moment later, I turned off my computer and practically sprinted to the elevator. The air outside felt as refreshing as cool water.

What I wanted to do was find the man, find Claypot, but of course I had no idea how to do that.

I had to walk four blocks to my bus stop.

I knew the way to go, but wanted to linger in the city. I wanted to soak up whatever it was that inspired Claypot.

I flipped open my cell phone and called Gayle.

"Hey gorgeous," she answered.

"Come into town," I said. "Let's have dinner somewhere."

"Where are you?"

"At work."

"Everything okay?"

"Yeah. Just don't feel like being home yet."

"This about that artist you were looking for?"

"I found him. His name's Claypot Dreamstance."

"And?"

"Come in. I'll tell you all about it."

"Okay," she said. "I'll meet you at—"

"*Maxies.*"

"*Maxies* it is."

We hung up. I picked *Maxies* because it was close to where Claypot had drawn the hole. I wanted to be next to his art. Or next to where his art had been.

I had about a half hour before Gayle would get into town. *Maxies* was only a few minutes away. Which meant I had some time to kill.

I noticed a man on the corner with a cardboard sign. It read: "Bet you can't hit me with a quarter." I'd seen him before. He always looked depressed. Who wouldn't be, begging on the sidewalk all the time? I had given him some money a few times. Today I felt an urge to give him a couple of dollars even though I had already contributed to the destitute with cigarettes and chalk. I walked up to the man and stopped.

"Spare some change?" he said.

I took out a dollar bill and handed it to him. He nodded and took the money.

"Can I ask you something?" I said.

He looked wary. His eyes snapped left, then right. "What?" he said.

"You know a guy named Claypot? He draws with chalk. On sidewalks."

"Yeah," he said.

I waited.

He waited.

I pulled out another bill from my pocket. Handed it over.

"Dreamstance."

"That's the guy. Do you know where he lives?"

"Lives?"

"Does he have an address?"

"He's one mean S.O.B.," said the man. "Why d'you care about him?"

"He's a friend."

He shook his head. "You don't know where your friend lives? What kind of friend is that?"

He had a point.

"We have a complicated relationship," I said.

He laughed. He doubled over and slapped his thigh. "You're a crazy motherfucker," he said. "Give me another dollar." I sighed and reached into my pocket for another bill. I handed it to him.

"He lives in the park," said the man with the sign.

"What park?"

"The park, the park. Over by the bridge. Forest Park."

Forest Park was a wild area north of town that the city had preserved for decades, despite the call from many to develop it. The people of Portland were unwavering in wanting it to remain forested and undeveloped except for hiking trails. The park sheltered numerous secluded spots, perfect for someone trying to live under the radar.

"How do you know?" I said.

"Man, you ask a lot of questions. How do I know? I know. People know."

"Okay," I said. "Thanks for the information."

"Yeah. Glad I could help you out with your *friend*."

I felt my face redden, then walked away, trying to affect a graceful and debonair demeanor. I was acutely aware that I was not succeeding.

But at least I had more information about Claypot.

I kept walking and arrived at *Maxies*. It looked like

a slow night.

"Mr. Miller?" A woman's voice behind me made me turned around. "Christopher Miller?"

She looked worried. I didn't recognize her.

"Do we know each other?" I said.

She showed me a business card.

The logo of *Visions*, one of the galleries I had called when I was looking for Claypot, adorned the left side of the card. The name on the card was Judy Dreamstance.

# *Refrain From Telling the Story of the Death*

I LOOKED UP at the woman. "I used to be married to him," she said.

"To Claypot?"

"Yes."

"Oh." My mind reeled as I thought about what domestic life with Claypot must have been like.

"Yes," she said. "Oh."

"I just met him."

"How much did he get from you?"

"Get?"

"He had you buy things for him, didn't he?"

I was reluctant to admit that he had.

"Never mind," she said. "Can we talk?"

"I'm meeting my wife here. We're having dinner."

"It won't take long."

She had a persuasive air about her, exactly like her

ex-husband. "You work at *Visions*?" I said.

"Yes," she said. "I didn't answer the phone when you called but I heard about you from my colleague who did."

"Okay," I said. "Come sit with me until Gayle gets here."

I got a table for four. Judy and I sat across from each other. We didn't say anything as the waiter brought us menus and we ordered drinks.

"So," I said. "How long were you and Claypot married?"

"Long enough. We met at art school when we were kids. Got married a couple of years later."

"Sounds romantic."

"Oh, it was. We were the romantic couple all right. We were going to live by our art and become famous. And rich. All of that dream."

"Was he always so wild looking?"

"No. See, we had a baby."

She said it like it was a tragedy.

"A baby," I said. "That's great. Claypot is a father?"

"Yes. A couple of years ago she died. Her name was Stacey."

"Oh," I said. "That's terrible."

"Claypot has never gotten over it."

Who *could* get over something like that? Judy? I didn't think so. I began to feel even more uncomfortable with her than I had with Claypot earlier that day.

"He thinks she's alive," said Judy.

I was confused. "But you just said."

"I know. He knows she's dead. We buried her. But there's something in him that won't accept it. He's still in grief and—I don't know. He thinks he can get her back."

I thought of that hole, the one Claypot had drawn that fascinated me so much. I felt like I had stepped into that hole by involving myself in Claypot's life. And now his ex was here to make things worse. I didn't need to be a part of this, but could not see a graceful way out of my entanglement.

"What happened?" I asked. "If you don't mind telling me."

She took a breath. She looked smaller than she should. Like she had pulled in on herself. Imploded, somehow. "We were at the fair," she said. "On the waterfront."

I nodded. I had been to that fair. It came every summer. Rides for the kids. Beer garden for the adults. Lots of booths with fried food.

"We had Stacey with us. She loved being there. She was eight. Perfect age for the fair. She ran everywhere. Loved cotton candy. And popcorn. We indulged her. Why not?"

I nodded. "Sure. Why not?"

"We were waiting in line for one of the rides. A carousel. Stacey got bored and wandered off. I told Clay to go after her. Didn't want her to get lost, you know?"

"Sure."

"He went. I stayed in line to keep Stacey's place. Stacey loved the carousel. There was an elf on this one. She really wanted to ride on the elf. She loved the elf's long beard. Don't ask me why. Who understands what kids like?"

The waiter brought us our drinks. Judy had a glass

of wine. Sparkling water for me. I felt like a kid with my non-alcoholic drink. She was the grown-up, with a grown-up drink, living a grown-up life with grown-up problems and grown-up pain. I felt completely out of my depth as I tried to understand her heartache. "You don't have to tell me any of this," I said.

"I've started. Let me finish."

"Okay."

"The grief counselors always say to tell the story of the death."

"I didn't know that."

She nodded. "Yup. Sounds crazy, doesn't it? Why relive it? But you're supposed to tell it over and over. Other things you're supposed to do, too. Like take time off work, volunteer for some worthy cause, start a new creative project, accept help from others. That sort of thing. It's all supposed to help."

"Does it?"

"I'm not sure. It still hurts, but maybe it would hurt more if I didn't do some of those things. Who can tell? It hasn't helped Clay to *not*. So maybe they have a point. Of course, with Clay, it's different. He blames himself."

I had guessed something like that was going on. I was pretty sure she probably blamed him too. At least a little, even if she wasn't conscious of it.

"So anyway, Clay goes after Stacey. She runs to the rail. You know it?"

I nodded. The fairgrounds were right on the river. The bank at that place had been replaced with a concrete wall about thirty feet above the surface of the water. A metal railing, like a fence, ran the length of the fairground at the top of the concrete wall. It was there to keep people from falling. However, if you wanted to, you could duck under the railing.

"So Stacey is at the rail," said Judy. "Clay calls to her. She wants to play. She runs along the railing. Clay doesn't see the danger. Who would, right?"

I didn't answer. Didn't need to.

"Clay gets into the playing mood. He runs after her. She runs faster. They used to do that. Run after each other. It was their game. But she runs too close to the rail. She stops. Clay stops. I'm coming up now. I left the line to go find them. I had this—premonition—I guess you'd call it. Something felt wrong. I come closer. Call her name. She looks at me, then at Clay. She's having fun is all. Playing. She takes a step back."

It was too awful to think about. I closed my eyes. Then felt stupid and forced myself to be there with Judy. Made myself open my eyes and pay full attention.

"She was so close to the edge," said Judy. "She didn't know. She fell into the river. I ran to the railing. I screamed and screamed. Hysterical. I couldn't stop. I saw Stacey already floating down the river. The current was so strong. Her arms were flailing, like she was grabbing at something. 'Save my baby. Save my baby.' Clay ran as fast as he could, didn't even stop at the rail. Stepped up and over it and boom! he was in the water. He tried to swim for Stacey, but the current was so strong. He couldn't fight it. The river took him in another direction. Not far off, but far enough. He couldn't get to her. Someone threw in a life preserver. There were all kinds of people at the rail now, watching, pointing. A cop came up beside me, called in for an ambulance. 'They'll end up on the other side,' he said. 'Come on.' I didn't want to leave, couldn't take my eyes from them. Clay and Stacey going down the river. It was awful. Like a dream. I didn't believe it was really happening. But I let the cop take me to his car. He drove me across the river, lights flashing, siren going full blast. We got on the bridge. We were on the other side in a few minutes. There was an ambulance. More police cars. Fire trucks. A lot of cars a lot of noise. I couldn't tell what was going on, exactly. Where was Stacey? All I wanted was Stacey. I thought: she has to be okay. She has to be okay. I thought about Clay, too, but he didn't matter. Isn't that awful? I wanted Stacey. No one else. Only her. It didn't matter if Clay was drowned. Didn't matter to me, right then, for even an instant."

She stopped.

I saw tears in her eyes.

"So even though he survived," she said, "even though they fished him out of the river alive, I lost them both that day."

I thought about the railing. That's all I could focus on. "They augmented the rail," I said.

She nodded. "After Stacey died they put a grating on it, so no other kid could fall through."

"Did he ever have her? In the river, I mean."

She shook her head. "He tried. Oh, God, he tried. He swam as hard as he could, but the water was so cold. And he had all his clothes on, weighing him down. He almost died himself."

I was fascinated in spite of myself. I wanted to know more. Which made me feel more than slightly ghoulish. "Where did they find . . . ?"

"You mean where was she?"

"Yeah."

"It's okay to be curious."

"I don't want to ask anything that's too hard to answer."

She looked away. "All of it is hard. Eating is hard. Brushing my hair is hard. Getting up in the morning is really really hard. It all hurts."

I tried to imagine the grief. It was beyond me.

"They found her close to where they found Clay," said Judy. "She wasn't breathing. The paramedics were right there. They tried to get her to breathe. Tried and tried. It didn't work."

I nodded.

"So," she said. "Why am I telling you any of this?"

"I was wondering that myself."

"Clay is not an ordinary man."

"I figured that out."

"I'm not talking about his foul language. He's on the edge. He's about ready to fall into a fantasy world and never come back."

I thought artists lived in fantasy worlds. Wasn't that the point?

"I don't understand," I said.

"He's had other friends since Stacey died."

"I'm not exactly his friend."

"Trust me," she said. "If he had you buy things for him, then he thinks of you as his friend."

"I had the idea he thought of me as more or less of a pathetic jerk."

"No, no. Not at all." She hesitated. "Well, maybe a little. But he thinks that of everyone. Only the thing is, he wants a normal life. He wants to be like everyone else."

"That's hard to believe."

"Tell him I love him."

"What?"

"He won't talk to me anymore. He used to. Even after we split. Not anymore. He avoids me. But I'm asking you to tell him I still care about him. I want him back in my life."

# *Spurn All Offers of Support From Others*

AFTER THAT, JUDY dropped her card on the table for me, then left. Quickly. Like she wanted to be gone before Gayle got there. Like she didn't want anyone else to see her.

I said I would pay for her drink, which remained on the table, untouched. I wondered why she ordered it. She accepted my offer, thanked me for my time, and disappeared into the city.

I sat in silence, a little stunned by our conversation. I picked up her business card and slipped it into my pocket.

Gayle came into the restaurant. I waved at her. Her face brightened and she came over. I rose and kissed her. She slipped into the chair, behind Judy's glass of wine.

"This for me?" she said. "Or were you expecting your girlfriend?"

"Very funny," I said. "Claypot's ex. She told me the story of their lives. Their daughter died. Drowned in the river."

Gayle's face softened. "Oh, that's awful."

"Caused them to divorce."

"That happens so often. When did she die?"

"I didn't get that," I said. "I think only three or four years ago. I'm starting to feel sorry I ever pursued this guy."

I had barely gotten out the last two words when I saw Claypot come in and stand next to the little sign that said "Seat Yourself." He scanned the restaurant. As soon as he saw me, he came over. He carried a box of his chalks. I expected him to start cursing me and Gayle. I was ready to stand up and defend my woman, a ludicrous feeling, but that's the kind of effect Claypot had on me. Before I could follow through, he was upon us.

Gayle looked up at him.

"Chris," he said, in the most mellow and resonant voice you could imagine, "you didn't tell me you were involved with such a beautiful woman." He put out his hand.

I didn't know what to say. Gayle looked at me, then at Claypot. She extended her arm. Claypot took her hand and kissed it, then bowed very slightly.

"Um," I said, "Claypot. This is my wife Gayle."

"Charmed," said Claypot.

"I understand you are something of an artist," said Gayle.

"Oh yes," said Claypot. "Your fine husband here has helped me immeasurably today by purchasing some much needed supplies for my creative endeavors."

"My husband is a generous man."

"Oh, indeed." He turned to me. "I was going to talk to you, Chris, but I had no idea you and your wife were spending the evening together. I will not impose." He stepped back, apparently prepared to exit.

"Don't be silly," said Gayle. "Sit with us. I'd love to get to know you better."

"If you insist," said Claypot.

This could not be the same person that sent a blue streak, several blue streaks, my way. Could it? He still had that impossible beard and that ridiculous hat. He took a chair between us. Gayle was obviously somewhat amused by the man. I was still wary, but my guard was relaxing. A little.

"I'm sure your good husband has told you a little about me already," said Claypot.

"He admires your work."

"Ah, yes," said Claypot. "My work. It moves people. I do not flatter myself that I am in any way responsible for it. I think of it as a gift that I am passing on. By the way, what did Judy say about me?"

An instant tension seized me. I was ready for an eruption.

No one said anything for a few seconds.

"My wife," said Claypot. "Surely you haven't forgotten her. She was just here. You know, she is always singing my praises. It's embarrassing. I never know how to react to her extravagant claims of my drafting ability. Did she mention our daughter, by any chance?"

No reason to deny it any longer. I cleared my throat. "Yeah, she did," I said. "It's so sad. I'm very sorry about what happened."

"Such a terrible thing," said Gayle. "So awful."

The waiter arrived. Claypot looked up at him with an expression on his face that made me think of a child. He seemed simultaneously wise and naïve. We placed our orders. I got a steak. Gayle asked for salmon. Claypot asked for a peanut butter sandwich.

The waiter, to his credit, did not flinch or make any kind of odd expression.

"With jelly?"

"Oh yes," said Claypot. "Definitely jelly."

"Very good," said the waiter. He gathered up the menus and walked back to the kitchen.

Claypot looked at us both. "Stacey likes peanut butter."

Gayle nodded. "Most kids do."

"Yup," said Claypot. "Did Judy also tell you she thinks I'm crazy?"

He looked at Gayle, who widened her eyes slightly. "I didn't talk to her."

Claypot swung his head around like a crane and stared at me. "She likes to do that, you know. Did she say anything to you?"

"What an odd question," I said. "She had nothing but praise for you."

"I'd like to impress upon you both that there is nothing wrong with me. Yes, I am very much involved with getting my daughter back, but such an endeavor is not only *sane*, but even noble. Don't you agree?"

Gayle nodded.

"Sure," I said. "We understand."

Claypot's eyes brightened as I watched him. I was ready to have him go off again.

But it didn't happen.

He relaxed. Something inside him deflated.

"It's sad," he said. "She is convinced Stacey is gone. But when I was in the river, trying to *save* her, I know she slipped away from me. That poor little girl they found is not Stacey, no matter what anyone says, even my good wife Judy, who has had only my welfare on her mind for a long time now. Even though she does not see the truth. We never buried Stacey. You understand that, do you not? Both of you? I feel you are on my side and I appreciate that completely. I need your support at this time. I need you as an ally. Judy has been—how can I say this—deluded into thinking something which is not true. You both see that, don't you?"

I'm reconstructing his speech as best I can. I make no claims that I am completely accurate, but I do believe I am conveying the essence of what he said. I'm not sure that I am also conveying the accompanying tension in his voice or his mannerisms. I know it made Gayle uncomfortable. But neither of us knew what to say to him.

"Both of you," said Claypot. "I want you to come with me tonight."

"Tonight?" said Gayle.

"After this fine dinner we are about to be served. I work at night. That's the best time. Not so many people about. You can be my lookouts."

"Lookouts?" I said.

"Yes, yes, lookouts. There are some members of the local constabulary who do not appreciate my work. Can you believe it? There is supposed to be a resurgence of appreciation for art in this country, and I get hassled merely for participating in this renaissance of interest by *making* art."

He had this odd mix of earnestness and vulnerability. It was so uncomfortable.

"Sure," said Gayle.

Claypot's face flushed. "Really?" he said.

"Of course. We wouldn't miss it. Right, Chris?"

"Yes," I said. "Of course, of course. We're there." I grinned. To my discredit, it was obvious I was not particularly happy about the situation. A few hours ago I would have wanted nothing more than to accompany Claypot on his art-making adventures. Now, I was beginning to think he was not only obnoxious, but also something much worse.

"Oh," said Claypot, "that is wonderful. You are both truly amazing people. Where's that food? I want to eat up and get going. How about you?"

Gayle nodded.

"It won't be dark for a couple of more hours," I said.

"You have a point," said Claypot. "Why not relax and enjoy the evening together? That's what you're saying, isn't it?"

"Something like that," I said.

"An excellent suggestion," he said. "We'll eat. Enjoy some conversation. Then enter the night. You'll love it. Truly. It will be an experience unlike anything you have ever known."

"I don't doubt it for a minute," said Gayle.

## *Shun Any Form of Creative Endeavor*

A COUPLE OF hours later we all three stood at the base of the Markham Bridge on the west side of the river near a massive concrete pillar that looked like a building itself, even though all it did was hold up one end of the bridge that took I-5 traffic over the river. The highway traffic above us sounded like a flock of birds at times, a rush of wings over air. Occasionally a truck passed by, creating a little storm of noise that threatened to collapse our ears.

Claypot stood right next to the pillar, a big piece of chalk in his hand. Some short distance away a warehouse's lights illuminated the area, though not very well. I wondered how Claypot would see well enough to do his work.

"It's cold," said Gayle. "She wrapped her arms around herself. I took off my jacket and put it over her shoulders.

Claypot hardly noticed us. He put his hands on the pillar, like someone about to mold clay. All his attention was on the surface. Beyond him, a few dozen feet away, the river flowed past. The water looked black. It seemed like a cruel thing to do to himself, to be here, next to where his daughter died.

Finally, he took a couple of steps away from the pillar and stood next to us. He kicked an old plastic bag at this feet. "What did I tell you before? People leave garbage everywhere."

"Do you know what you're going to draw?" I said.

He gave me a sharp look.

"What?" I said.

"What do you think I should draw?" he said. "A Monet?"

"Monet didn't do trompe l'oeil. Did he?"

Claypot laughed. The first time I heard him laugh. "It's going to be a long night," he said. "Are you ready?"

"I am," said Gayle. She seemed to be enjoying her time with me and Claypot, like she didn't have work in the morning. Like she could afford to squander her time here in a place neither she nor I would ever in a million years have thought of coming to on our own. But Claypot gave us both that invincible feeling, like his mere presence was protection from everything. I could see that in her, that ease in the world. It felt like her relaxed attitude was a gift from Claypot. To Gayle and to me.

"Okay," said Claypot. "Let's have some ideas. What's on the other side of this surface?"

"The interior of the column," said Gayle.

"In my business we call that answer N. I. No imagination."

Gayle laughed.

"Try again," said Claypot.

"You want to know what kind of trompe l'oeil to do on this, right?"

"In a crude way, yes, you're right. But I don't want you to think about trompe l'oeil so literally. This isn't about technique. It's about what you see. When you lose your preconceptions, what do you *see* when you look through this surface?"

Gayle got into the spirit. She regarded the concrete, studied it. She put her hand on the surface, exactly as Claypot had done.

"It feels smooth," she said. "Mostly. It's got some crevices in it. A few rough spots."

"What do you think of it?" said Claypot. "As a surface?"

"It's solid," said Gayle. "Even with all those cars going over us, it doesn't shake or tremble at all."

"Chris," said Claypot. "Your wife knows what she's doing. Get over here and follow her lead."

I got over there and put my hand on the surface opposite Gayle's hand. "There's a kind of dust on it," I said.

"Yup," said Claypot. "Now you're getting it. Outdoor concrete is a different medium than paper or canvas that's been coddled in climate controlled comfort. You ever think of the first artists? They were probably people in caves. Drew on walls. Ever think of that? No framing, no portability. Simply *there*, stuck to immovable rock."

"Why are we getting this art lesson?" I said.

"Christ," said Claypot. "Sometimes you ask the most stupid fuck ass questions."

Oops.

Claypot sighed and lowered his head.

"My apologies," he said to Gayle. "Such language is not suitable around a woman."

"It sure the fuck is not," said Gayle.

Claypot smiled at her. "Chris," he said, "you are not the least bit worthy of this extraordinary woman."

That was nothing new. Most men aren't worthy of their women.

"Don't be dissing my man," said Gayle. "That's my job."

Claypot tilted his head and laughed long and hard. "Now tell me," he said. "What's on the other side of this surface?"

"The river," I said.

Claypot bowed to me. "Well done," he said. "What color is the river?"

Color? "Um," I said. "It's too dark to tell."

"Wrong answer. We're using our imaginations here."

How could imagination tell you what color something was?

"It's the same color as the concrete," said Gayle.

"Bingo!" said Claypot. "We're seeing it through the screen of the pillar. It's like looking through a pair of sunglasses. It's going to tint the world the same color as the glasses, yes?"

"Yes," I said. "But the hole you drew in the sidewalk, it wasn't the same color as the sidewalk."

"Different location, different solution to a problem," said Claypot. "Try to keep up with us, hmmm?" He turned to Gayle. She smiled at him, which at first I thought was a flirty thing, which I didn't much care for right there, but then I saw it was more of a pity thing, like she felt sorry for Claypot. I completely understood. He was working hard to be light and friendly, but it was starting to feel forced. Like he was already losing his patience with us.

"Chris," he said. "Remember all that chalk you so graciously purchased for me today?"

"Yes."

"Find a big thick gray piece."

I fumbled around with the boxes, trying to see the colors in the shadows. I found the one he wanted, pulled it out of the box, and handed it to him.

He took it between thumb and forefinger. "Very good," he said. "Someday you will make an excellent assistant."

I blushed.

Ridiculous. But I liked his approval.

"Now step back," he said. "This could get dangerous."

I walked over to Gayle, who had retreated from the pillar slightly. I put out my hand next to her. She took it and gripped it tightly.

Claypot attacked the pillar.

There's no other way to describe it. He took the piece of chalk and launched himself into a mad scramble of scrapings and scratchings. His hair flew around his head. His hat fell off. His beard trembled and swayed as he worked. The chalk quickly crumbled to dust.

"More," he said curtly.

I handed him more gray chalk. He moved to the next side of the pillar and began the same campaign, assaulting the surface like it was an enemy he needed to vanquish.

Gayle and I stepped forward to examine Claypot's work. We saw a ragged line above and below. The space between the lines displayed the contours of a river and some buildings. I couldn't be sure, but they appeared to be the buildings visible on the other side of the river. Or what would be visible if it wasn't dark.

Claypot moved to the third side. He didn't speak. He put out his empty hand so it appeared at the side of the pillar. I put a piece of chalk in it and his hand disappeared behind the pillar again. We heard the sound of chalk scraping over concrete. He continued to make the picture he needed to make.

I say needed because that is exactly how it appeared to me. This was not an activity he chose to do. It chose him. Like a puppet, some other power animated his hands and heart. Who or what that puppet master was, I couldn't begin to imagine.

He moved to the fourth side. Gayle and I followed him around the pillar. I saw that the jagged tops and bottoms of the four sides were connected, and he had different shapes between the edges at all four sides.

The images were ghostly representations of what was behind the pillar, viewed from each side's perspective.

"Black," said Claypot. "Thick."

I found a big black piece of chalk. I put it in his outstretched palm. Claypot danced the chalk over the concrete. He filled in the shapes, gave them depth and body. Occasionally he stuck his head around the pillar, looked in the distance, seemed to contemplate the significance of the scene, and returned to his dance. The chalk scraped and screamed. Gayle and I watched, both mesmerized by the performance.

It lasted about forty-five minutes. As it progressed, Claypot slowed down and the chalk he used diminished in size and he began to fill in details and fine points of the scene.

Near the end, Claypot looked worn out. All the energy had drained from his face and body. He stood slumped, with his shoulders low and drooping.

"Do you need something?" said Gayle. "Water?"

Claypot shook his head. "No water," he said. "But thank you for asking. You are very kind."

He worked for a few more minutes. He asked for thin pieces of red chalk, thinner pieces of blue, yellow, and green. Then the thinnest piece of black chalk. I gave him what he asked for each time. Finally, he took a piece of chalk, and walked around the pillar.

Gayle and I held our breaths. The thing looked finished to us. Claypot made two slow circuits of the pillar. He stopped, twirled the chalk in his hand.

He raised it and held it steady, inches from the pillar, then dropped it.

"No," he said. "No more. It's done."

He stepped back so he stood between us.

We didn't move.

Claypot had created a masterpiece of illusion. It was as though we could look through the pillar to the other side. It was like a whole chunk of the pillar had simply gone missing.

"I can tell you like it," said Claypot. "People can't hide a physical reaction."

"I feel like I can put my hand through it," said Gayle.

Claypot nodded.

"My only regret is that it is protected from the elements here. The road bed will keep a lot of the rain from hitting it. It'll probably last for a few weeks, maybe even a few months. I usually like my work to be more ephemeral than that."

Was this an invitation to a debate about the permanence of art? Or only a statement of his wishes? I couldn't tell. I plunged in anyway.

"Is there a reason you don't want the pieces to last?"

"Oh fuck," said Claypot.

Oh oh.

He put his hand to his pocket. "I forgot my fucking cigarettes. You have any?"

I shook my head.

"Of course not. You're some kind of son of a bitching health nut, right?" He grinned at me.

I stepped back. Not a lot, but enough for him to notice.

"Still scared? You just watched me create a masterpiece, and you're still scared of me?" He turned to Gayle. "How do you put up with such a milquetoast?"

"He's good in bed," said Gayle.

Claypot's face contorted into a grin. Then he put his head back and laughed. He picked up his hat from where it had fallen to the ground and placed it on his head, then grabbed it from there and hit his thigh with it, then returned it to his head. All the while he just laughed and laughed.

"Come on," he finally said. "Let's get us a drink. I know a bar where they still let me in. Stacey needs her sleep now."

He and Gayle began to walk back to the city. I followed.

*Stacey needs her sleep now.*

# *Do Not Search for Meaning*

BY THE TIME we left the pillar it was close to midnight. Gayle and I both had to work in the morning, so we said good bye to Claypot. Gayle kissed him on the cheek. He turned red. "Don't drink too much," said Gayle.

"Ah hell," said Claypot. "How can I refuse a request like that from such a beautiful woman?"

"You can't," she said. "Stacey wouldn't want that either."

He took a breath. His eyes moistened. "No," he said. "She wouldn't. You are absolutely right."

"And the smoking," said Gayle. "You have to stop smoking."

"You're making me question my previous extolling of your virtues," said Claypot.

"I'm serious," said Gayle.

Claypot didn't answer. He nodded to us both, then

took several steps backwards, turned, and walked away from us. We watched him for a few moments until he disappeared around a corner.

We began to walk in the direction of the car. "Hey," I said, "I won't have to take the bus home."

"Is that why you invited me out tonight?" said Gayle. "So you could get a ride home?"

"You figured me out. What did you think of him?"

We walked to an intersection, turned down the street toward downtown, and adopted a leisurely pace.

"He's sad."

"Yeah. Anything else?"

"Are you sure you want to associate with him?"

"Do you think he's dangerous?"

She considered my question for a moment. "I'm not sure. I don't get that particular vibe from him, but he is, at the very least, wildly eccentric."

"All artists are eccentric."

"How do you know that? You don't."

She was right. I had no idea. "On TV they always are," I said.

"Where does he live?"

"A homeless guy told me he lives in Forest Park."

"A homeless guy? You know a homeless guy?"

"What can I say, my dear, it's been an eventful day."

"I'm worried that he might, I don't know, explode or something. He's wound up tighter than anyone I've ever seen."

We passed a woman with a cup. She held it out toward us. She looked at least sixty years old. What was someone her age doing begging for money at this time of night? I was ready to walk right by here, but Gayle stopped.

"Honey," she said, "don't you need to get inside for the night?"

"No room," said the woman. "Can you spare some change?"

Gayle opened the wallet in her purse and pulled out a twenty dollar bill. I raised my eyebrows. I had never seen her so generous with someone in the street asking for money.

She pressed the bill into the woman's palm. The woman thanked her.

Then we walked on.

I wanted to ask her why she did that, but a strange silence came over us that neither one wanted to break. We arrived at our car. Gayle beeped it open and I got in the passenger seat. She got in the driver's side and started the engine. She eased out of the parking space and into the sparse late night traffic.

In a few minutes we were on the expressway, only fifteen minutes or so from home.

The odd silence no longer felt so forbidding.

"I guess it was Claypot's influence," she said.

"What?" I asked.

"You were wondering why I gave her the twenty."

"How did you know?"

"Because I was wondering myself."

"So why did you?"

She stared at the road ahead. "He did something to me. Opened my heart, I guess. I couldn't walk by her. Didn't you feel it? From being around him?"

I didn't. Claypot was interesting and I enjoyed the evening, I think, but he didn't make me want to give away my money to a total stranger. Oh, wait. Scratch that. He made me want to buy things for a total stranger.

"I see what you mean," I said. "There's something about him. His energy."

"It's wild," she said quietly.

"Yeah, wild."

Gayle took our exit and we went down a few side streets until we got to our house. We pulled into the driveway. She put the car into park, turned off the engine. We sat in the dark and stared at the front of our house.

"How come we don't want to go inside?" I asked.

"It feels like it'll be boring inside," she said.

"So, what?" I said. "Claypot made us realize our lives are boring?"

I looked at the garage door in front of us. I didn't want to pull down the sun shade which had the garage remote clipped to it. That seemed like too much work, suddenly. And it would only have afforded us access to a boring garage for our boring car.

"Our lives aren't boring," I said.

"Put them up against Claypot's," she said, "and they're boring all right. But there's nothing wrong with that."

"You're saying you *want* a boring life?"

"I'm saying a certain amount of complacency is inevitable in any life. It's not the end of the world."

Not only did I not want to open the garage door, I didn't want to get out of the car either. It felt good to have the shell of it around me. Gayle slid over from her side and put her arm around my mine.

"It's a strange night," she said.

"Yeah."

Her weight against me brought back memories of the time we went to the Grand Canyon. We stood on the edge and looked at the striated walls, all pink and red, sandy textured. The Grand Canyon was as spectacular as everyone had always said it would be. It was no disappointment in any way and I was glad we went there. We went a few years into our marriage. It was our grand adventure, but not an adventure that anyone else would think of as spectacular or even that interesting. Did that make us boring? I suppose so. The morning we were there we heard about a man who had fallen from one of the observation rocks. He fell a long distance, hit the canyon wall on the way down, and ended up on the bottom. I forget how many feet he fell, but as I thought about it, while Gayle and I stood side by side on the lip of the canyon, it made me see how transitory my life with her was. The park officials sent a rescue team down to get the man. That was what they called it, but they must have known no possibility of rescue existed. Maybe they called it that because it was too hard to think of going down there for a dead body. We never saw the man come up. Later we heard that at least a couple of such deaths occur at the canyon every year. We had no idea. None of the guide books mentioned anything like that. Probably just as well. I'm not sure we would have gone if we had known. Statistical safety is not a particularly reassuring mode of shelter.

"What are you thinking about?" said Gayle.

"That guy at the Grand Canyon."

"You often come back to that," she said. "It still bothers you that he died."

"Yeah," I said. "Always makes me think about how fragile life is."

She nodded. "I've been thinking about Stacey."

I wondered if Claypot would ever admit that his daughter was gone. That would be hard, to lose your child. I could not imagine it. Did not want to imagine it.

"Her memory is the only thing driving him," I said.

"Yes, but it's not a memory to him. He thinks she's still with him."

"I suppose so."

"I have a picture of her in my head," said Gayle. "I see her wearing a red shirt. She's got long blond hair, thin, like kids have. Maybe a bow or two in her hair. She's got purple pants and dirty white sneakers. She's a kid that likes to get into stuff, you know. Mud and dirt. Her parents don't give her too hard a time about it. They like to see her having fun. She draws. All the time, like her Dad. She's got a tree house out back, and she lets her friends in."

Gayle and I never had children. Neither of us was ever interested, but we sometimes talked about what our children, if we had any, might be like. This fantasy about Stacey sounded like one of those imaginings.

"I see her as very outgoing," I said.

"Oh sure," said Gayle. "Very. She's a natural born leader. The other kids flock around her."

"Plus," I said, "she's smart."

"Of course. Very smart. But she doesn't use her brains to lord it over anyone. She's kind. She tries to make things better for everyone."

"Why is it," I said, "that whenever we do this we come up with some kind of super kid? Most kids aren't like that. They're just kids and they grow up to be ordinary adults."

She shrugged her shoulders slightly. "Ordinary like us?"

"Yeah," I said, realizing how sad it sounded. "Like us."

"I don't know. If we're going to imagine, why not imagine the ultimate?"

"I suppose."

"You want to walk around the neighborhood for a while?"

"That might be nice," she said.

We got out of the car and stood in the driveway. The stars were sharp in the sky. The lingering effects of the rain from the day before: the smog had not had a chance to come back in.

I stood next to Gayle and made a little teapot handle with my arm. She put her arm through it.

The street lights made me think: Claypot could do one of his trompe l'oeil paintings right here in front of my house.

# *Resist the Urge to Develop a New Self Identity*

BARELY THREE HOURS later a massive and incessant pounding at the front door roused us from sleep.

Gayle sat bolt upright. "What is that?"

I reached for the alarm clock next to the bed. 4:20.

I groaned.

"You better go down and see," she said.

I got out of bed and put on my pants. I went down the stairs and looked through the peephole. Claypot's face loomed like a giant bug.

I heard his muffled voice. "Hey, anyone in there? Wake up."

I pulled the door open.

"What the fuck took you so long?" he said.

"Claypot," I said, "it's not even five o'clock."

"Not my fault," he said. "What you got going for breakfast?" He stepped inside and zipped right by me, through the living room and into the kitchen. He carried a plastic bag full of chalk, which he dropped onto the kitchen table.

"Nothing," I said. "We were asleep. How did you find us?"

"How did I find you? What the fuck, you think you're invisible or something?"

He pulled cupboard drawers open and left them open as he continued down the counter. "You got corn flakes? I love corn flakes."

Gayle came down the stairs. She had put on her robe and tied it as she walked.

"Claypot," she said. "You better not be smoking in here."

He held up his hands to show he was clean. "No, Mom," he said. "And I haven't been drinking either."

She walked right by me, obviously not the least bit outraged by Claypot's intrusion, and smelled his breath. "Huh," she said. "You're right."

"I told you."

"Would you like some bacon and eggs?"

"Hell yes," said Claypot. "You don't have corn flakes."

"No corn flakes," said Gayle. "We're not a corn flakes kind of family. We'll have oatmeal sometimes."

"Hate oatmeal," said Claypot.

"Chris," said Gayle, "how about rustling us up some breakfast while I show Claypot to the bathroom?"

I blinked. "Sure," I said. "We didn't want all that sleep anyway."

"Don't be difficult, Chris. We have a guest." She turned to Claypot. "When was the last time you bathed?"

"Am I under oath?" he said, grinning.

"March right over to that bathroom, mister, and get into the shower. I'll bring you down some clean clothes."

Claypot disappeared into the bathroom. I got some bacon from the fridge, slapped it onto a pan, and put the pan on the stove. I heard the shower come on. Gayle came back through the kitchen.

"The smell was starting to get to me," she said.

Funny, I hadn't noticed an odor from Claypot. "Do we want to be encouraging him to become a part of our lives?" I said.

"I believe that precedent was set by you," she said.

She had a point. "But still," I said. "I never told him where we lived."

"He must have found out from a homeless man." She smiled.

"Seriously," I said. "It kind of gives me the creeps."

"He's mostly harmless," she said.

"Mostly?"

"He's going to explode, one of these days. It'll be messy, but probably not dangerous."

Gayle generally had a good instinct about people. I supposed I should accept her judgement. It rarely ever failed in the past.

"If you say so," I said.

"I'm going to give him some of your clothes."

I pushed the bacon around in the pan with a wooden spoon. "Fine with me," I said.

She went up the stairs and returned with a shirt, a new package of unopened underwear, a pair of pants, and some socks. She went to the bathroom. A couple of seconds later she came out with Claypot's dirty clothes in a hamper.

"Did you know he puts his ashes in his shirt pocket?" she said.

"I had kind of noticed that," I said.

She shook her head. I couldn't tell if she was amazed or repulsed.

I put four slices of bread in the toaster and pushed down the handle. It hummed to life. The wire inside glowed red.

Gayle stuffed Claypot's clothes into the washer, added some detergent, and started the load running.

She came into the kitchen and sat at the table.

"Did you use extra detergent?" I asked.

"Very funny."

"Did you disinfect yourself?"

"Even funnier."

"How about getting us some plates?"

She pulled out a stack of dishes from the cupboard and arranged them on the table.

Claypot came out of the bathroom and into the kitchen. He vigorously rubbed a towel over his hair. "Something smells good," he said. I tried not to look at his lower half.

"Clay, honey," said Gayle. "House rule: no walking around naked."

Claypot grinned, then backed away. "Sorry," he said. He retreated to the bathroom.

Gayle and I looked at each other. "We don't need children after all," I said. "We have Claypot."

He returned fully clothed. He was a size or two larger than me, but he would get by fine.

"Go ahead and sit down," said Gayle.

I filled each of three plates with bacon, eggs, and a slice of toast. Gayle put out butter and jam. Claypot wasted no time digging in. Despite his usually unruly behavior, he was a polite and fastidious eater. No loud chewing or spitting involved at all. I poured him an orange juice and he sipped at it almost daintily.

"After breakfast," he said, "I'm going to the petroglyphs at Horse Thief."

"That's nice," I said. Horse Thief is a park in the gorge, a good hour and half east of the city. Many Native American rock paintings are accessible for public viewing there.

"You're going to have to come with me," said Claypot. "I can't walk that far and I don't have a car."

"Impossible," I said. "We both have work. I have to be at the power administration office in a couple of hours. Gayle has to be at the library."

"Call in sick. This is more important."

I was willing to accept his intrusion in the household as endearing eccentricity. I was happy to have him eat my food. I was even okay with him wearing my clothes; I had lots of clothes. But ordering me to drive him around was going over the line.

"I can't call in sick," I said.

"Sure you can. Gayle, you too. Call in sick. We should all three go. Have you been to see them?"

Gayle shook her head. "I've heard about them, of course, but never been."

"That is a real shame," he said. "But we will correct that today."

She glanced at me, as if to say, let me handle this. Then she looked back at Claypot.

"We'll be happy to take you," she said. "Just let me get dressed." She stood and went back up the stairs. I was too stunned to even acknowledge her as she brushed past me.

Claypot looked at me with deep pity.

"You do not deserve her," he said.

I didn't want to argue with him. "How did you find me?" I said.

"Judy told me."

"Judy?"

"My wife, remember? You had drinks with her."

He got that look I had already come to understand as being somewhat dangerous. Like he was about to uncoil and strike.

"But I never told her where I lived."

"You ask a lot of questions," said Claypot. "Look, you wanted to find out about an artist, right? Well here I am. You can find out all about me. You can watch me for a day. I'm going to a gallery for professional reasons. I'm going not as a viewer but as an artist looking at other artists. Now go call your fucking boss and tell him you're sick. Jesus. I know *I'm* sick of you."

It is an odd sensation to have some derelict telling you off in your own house, and then not having the balls to tell him to go fuck himself. Somehow I could not muster the courage to tell him to clear out of my house. I'm not trying to make excuses for myself, but he had something about him I could not defy.

Gayle came down the stairs. She had put on some light summery clothes.

"We ready to head out?" she asked us both.

Claypot spread his hands and looked at me. "There, you see," he said. "Now that's an attitude we can all emulate." He stood up and grabbed his bag of chalk.

"I'll call in sick on our way," said Gayle. "No one's at work right now."

"Me too," I said.

A few minutes later and we were on the road traveling east on Highway 14 with the sun, unseen below the horizon, just beginning to lighten the sky. Me driving, Gayle beside me, and Claypot in the back seat, leaning over so his head floated between the two of us. The gorge air practically glowed clear and fresh. The hills radiated a deep, dark green. The Columbia River flowed beside us on the right, the gorge cliffs rose on our left.

"It's always great to be here early in the morning," said Claypot. "Not so many tourists."

"When was the last time you went?" I said.

"Years ago. It's hard to find anyone who will take me now."

Like it's hard to find stores that will sell you cigarettes, I thought.

"This is a great idea," said Gayle. "Fun to do something spontaneous for a change."

"Yeah," I said. "Everyone should indulge in a little occasional spontaneity."

We drove along in quiet for a few miles. We came up on a train loaded with wood chips on the tracks next to the highway, slowly overtook it, and finally passed it. Claypot watched it intently the whole time.

"I've seen better," he said.

"What's that?" said Gayle.

"The graffiti on the box cars. I've seen better. Too many of them only do lettering now. Used to be you'd see all kinds of stuff: landscapes, mythical creatures, dirty pictures. But artistic, you know. They'd try to do something interesting. Now, pfft. Hardly worth looking at."

*They?* Who were *they?*

"You ever do one of your trompe l'oeil pictures on a box car?" said Gayle.

"Not my medium," said Claypot. "I prefer surfaces that don't move."

"It would be interesting, though, to do a picture of the interior of a box car on the outside of a box car," I said.

Claypot didn't answer, but I felt him smolder with resentment, like I had said something I shouldn't have. Gayle glanced at me. Claypot fell back against the back seat. I saw him in the rear view mirror staring out the window of the car. The sun had risen, and hung low in the sky in front of us. Its light fell on Claypot's eyes and beard. It made him look harsh and angry.

We came to Bingen, a small town where the landscape began to shift from lush green to a dry and desert-like yellow. The hills suddenly supported far fewer trees, and dry grass prevailed. Everything looked more stark than before, like we were seeing an X-ray of the gorge instead of the gorge itself.

I pulled into a bakery parking lot. By now it was a little after seven o'clock.

"Thought it might be nice to get some sandwiches or something for later," I said.

We all got out of the car and walked into the bakery.

Claypot wandered over to the restroom. "I need to take a leak," he said. I ordered three sandwiches and some pastries to go. The person behind the counter began making up our order.

"Have we ever in our lives done anything like this?" said Gayle.

"We must have," I said. "At some point."

"I don't think so," she said. "There's something about him. It makes me want to ignore my responsibilities."

"I know what you mean, but I feel like I have to be careful around him."

The bathroom door slammed open. Claypot stepped out and came to stand by us. I saw a spot of moisture on the crotch of his pants. My pants, I corrected myself. Except maybe they were his now, for good.

"They have doughnuts," he said. "Let's get some doughnuts."

"Sure," I said.

"I didn't get any sleep last night," said Claypot in his loud voice. There were a couple of other customers in the bakery. They looked at Claypot like he was an annoying dog that needed to shut up.

"Chris," said Gayle, "you get the food. I'll wait outside with Claypot." She took his arm and guided him to the door.

"What?" he said, even louder than before. "Am I embarrassing someone? Am I making someone the fuck uncomfortable?" He grinned. Gayle hurried him out.

The woman behind the counter gave me a glad-it's-you-and-not-me look, which I found not annoying at all, but actually quite charming.

She handed over a bag of sandwiches and a few doughnuts. I paid her and took the bag outside.

Where I found Claypot smoking a cigarette and dropping the ashes into my shirt pocket.

Gayle, already in the car with her arms crossed in front of her, pointedly did not look at or acknowledge Claypot.

Claypot held up his hand with the cigarette. "What can I say?" he said. "I loves me my smokes." He tapped a column of ash onto the ground. Not into the pocket this time. He took another puff, then tossed the butt to the ground and stepped on it. "I'm a litter bug, too," he said.

Then he got into the car.

I got behind the driver's seat.

"Those cigarettes are going to kill you," said Gayle.

"It won't be soon enough for me," said Claypot.

I handed the bag of food to Gayle and pulled out of the driveway of the bakery and drove slowly through Bingen, then increased speed as we left the town behind.

"How about one of those sandwiches," said Claypot.

"I thought we would save them for after the petroglyphs," said Gayle, but she handed Claypot a roast beef sandwich anyway. He pulled off the wrapper and ate the sandwich with gusto. Like he did everything. When he was in the mood. Apparently he was in the mood now.

When he was finished he asked where he could put the wrapper.

"There's a paper bag next to the seat," I said.

"Oh, yeah, I saw that. Didn't know what it was. You always have a bag of garbage in your car like that?"

"It's just for incidental trash," I said.

"But it's a bag of garbage. That you leave in your car all the time."

"What would you have us do?" said Gayle.

Claypot put up his hands. "Whoa," he said. "Didn't mean to get on anyone's *nerves* or anything. Excuse the fuck out of me."

By this time I had decided it was something of a mistake letting Claypot talk us into a road trip. And now there was no easy way to terminate the expedition. We couldn't just decide to go back and leave him out here. I had no doubt that he would find his way back to town and his tent in Forest Park, but it would still be a crummy thing to do to him.

"Oh," said Gayle. "Dammit. I have to call work. So do you." She flipped open her cell phone and pressed the speed dial number for her office.

"Hi Frank," she said. "Is Evelyn in yet? Great. Let me talk to her."

Claypot had the biggest grin on his face.

"Hi Evelyn. Yeah, everything's okay, except I feel like I'm coming down with something. Need to stay home. Yeah. Thanks. I'll be fine."

Claypot leaned forward. "She's *lying*," he said loudly. I wasn't sure if it was before she closed the phone or after. Neither was Gayle. So maybe her boss heard it and maybe she didn't.

Gayle turned around and hit Claypot on the arm. "What did you do that for?" she said.

Claypot raised his arms like a boxer protecting himself in the ring. He laughed. "I was telling the truth," he said. "That's what we do, we artist types. We're truth tellers."

"You can't do that," said Gayle. "Don't screw up my work like that."

"How can truth mess things up?" said Claypot. "Truth is what makes us human."

"What?" said Gayle.

"The only way to become a new person is by dedicating yourself to the truth. Don't you agree?"

"I might agree if I knew what you were talking about."

"Never mind," said Claypot. "Chris. Your turn. Call up the man and lie to him. Which is about the extent of your rebellious spirit, I think. Let me see you in action. Make me proud."

"I'm driving," I said.

"Don't bother pulling over," said Gayle. "I'll call for you."

"Oh," said Claypot. "This should be good. Lying by proxy. Always an excellent strategy to deflect responsibility. You know, for being upstanding middle class folks, you two do a few things that are not so upstanding."

Gayle held up her finger and pointed at Claypot. "For the next two minutes you are to remain absolutely silent. Got it?"

"Oh sure," said Claypot.

"Promise me," said Gayle.

"I said I would be quiet."

Gayle wanted to say something else, maybe get a more explicit pledge from him, but decided to accept his word. She stared at him while she placed the call.

"Hi Dave. It's Gayle, Chris's wife. No no, we're fine. Just wanted to let you know Chris is a little under the weather today. He needs to take a sick day. No, nothing serious. Just want to nip it in the bud and not infect anyone at the office, you know. Right. Yeah, thanks. Sure. He'll call you to let you know."

She closed the phone.

"See," said Claypot. "I can play nice when I want to."

"Thank you," said Gayle.

"Don't mention it. So how come you two never had any children?"

Gayle looked at me with a "now what?" expression.

"I mean, is it something physical? Does Chris shoot blanks? Or you, Gayle, something wrong with your eggs?"

Neither Gayle nor I answered him right away.

"I mean," said Claypot, "you do fuck, right? It's not like you don't do what it takes to make a kid?"

"What business is it of yours?" said Gayle.

"I'm just asking is all. Trying to get to know my traveling companions."

"Some things are personal," said Gayle.

"So the whole baby thing and fucking and all, that's one of those *personal* things?"

"Yes."

"Because you seemed *real* interested in what my kid would want or not want. I mean about me smoking. You seemed *real* interested in that kind of *personal* stuff about me and *my* life."

"I didn't mean to pry. I was trying to let you know I was concerned about you."

"Oh," said Claypot. "I see. Concern, was it? Hey," he said to me, "watch that guy." He pointed ahead. I looked down the road and saw a car weaving toward me, going over the center line into my lane. I leaned on the horn and eased my car over to the right edge to give the other car more room. My horn seemed to wake him up. The other car moved back to its own side.

"Jerk," said Claypot. "Probably on his cell phone. Which reminds me, you guys know those are cancer machines, right? You shouldn't put them up to your ear. Unless you *like* having tumors grow in your brain. I guess some people are into malignancies. I don't know."

Neither Gayle nor I felt inclined to answer him.

"Just saying," said Claypot. "Just trying to show my concern for you. You know, that's who I am. I have love for all God's creatures."

We drove in silence for a few miles. The river widened and the road rose on the hilly terrain. We were a few hundred feet above the water. I looked out the side window and saw a train way down on the other side of the river, a toy chugging along the shore. The river also held islands, some with vegetation, but most that looked like piles of sand in the current. A barge carrying wood chips from a mill far upstream left a faint wake behind it, a long V that rolled across the width of the river.

The road still climbed higher and wound around with sharp curves. We passed eighteen-wheelers going way below the speed limit to protect themselves from toppling around some of the corners.

"Hey!" said Claypot. "Stop the car. Pull over."

"Why?" I said.

"Stop the car. Fuck. What's it going to cost you? Right here. At the viewpoint."

I looked ahead. A turnout was less than a mile away. "Okay okay," I said. "I'll stop."

"I haven't seen a view like this in ages," said Claypot.

I slowed down even more and turned off when we got to the viewpoint. We were at the summit of the road here. I estimated we where about 900 feet above the river. The viewpoint had room for several cars, but we were the only ones there. We all three got out of the car and stood at the fence, a sheer drop below us to the river below. To the left, across the water, the city of The Dalles hugged a big curve of the river. To the right we saw the mountains we had just left. Portland lay too far to see, but we could imagine it at the far end of a series of curves the river took through the mountains.

Gayle and I stood next to each other. Claypot moved down along the fence, getting farther from us.

I whispered to Gayle. "Maybe we should run for the car and drive off."

"Not a bad idea," she whispered back.

We took in the view in silence for a few minutes. Presently we heard the sound of liquid splashing on pavement. I looked at Claypot. He had his back to us, but I saw a thin arc of yellow, like a rainbow, flow away from him.

"Is he *pissing*?" said Gayle.

"It appears so."

Claypot had a lot of urine in him. The flow went on for some time. Gayle and I put our heads together and giggled, unable to control our incredulity. When Claypot spit and shook his behind, preparatory to zipping up, we turned from him and pretended to be absorbed in some of the orange California poppies that lined the fence at our feet.

"Okay," said Claypot as he walked up behind us. We turned around. He carried a clump of dirt which he used to scrub his hands. "Soil is nature's disinfectant," he said.

"I've heard that," said Gayle.

"I had to go, you know."

"Sure," I said.

"You guys ready?" He slapped his palms together several times. A cloud of dust briefly stained the air around his hands.

We piled back into the car and kept going. We weren't too far from the petroglyphs.

"Either of you guys want to go to Stonehenge after the petroglyphs?" he said.

"Maybe," I said. "We haven't been there in a long time."

"You know there's a copy of Stonehenge in England, don't you?"

"Um," said Gayle. "Don't you have that backwards?"

"No, no. I'm serious. The druids could time travel. Well known fact, although there have been numerous attempts to suppress that particular bit of knowledge. Thing is, way back in however many centuries ago it was, the druids time traveled to here and they saw our Stonehenge and liked it, so they went back to their time and built one of their own. Of course, since it lasted so long people naturally assumed their Stonehenge was the first, but that's not true. Never was true. I wish people would stop spreading false information about that stuff. Our Stonehenge was the first one."

"I've never heard that explanation before," I said. "Didn't some guy in World War I make ours. He modeled it on the one in England. I'm pretty sure."

"You must believe everything you read," said Claypot. "How do you ever expect to become a new person if you keep listening to old explanations for everything?"

I listened for something in Claypot's voice that would indicate his Stonehenge theory was a joke, but I couldn't find it. He sounded as serious as a newscaster describing the devastation of a hurricane's landfall on a highly populated shoreline.

"Stonehenge is a lot farther past the petroglyphs," said Gayle.

"Not that far," said Claypot. "Forty miles."

"That's a lot."

Claypot shrugged. "It's your car," he said. "Only, we came all this way, why not go a little farther, you know?"

"We'll see," said Gayle.

"I mean," said Claypot, "what else do you have to do today? You got some important business back in the city? You blew off work."

"Like I said," said Gayle. "We'll see."

Claypot heaved an audible and long sigh. He fell against the back seat of the car like a petulant child.

We came to the turnoff for Horse Thief State Park. I slowed the car and eased into the long narrow driveway. By this time we had descended almost to the river level. The driveway took us even lower. No vegetation thrived here. Black rocks spread out like a moonscape on either side of us. It felt like a completely alien world. Gayle and Claypot felt it too. They were silent, taking in the surroundings.

I pulled into a small gravel parking lot by the entrance to a trail that looked like it snaked up the side of the rocky hill. I had been here years ago, but there was no parking lot or marked trail then. You had to know where the petroglyphs were and find the trail on your own. People used to park their cars on the side of the road, half on the shoulder, half on the pavement.

Claypot was the first one out of the car. He pulled out a cigarette from the pack he carried in his back pocket and lit it. He took a couple of long drags and exhaled enormous clouds of smoke. Gayle and I got out of the car and stood a slight distance from him.

"May I dust you with some smoke?" he said. Incredibly polite.

I expected Gayle to cringe. Or say something insulting. But she surprised me. "Why would you do that?" she asked. Not in a nasty tone or attitude, but out of genuine curiosity. I wondered myself why Claypot would want to do that.

"We're going to a holy place," said Claypot. "It's best to prepare yourself. It's a sign of respect. A cleansing."

"Don't people usually use sage for that?" said Gayle.

"Very good," said Claypot. "You know your theology."

"I pick up stuff," said Gayle. "Here and there."

Claypot nodded. "You're right. We should be using

sage, but I didn't have any handy, so here we are. Tobacco's a holy plant too."

Gayle held her breath and stood with her arms outstretched. Claypot took in a good long drag and then blew smoke over Gayle's arms and hair and back. She dropped her arms. "Thanks," she said.

"Don't mention it," said Claypot. "Chris?"

I was still stunned by the spectacle of my woman accepting cigarette smoke applied to her person. But I composed myself. "Okay," I said. I put out my arms like Gayle had done.

Claypot blew smoke over me.

I didn't feel any of it but I smelled it. Made me a little lightheaded right away.

"Okay," said Claypot. "Now me." He held out his cigarette for one of us to take.

"We don't smoke," I said.

"Learn," said Claypot.

"Even if we wanted to, we couldn't do it like that."

"I need to be cleansed too," he said. "This is a sacred Native place. I can't walk in without being cleansed."

Gayle went to the car and came back with an empty plastic bottle. "Blow smoke into this," she said to Claypot. "I'll release it over you."

"You're a genius," said Claypot. He took the bottle, inhaled a lot of cigarette smoke, and exhaled it into the bottle. Gayle put her hand over the top. Claypot stood facing me, with the river in front of him, and put his hands out as wide as they would go. He closed his eyes and lifted his chin slightly, enough for me to see that he believed this moment to be important. Gayle put two fingers over the top of the bottle, then separated them enough for a thin column of smoke to curl up into the air. She moved the bottle along the under part of Clay's arms. The smoke rose up and around his elbows, forearms, and hands, then dissipated into the air. She ran the bottle up and down his legs and torso. She turned her head for much of this, to keep the smoke out of her eyes.

When the bottle was empty of smoke she stepped back. "There," she said. "All done. We're all cleansed now."

"Touched by fire," said Claypot. "Let's go."

We crossed the road and stopped at the sign erected at the trailhead. Written in bureaucratic language, it told us we were in a protected area that Natives had consented to be open to the public. We were to respect the petroglyphs as they were more than art. They were historical artifacts.

We each looked at the sign for a few seconds, then stepped onto the trail. It ran close to the base of a high basalt cliff. Swallows flew in swoops and circles above us. The sun warmed the cliffs. On the other side of the trail the river crawled along beside us, placid and smooth. The trail had been built a short distance upstream from the dam at The Dalles, which greatly quelled the river's current.

I got hot right away. I regretted not bringing a hat. Claypot was obviously hot too. A sheen of sweat covered his face and arms.

Soon the trail angled up on a steep rise, which put us on the edge of the cliff. We continued through a boulder-strewn field, then dropped down again. Now the trail took us along a shorter cliff. I remembered the petroglyphs started somewhere near here.

Claypot had gone far ahead of us. He tapped a reserve of extra energy and used it to leave us behind. He stood on the trail and faced the cliff. He looked like he was gazing up at the sky.

As we approached he glanced over at us, then looked back. We stopped next to him and saw what stopped him: a small painting on the rocks. It was a petroglyph of a stick figure, male or female, no way to tell for sure. The figure stood under a rayed arc that floated above its head. A large expanse of rock extended above the image. It was as though the figure had been placed beneath a rock sky and the rock sky had been placed to make the figure look small. Claypot seemed to be spending a lot more time at this petroglyph than was necessary. I knew of much more elaborate and interesting ones farther down the trail.

"No one knows how old this is," said Claypot. "They made them on these rocks overlooking the river. It was like they were making guardians for the river."

"I like this one," said Gayle. "It's so childlike."

"Yup," said Claypot. "You could imagine a kid painting it on a wall at your house. If you had kids, which you don't. I could see something like this on a piece of paper that a mother or father taped to the fridge door."

"Yes," said Gayle. "That's exactly it, isn't it?"

"The thing is," said Claypot, "you have to imagine the river as much more wild. Before the dams tamed it there were wicked currents between those banks. Water flowed like gangbusters and it was dangerous to be on it. They would go on it, though. All the time, for the fish."

I turned and looked down at the placid waters. The river was only a shadow of what it had once been. The water was a good sixty or seventy feet above its undammed state and the higher water submerged lots of petroglyphs closer to the dam. When the dam got built back in the fifties, the Army Corps of Engineers cut some of the images out of the rock and moved them to a museum. I never went to see those, though they were still on display. It felt wrong to go look at them out of their original location.

"So these images are here for a reason," said Claypot. "They aren't art for art's sake. These are guardian images. They're here to protect the river."

Claypot seemed right at home as the genial lecturer. He threw off bits of trivia like a welder threw off sparks.

"Now here's the most important thing," said Claypot.

"Yes," said Gayle.

"There's good reason to think that these images were made under the influence."

"What do you mean?" said Gayle.

"Here's what happened," said Claypot. "They'd take some mushrooms and get high. They'd come up here and watch the river. They'd have these crazy visions, like an acid trip, you know. Then they'd turn to the rock. Rocks are potent symbols. They appear completely lifeless, but that's an illusion. They have a lot of life in them and under the influence these artists could actually look into the rock and see the interior. They'd draw what they saw inside the rocks, which was, more often than not, some sort of person."

Gayle got it right away. "You're saying these are like trompe l'oeil," she said.

"Damn right trompe l'oeil," said Claypot.

"Like what you do," I said.

"Like what I do. Like what I started doing after the accident."

Neither of us knew how to respond to that statement, so we chose not to. We studied the rayed arc figure for a few more minutes, then Claypot patted the rock next to the picture and moved on down the trail. Gayle and I followed.

We passed other images. More figures. Some creatures: fish, deer. They were mostly done in white. Many were faded, a few almost indecipherable against patches of light colored rock. Claypot paused and studied these the longest. I thought of his own art, chalk pictures that disappeared soon after they were made. These fading petroglyphs were like that, only the disappearing took a lot longer to happen than with Claypot's images.

At one image, a picture of two stick figures standing beside one another and holding hands, Claypot stopped and stared for a long time.

By then, I have to say, I was getting a little tired of petroglyphs. I get that they are important artifacts of a lost era; I understand that they display a deep understanding of artistic principles; blah blah blah. But there's only so much art I can take in at one time. After a while it gets repetitive and boring.

Claypot moved very close to the image. "Is that what I think it is?" he said under his breath. His nose almost touched the rock.

"Jesus motherfucking Christ," said Claypot. "Those

cock *sucking* cunt *licking* goddam mother *fucking* pieces of *shit*. Do you see this?"

"What?" I said.

"Right here." He put his finger next to the image. I looked where he pointed. I thought I saw a small fleck of something red, like a bit of paint or something. But I couldn't be sure. It might have been a variation in the rock color.

"Let me see," said Gayle. She moved in next to me and put her face close to the rock.

Claypot bent his head back and cursed at the sky. Loudly. Then: "Some punk ass motherfuckers came and vandalized this picture."

"I think he's wrong," Gayle whispered to me.

"I think you're right," I said.

I turned to Claypot. "I'm not so sure," I said to him. He stared at me. "What?" he said quietly.

"I think it's a coloration in the rock."

"You don't know what you're talking about," said Claypot.

"I don't know about art or rocks," I said. "That's true. But I'm sure this isn't paint. Look at it again."

"I've *looked* at it, electro man. That isn't rock. I draw on rock. You think I don't know about rock?"

What was I supposed to do or say at that point? Tell him he drew on concrete, not rock? Did I want to get into that argument with him? He was convinced someone had been here "vandalizing" petroglyphs. Any facts in the matter were not going to dissuade him from his conviction.

I *wanted* to tell him he was full of shit. I *wanted* to curse him out, the same way he had cursed me out the day before, and some fictional vandals just now.

Looking back on it now, I wish I had. It might have transformed our relationship and put me on a more even footing with Claypot. Instead of him always being the alpha, I might have had some parity with him and maybe I would have gotten more out of my relationship with him. All those things would have been good.

But none of that happened.

Instead, after a few seconds of us staring at each other, I shrugged my shoulders and said, "you're right Claypot. I don't know what I'm talking about."

"Damn right you don't. We need to report this."

"We passed a ranger station on the way in," said Gayle. She didn't want to argue with Claypot either. "We can tell them when we leave."

Claypot made a move to go back along the trail. "I think we should tell them now."

"This was done a long time ago," said Gayle. "We can wait a few more minutes to tell them. Don't you want to go on and see She Who Watches?"

She Who Watches is a large, well-preserved petroglyph at the end of the trail. She looks like some kind of creature, perhaps a bear, maybe an owl, maybe something else, no one is exactly sure and theories abound as to what she actually represents. She has big eyes. A lot of people believe she watches and protects the river. Whoever painted her purposely placed her in a spot overlooking the water, near where Natives have fished for centuries. A visit to She Who Watches is a pilgrimage for many people in the area.

"Yeah," said Claypot. "She Who Watches. I should see her." He looked up the trail. I thought I knew what he was probably thinking: what if She Who Watches had been vandalized like the other image? What if he got all the way to the end to find her marred by some spray paint wielding yahoo?

I didn't think that was likely. For one thing, She Who Watches was revered by anyone I ever talked to about her. Even people who had never seen her, and who had no real idea of where she was, thought of her as an amazing and sacred image. And for another thing I didn't think the other image had been vandalized either.

"Let's go to her," said Gayle. "She'll make you feel better." She took Claypot's arm and nudged him to keep going on the trail.

"Yeah," said Claypot slowly. "I guess we can keep going. But we're going to stop at the ranger's on the way back."

"Of course," said Gayle.

"I'm sorry I swore around you. I try not to swear around women."

"That's okay," said Gayle.

"It was so fucking upsetting seeing that. Do you think they can fix it?"

"I'm sure. They'll get people out here who know what they're doing and they'll take care of it. No one wants to see these images damaged or destroyed."

Gayle and Claypot kept going down the trail. I followed, slightly bewildered. Why was Gayle able to have such a rapport with this nut case? And he was a nut case. My inability to effectively confront him on his issues did not make him any less of a nut case.

We continued on the trail for another ten or fifteen minutes. We passed more petroglyphs, small ones. All the images were simple stick figures with very little background, but something about them made you believe they were a true representation of life. Not the specific lives of Natives, but something about life itself. Life the way it is lived and has always been lived.

Their simplicity lent them this air of authority. Figures stood by themselves or with one or two other figures. Simple animals. It was easy to imagine them about to be killed and eaten by the people.

Somehow Claypot, despite his smoking habit, had more wind than Gayle or me. He shot ahead of us on the trail. By the time we caught up to him he had stopped and was looking high up on the cliff. A few feet above him a flat rock face displayed She Who Watches. She was magnificent, much bigger than the other images we had passed that morning. Easily three feet wide. The eyes were big. The mouth reminded me of a bear's mouth, but the head was not shaped like a bear is. She looked over the river, like she was its guardian.

Below the image, at waist height, a rock ledge bore bundles of burnt sage and other offerings: a ring, an origami crane, a few candles, a bottle cap, some wallet-sized photographs, and a child's tooth.

Claypot retrieved a cigarette from the pack in his pocket, lit it, and wedged it filter side down in a small crevice next to the candles. Gayle didn't say anything.

"I didn't bring a candle," said Claypot.

"But tobacco is a sacred plant," said Gayle.

"Now you're learning," said Claypot.

We stepped back on the trail to get a better look at the image. Before long Claypot began chanting. It sounded like a cappella drumming, with a strong thumping rhythm. His low voice gave the sound a real sense of authority. It came from deep in his belly. I felt immediately uncomfortable. Not because of his chants, but because of how the sound crawled into me. I felt it in my chest and my own belly.

He chanted for a few minutes. I wondered if he had some Native blood in him, he seemed so at home here in front of She Who Watches.

Gayle closed her eyes and swayed, taking in the chants. Claypot didn't notice. He was completely intent on the petroglyph. He never look away from the image. I'm not sure he even blinked.

Finally, after a few minutes, he stopped. We all three of us stood in the silence.

"I come here," said Claypot, "to be someone else for a few minutes."

# *Complicate Your Life*

"WHAT IMAGE ARE you referring to, sir?" asked the park ranger. His name tag read Gene Franklin.

"The one on the way to She Who Watches," said Claypot. "Which other one would it be? You got petroglyphs somewhere else in this park?"

Claypot and I were at the ranger's office after our hike back from the trail. The ranger wanted to help us, I could see that, but he didn't know how to deal with Claypot.

"There are lots of petroglyphs on the way to She Who Watches," he said. "Can you be more specific?"

I stepped in, wary of Claypot's temper. "It's the one with the rayed arc," I said. "It looks possible that it has been tampered with. Some paint." I shrugged.

"I think I know the one. I'll take a look at it."

"When?" said Claypot.

"I'll look at it, sir, don't worry."

"Yeah, but when? Tomorrow? Next year? Don't you take your responsibility seriously?"

Gene didn't respond immediately. It looked like he wanted to say something, but it was clear he was not sure how to proceed with the man in front of him. He glanced at me for some guidance. I felt lost, like Claypot was my charge and I didn't know how to manage him properly.

"Don't look at him," said Claypot. "He's not my fu—"

Gene stiffened. He looked wary. Claypot stopped. He knew as well as I did that if he resorted to profanity the little meeting with the park ranger would be over.

"Uh, that is," said Claypot, "he's not my fa—ther. Can't you just answer a simple question?"

"We're just trying to make sure nothing happens to these petroglyphs," I said.

"We all want to protect them," said Gene. "That's part of my job. And I will do my job. They have been vandalized in the past. We try to keep visitors well-informed of their importance and their fragility."

"Fragility?" said Claypot. "They aren't fragile. They've been there for a long time. I just don't want to see them spray painted with some freaking logo or with Ralphie hearts Tiffany or some such crap."

"Rest assured," said Gene. "I share your concern. I will take care of it."

Claypot still didn't have the answer he wanted, but I wanted us gone. Gayle stood near the car, waiting.

"Thank you for your time," I said to Gene.

"Not at all," he said to me, pointedly avoiding Claypot. Then he thought better of it. He turned to him. "I truly appreciate your concern," he said.

Claypot grunted. I grabbed his elbow and guided him out the door of the ranger station.

As soon as we were outside Claypot let loose. "That motherfucking piece of shit," he said. "He doesn't give a good goddam about the petroglyphs. Only thing he cares about is his precious cocksucking job. That's *all* he cares about. Asshole."

Gayle, who had been standing next to the car admiring the golden hills across the river, smiled at us both. "So it went well, I see."

Claypot glared at her.

Gayle glared back. "You don't scare me," she said.

"Well, I should."

"Well," she said, perfectly mimicking his voice and mannerism, "you don't."

I thought he was going to laugh. I was ready to. Instead he picked up a rock from the ground, walked over to the ranger's truck, and quickly scratched a picture onto the driver's side door. It looked like She Who Watches in stark outline.

Gayle and I both ran to try to stop him. We each grabbed one of his arms. He pushed us both away with a grunt and a powerful lunge of his back and kept scratching.

"Clay." I said. "What are you doing?"

Claypot threw the rock on the ground and stepped away from the ranger's truck.

"There," he said. "That'll remind him of what's important." I looked at the image. Claypot had gouged his way through the paint completely, revealing the silvery metal underneath. He had captured She Who Watches in a stunning image. And he had done it in less than ten seconds.

I turned around and headed back to the station door.

"Where you going?" said Claypot.

"I have to tell him what you did. We can't go now."

"The fuck we can't. Screw that asshole jerk. Let's go."

I had my hand on the door. I was about to step inside the station.

Then I stopped. I released the door handle, turned around, and got into the car. Claypot and Gayle, still standing outside, looked at me with big grins on their faces.

"We can't do this," said Gayle.

"Am I going to be driving home alone?" I asked.

They scrambled to jump into their seats. I started the car and drove up the long driveway back to the state road. I saw the ranger in the rear view mirror step out of the station and look in our direction. I wondered if he noticed the petroglyph carved into his truck. I also wondered if he had time to see our license plate and if he had a good enough memory to recall it later when he reported the vandalism to the police.

What felt like an exciting risk-taking move only half a minute ago suddenly became the stupidest thing I could ever have done.

"I should go back," I said.

"No way," said Claypot and Gayle in unison.

"You trying to get me put in jail?" said Claypot.

"We'd all go to jail," I said.

"No," said Gayle. "We wouldn't. Me and you, we'd get a fine and a slap on the wrist. The only one in this car that would be facing a jail sentence would be Claypot. No income, and living on the street. He's fair game for the justice system."

"Yeah," said Claypot. "What she says."

I didn't have an answer for that. They were right, but the man was a menace. Maybe not truly dangerous, but not exactly the most social guy around. And now I was mixed up in his petty crime.

"Well well well," said Claypot. "First you lie to your employers, now you're on the run with a criminal. And it's not even noon! You two have had a full day already. Aren't you proud?"

"Not exactly proud," said Gayle. "Energized, maybe. I don't know."

"I tell you what I found out," said Claypot. "I could really get into rocks as a medium. That stone I used to carve on the truck. It felt good in my hand. It was like I was back in a cave somewhere, covered in animal skins and working the wall. Solid."

I only half listened to him. I kept checking the mirror to see if any police were after us.

Claypot noticed. "What are you so worried about?" he said. "I'm the one who did the bad thing."

"I drove you away from the bad thing," I said. "I'm in as much trouble as you are."

He sighed and turned to the window, apparently unwilling to abide my fretting any longer.

"Clay's right," said Gayle. "We shouldn't have done that, but we don't need to worry about it anymore now. That ranger should be happy he got an original Dreamstance on his truck."

"Listen to her," said Claypot. "She's the only one in this car besides me who makes any sense at all."

"Let's go to Stonehenge," said Gayle.

"I think I want to get home," I said.

"No," said Gayle. "We're out for an adventure today, let's keep adventuring. We haven't been to Stonehenge in years."

I pulled over to the shoulder, made sure no traffic approached, turned the car around, and sped off in the opposite direction. I pressed the gas pedal almost to the floor. I pushed the car to go much faster than I normally ever did. In no time at all I was a good thirty miles over the speed limit.

"Wooo Hooo," said Claypot. "Someone's feeling his oats."

"Chris," said Gayle. "What are you doing? This road is too curvy for going this fast."

I slowed down.

"Sorry," I said. "Don't know what got into me."

"I do," said Claypot. "You're a criminal now, so you don't care about rules or the law. It's kind of cool, isn't it?"

I wasn't sure about cool, but it did feel good. We zipped by the entrance to the park. I glanced over and saw the ranger's green truck way down, still in the place we last saw it. Claypot and Gayle also looked down there.

"I don't think he's left the building," said Gayle.

"Told you," said Claypot. "He doesn't give a shit about the petroglyphs."

We were past the entrance in a flash. A few miles

ahead I saw a gray dot on the horizon. Claypot pointed at it. "There it is," he said. "There's Stonehenge."

"I see it," I said.

"Go in the back way."

"There's a back way?" said Gayle.

"Yeah, there's two entrances. One goes up the hill from the river, but the other one is cooler. You approach it from behind and see the hills on the other side of the river as a back drop. Way more dramatic."

"Okay," I said. It didn't matter to me either way.

A guy named Sam Hill built Stonehenge on the cliff over the river back in the 1920s. He modeled it on the one in England so it looked how that one would look if all its stones were still intact. Hill intended his Stonehenge as a memorial to the soldiers of World War One. He was a pacifist and wanted to remind people of the folly of war.

I took the route Claypot preferred and approached the circle of concrete pillars by way of a gravel road, driving slowly to see the mass of them all gray and stately against the hills across the river. An empty gravel parking lot surrounded Stonehenge. I stopped the car a respectful distance from the pillars and we stepped out.

The three of us were suddenly not a group anymore, but rather individuals. We stepped away from each other and we each approached the monolithic structure on our own. Claypot walked under one of the cross stones and stepped up onto the center stone. He stood with his hands stretched out for a few minutes. Gayle walked the perimeter of the ring of pillars. She was in a dreamy state. She put out one hand and ran it along the pillars. They weren't stone, like the ones at the Stonehenge in

England. Sam Hill made his pillars of concrete, some of which had crumbled at the corners and edges over the years.

I walked through the structure and out the other side. I liked the view from there. Stonehenge sat on a high cliff, several hundred feet above the river. I looked way down to the left. A dam, one of several on the river, held back a lake of water. To my right a bridge spanned the river to Biggs, a small settlement on the Oregon side, more of a big truck stop than a town. Eighteen-wheelers and their drivers refueled there before continuing on to Portland to the West, or Salt Lake and other cities to the east. Wildflowers decorated the hills beneath me. Orange California poppies, mostly, but also some blue chicory.

A little farther below me, right on the near bank of the river, a series of fruit orchards stretched along the river. People grew peaches and pears down there. Some cherries, too. I thought we should go down after our visit and buy some. A tiny town, home to no more than a couple of hundred people, clung to the river bank. Its biggest structure, a small white church, sat to one side in a large green lot, its cross rising like an elongated plus sign against the greenery.

And then, across the river, a quilt of cultivated squares stretched away for miles. Each square represented a different crop, wheat, mostly, but probably other agricultural products as well. The air was so clear today that it was easy to see a long distance. It felt like looking into infinity.

Claypot crunched up beside me.

"Quite a view," he said.

"Yeah," I said.

"Where's Gayle?"

She was still circling the perimeter. Her feet on the gravel went scrunch scrunch scrunch. I liked the sound. A little bit like strange music.

"Walking the circle," I said.

"Did you see all the names of the dead in here?" he said.

I turned around. "Where?"

"I'll show you," he said. "Come on."

We entered the interior, passing some inner ring pillars. Claypot led me to one of the bigger pillars. A bronze plaque with a male name and dates: 1900-1918. A soldier lost in the war. Claypot showed me another pillar. 1893-1919. And more pillars with more plaques. More dates, more early deaths, all in World War I. Eight plaques in all. They were the names of soldiers from this county that died in the war to end all wars.

"It's so fucking sad," said Claypot.

I nodded.

"They were all so young. Not a one of them made it to thirty. Some were just kids."

"Any of these guys related to you?" I asked.

"Not that I know of," said Claypot.

"Sam Hill wanted people to remember them. I guess he got his wish."

"I'm going to get my chalks," said Claypot. "Be right back."

His chalks?

"Wait a minute," I said. "You aren't going to do one of your trompe l'oeil here, are you?"

"Yeah, why not?"

He thumped my shoulder and turned and walked briskly toward the car. I thought maybe I should follow him, to try to talk him out of drawing a picture here, but then I thought, why? Why stop him? Who would care if Claypot Dreamstance did one of his pictures on one of the pillars of Stonehenge?

Gayle came into the circle and stood beside me.

"Where's Claypot going?" she said

"For his chalk. He feels inspired."

"Oh, that's great. I think it's always good when he's being creative. Better for everyone. Us and him both."

Claypot crunched back and threw his bag of chalk down on the gravel.

"Do you know what you're going to draw?" said Gayle.

Claypot sorted through his chalk and held up a black piece and a purple piece and regarded them both in turn, one after the other, like each piece was a sandwich and he had to decide which one to take a bite out of first. He finally settled on purple and tossed the black piece back into the bag.

"I've got an idea," he said.

He went at one of the pillars with the same gusto he displayed earlier when he did the picture under the bridge. He took that thick piece of chalk and slammed it into the pillar, then scraped it over the surface, like he was scratching an itch and the pillar was his own skin. I immediately saw what he was drawing.

And I noticed something funny.

I didn't want to watch him. I'd already seen the process. I didn't need to again.

I stepped back from him and let him go. He dropped

the purple chalk and grabbed up a few other pieces and went back at the pillar. Gayle and I retreated to the spot where we could see over the river to the quilt-work fields across the river.

"Where to after this?" I said.

"Home, I guess," said Gayle.

"Or we could keep driving."

"Keep driving? There's nothing to see after here."

"There's the wide open country," I said.

Gayle followed my gaze to the road snaking east along the river.

"Hmmmm," she said. "Do we have to take Claypot with us?"

I laughed. "Maybe we should jump in the car and drive away. Leave him here. He could do his trompe l'oeil on all the pillars of Stonehenge. That should take him a few days at least."

She liked the idea. "We'd come back and he'd have every pillar covered in chalk, a Stonehenge gallery."

That sounded good to me. We did not usually take the time to think about the future. Our friends with children told us that was because we didn't have kids. Children change everything. How many times did we hear that over the years? Too many to count. So you have a kid or two. They grow up and go away. Then you're on your own again, just you and your spouse. It's like owning a business that you then sell. You had this big project in your life for a while, but then it disappeared. That's how it looked to me, from the outside. I never told any of my friends my thoughts along these lines, however. It would have gotten me into trouble. Also, even I knew it was a completely flip and cynical attitude. Then I thought of Claypot, losing Stacey like he did. That had to be awful. Claypot obviously still had not completely processed it. If at all. I wondered if that's what all the trompe l'oeil was about. Did he think a view into walls and sidewalks could help him discover what his own life concealed? He gave up his life: he didn't want to be with his woman anymore, spurned traditional housing, and kept few possessions. Was that a way to relieve himself of the burden of dreams and life? Since Stacey died, maybe he wanted everything else in his life to go away too. Even the walls all around him. Did they press on his psyche? Did he need to obliterate all walls to feel free? Or whole?

"You're deep in thought," said Gayle.

"I was thinking about Claypot," I said.

"I like him," she said. "Sometimes. Other times he can be so deliberately mean that I want to smack him."

"He's obviously in great pain."

"I know, that's why I try to give him some slack. But there are limits."

I knew what she meant. Even the most troubled person can test you with their neediness. There comes a time when you want to tell them to get over whatever it is, no matter how heartbreaking or challenging.

"Think he's done?"

I didn't even want to turn around to see. "I don't think he'll ever be done," I said. I meant his grief, not the picture.

"I think you're right," said Gayle. "Not unless he does something different. All this trompe l'oeil is a strange obsession. I don't pretend to understand it, but it's keeping him going in some wounded way that can't be good for him in the long run."

"Listen to us," I said. "Talking about him like we know what we're doing."

"Oh," said Gayle, "we're just thinking about him. He's an interesting problem. I don't like that, thinking about him like a problem. He's a human being, after all. He has some independence beyond our ideas about him, I know that. But it's still interesting to think about him."

We turned around. Claypot wasn't there. I groaned.

"That's funny," said Gayle. "Where could he have gotten to?"

We crunched across the inner circle. No Claypot. We scanned the perimeter of Stonehenge. No sign of him at all.

We looked at the pillar he had been working on. He had drawn hills on it that perfectly matched the hills in the distance.

I moved back from the pillar, keeping my eye on it. I backed right to the center of Stonehenge and that's where Claypot's picture clicked into place. I could almost hear the sound of gears meshing. "Hey," I said. "Stand over here."

Gayle looked at me like I was crazier than Claypot. "Are you serious? We need to find him."

"I know, but come over here. It's a great effect."

She came and stood beside me and looked at Claypot's picture.

"Whoa," she said.

"Didn't I tell you?"

"It looks like it's not even there."

Absolutely right. It felt like whoever built this Stonehenge forgot to put in a pillar. It looked like a gap in a row of teeth.

"How can he *do* that," said Gayle.

*"Why* does he want to?" I said.

We were silent. Disappearances. Vanishings. It felt like we were being presented with both, and for different reasons.

"So he finished this, then he walked away," said Gayle.

"Are we supposed to go find him?"

"Does he want to be found?"

"I don't know," I said.

# *Deny the Reality of Death*

WHILE WE TALKED about what to do next, a couple of cars drove up to the parking lot and a few people got out and wandered around the perimeter of the pillars.

They saw us and waved. We waved back.

A dog came out of one of the cars. From the way it pawed at the gravel and ran around frantically, I thought it must have been cooped up in the car for a while.

Gayle and I stepped away from the pillars to avoid the dog, who only got more and more lively, running in circles and kicking up dust and gravel. The dog paused long enough to smell us, then went on, throwing up gravel as it ran.

We looked at each other and shrugged.

We scanned the horizon for some sign of Claypot. I saw only yellowing vegetation. "Look," said Gayle. She pointed at the grass. "Some of the blades are bent down.

He's been through here."

I looked along the grass and saw a trail of bent stalks.

"Shall we?" I asked.

"Yes, let's," said Gayle.

We stepped down from the plateau that held Stonehenge, leaving it to the family with the dog, and began a descent into the valley below. The air was hot and scratchy. Neither of us liked it.

"Do you suppose he wanted us to follow him?" said Gayle.

"Who knows what Mr. Dreamstance wants from us," I said. "Or from anyone for that matter."

The cliff face, if it is quite proper to call it that, became much steeper. The bent grass gave way to an actual trail. Rocks studded our path. The ground rose up and enclosed us in something like a canyon. We lost the view of the river and of the opposite bank of the river. Any hint of breeze suddenly disappeared. The air got hotter. I regretted not bringing water.

"How you doing?" I asked.

"This is not exactly my idea of fun," she said. "Actually, it's my idea of misery."

I could not disagree and we both paused for a couple of minutes to catch our breaths and survey our surroundings. The trail continued down for a distance. I could not see the end, but evidently it emptied out into the town below. Did Claypot want to go to this town? Why?

I looked at Gayle. She knew what I was thinking.

"I have no idea," she said. "The man's an enigma."

"Wrapped in a mystery," I said.

"But is he our mystery?" said Gayle. "Do we need to keep going here?"

"I worry about him."

"I think he can take care of himself just fine."

I raised my eyebrows.

"Okay," she said. "Not very well, but well enough."

"So maybe we should go back?"

She held her hand to her forehead and looked down into the town. "Oh, I don't know," she said. "What do you think?"

"Let's go back up, get in the car, and *drive* to the town."

Gayle thought that was a good idea. We reversed direction and began ascending. It was a lot more work and we got even warmer. Sweat popped up on my forehead and tickled my back.

We got to the lip of the cliff and saw the family clustered around Claypot's chalk drawing on the pillar. They put their palms up to the drawing, like they wanted to move their hands through the concrete. The dog had calmed down considerably and was stretched out on the ground behind them, panting.

The father must have heard our feet on the gravel. He turned around. "Hey," he said. "Did you do this?"

We shook our heads. "No," I said. "We're not artists."

"Artist?" said the man. "This isn't art. It's vandalism."

Oh, oh. "Forget about it," muttered Gayle under her breath. "Let's get out of here."

"I wouldn't exactly call it vandalism," I said. "It's chalk. It'll wash right off in the first rain."

The man looked at us through hooded eyes. "How do you know it's made of chalk?

"Um," I said. "It's obvious."

"Do you know who did this?"

"It's an artist. Obviously."

"I've called the police to report this."

"That's a good idea," I said. "They need to know about this."

The man looked upset, like I had wrecked his day and he wasn't going to have it.

"You trying to be a smart guy?" he said.

"*Chris*," said Gayle. "Why are you still *talk*ing to him. Get in the car."

Gayle stood next to the open passenger door. I waved at the man and got into the car. Gayle slid onto the passenger seat and closed the door. I started the engine and turned on the air conditioner. The blast of cold air felt as refreshing as a dip in a pool. I backed out of the parking place and drove slowly toward the way out. The man eyed us suspiciously as we passed by him.

"You know," I said to Gayle, "he could make things difficult for us."

"I know," said Gayle. "Let's get Claypot and get out of here."

We got back on Highway 14 and took a turn to go down to the town. We drove along the main road, lined with fruit stands.

We got to the center of town. A few houses clustered around an intersection, the white church on one corner. And something else: my clothes strewn haphazardly on the lawn in front of the church.

"Oh no," said Gayle.

I stopped the car and got out. Gayle followed. I pushed the door open and stepped into the church. I gave my eyes a few seconds to adjust to the darkness. Claypot stood at the front of the church, completely naked. He curled his hands into fists and held them above his head.

"Come on down, you motherfucker," he said. "Don't sit up there like a cocksucking asshole, pissing on us down here. You shithead! Come on down and breathe life into this creature. I know you're supposed to be able to do it, motherfucking almighty piece of shit."

He waved his fists in the air.

Was the man drunk? How could he be?

I looked past him to what looked like a pile of fur on the altar. A dead animal? Claypot brought a dead animal into the church?

Gayle came up behind me.

"What do we do?" I said.

She held the clothes in a pile. "Try to get him back into these," she said.

Claypot paused his ranting and looked down at us. His breaths came in great gulps of air. "I'm not putting those on," he said. "I was born naked and I'm going to be naked when I meet the fucker who made me."

"You are not going to meet God," said Gayle.

"Fuck you, bitch," said Claypot.

I felt an animal need to punch Claypot in the face. I stepped forward. Gayle grabbed my arm. "Don't," she whispered. I stopped.

"Yeah," said Claypot. "You heard me. Fuck you and your cocksucking husband. How about that? Now get the fuck out of here. I have business to attend do."

"Okay, Clay," said Gayle. "I can see you're busy. I'll leave these here for when you're done with your meeting." She put the clothes down in one of the pews. Claypot glared at her, then at the clothes. Gayle waved at him. "We'll be waiting outside when you're ready," she said. "Don't leave the building until you've put on something, okay? It tends to scare the neighbors."

Claypot still glared at her, but he nodded. That had to be a good sign.

Gayle put her arm around me and we walked out of the church.

We stood on the front lawn. "How do you suppose he got in?" said Gayle.

"Maybe they left the front door unlocked?"

"Unlikely. He probably broke in. This isn't going to be good, Chris. He's vandalized two places. He's going to be in trouble. Probably go to jail."

"Not to mention the dead animal."

"Yes. He must have found it on the trail on his way down here."

"We should get him out, take him back home. What was it? Looked like a raccoon."

"I don't want him in our house," said Gayle.

"No, I mean his home. In the park."

"But do you want to go in and grab him? He's a big guy and he's pissed."

We heard his muffled voice, still challenging the almighty to a duel.

"You don't like fists, motherfucker? Is that it? Okay. Whatever you want. Harsh words, then? You're good at that, aren't you? The word of God, right? I can take you on you cunt licking cocksucking motherfucking piece of shit. Come on!"

As we listened, a few men from town came up to us. They didn't look angry, so much as puzzled. I waved at them. They didn't wave back. "Our welcoming committee," I whispered to Gayle.

"Looks like it," she said.

They stopped a few feet from us. Four of them.

"Hi," I said, trying to sound as bright and lively as I possibly could. "Sorry for the disturbance."

"That a friend of yours?" said one of the men.

"Yes sir," I said. "He's going through a rough patch right now. Lost his daughter."

The man nodded. "I can understand how someone might go a little bit crazy over that, but he broke into our church. We've already called the sheriff. His foul language is getting out everywhere. If you can get him into some kind of presentable shape, it'll go better for him."

While the man talked, his three companions went to the church entrance.

"Damn," said one of them after peeking inside, "the guy's completely naked. And he's got a dead raccoon."

I heard Claypot through the open door. "Look, motherfucker," he said. "I've got a dead animal here. You want to reanimate the fucker or don't you? Simple question. Show me what you got, asshole."

The man looked at me with an expression that said he was about fed up. I understood. I was ready to be done with Claypot myself.

"There's a pile of clothes in there," said Gayle. "It would be nice if you could get him to put them on."

"He's your friend?" said the man.

"Yes, but he's not interested in listening to either of

us right now."

"And you think he'd listen to me?"

"It's worth a try," said Gayle.

The other three men came over to stand next to him. The man looked very doubtful about the whole thing.

"He's nothing to me," he said.

"Please?" said Gayle.

"The guy's obviously disturbed," said one of the other men. "He isn't going to want to put any clothes on, but if we all hold him down, then maybe we can get something on him so the sheriff doesn't find him like this."

They seemed to come to a group decision. "Okay," said the first one. The four of them went into the church.

Gayle and I followed.

We saw Claypot at the front of the church, still raging against the powers that be. He looked up at the ceiling. He glanced over at the four men. I expected fireworks. Resistance and more foul language.

Instead, he slumped into a relaxed disarray.

The four men walked up to him. One of them took the clothes from the pew where Gayle had left it.

"You shouldn't be bringing dead things into church like that."

"I know," said Claypot. "I didn't think it was dead. Nothing is ever really dead."

"I can't quite agree with you on that," said the first man. "But I take your meaning. You want things to be different. We all do."

Claypot looked dazed. He caught my eye and I saw pleading in his. It made me uncomfortable that he wanted something from me.

One of the men picked up the raccoon and took it out of the church. He didn't look disgusted or upset by the task at all.

Claypot took the clothes from the other man and began to put them on.

"I'm sorry about your daughter," said the first man.

"Yeah," said Claypot.

"You seem to be an okay fella. Maybe we shouldn't have called the sheriff, but you did break into the church. If you need anyone to help you out with the law, tell them they can talk to me."

"I'll do that," said Claypot.

I heard a car crunch up on the gravel behind me.

Gayle and I turned around. A sheriff's car was stopped a short distance away.

A slim young man in a brown uniform got out of the car. He had a pin on his uniform that indicated he was a deputy.

"You call in a complaint, Sam?" he asked the man we had been dealing with.

"It's all taken care of," said Sam.

The sheriff raised his eyebrows. "Report said something about a break in at the church?"

"A big misunderstanding. The gentleman was a little disoriented. Didn't quite know where he was. That's all."

The deputy looked doubtful, but also inclined to believe Sam.

"What about the damage?"

"These fine people, who are friends of the man in question, have agreed to pay for any damage."

Very smooth of Sam.

The deputy looked directly at me. "That right?" he asked.

"Absolutely," I said.

"Okay," said the deputy, "let me go talk to him."

He went into the church.

"Should we follow?" I asked Sam.

"Probably best not to," he said.

"Thanks for that," I said.

"You seem like okay people. I expect the damage will come to a thousand bucks, give or take."

"Oh," I said. "Of course. I can write you a check."

"That would be fine."

I went to the car to retrieve the checkbook. Gayle followed me. "We're going to hand over a stranger a check for a thousand dollars?"

"He did us a favor," I said.

"He did *Claypot* a favor. That's not the same thing."

"Claypot can't pay anything."

"And that's *our* problem?"

She had a point, but it still felt like we should take care of the damage Claypot had done.

I heard the door of the church swing open and slam against the wall.

I looked up.

Handcuffs secured Claypot's wrists behind his back. The deputy hustled him away towards the police car.

# *Behave in a Grown-up Manner at All Times*

"HEY," I SAID. "What's the idea? We were going to let well enough alone."

The deputy looked right past me, like I was air.

"Easy, there," whispered Sam.

"What are you doing with Claypot?" I said, ignoring Sam completely.

Gayle took my arm and tried to pull me back. I didn't let myself be pulled.

"Sir," said the deputy, "unless you are his lawyer I have nothing to say to you."

Claypot had on my clothes. He didn't look like he was in distress, despite the handcuffs. If I was cuffed like that I would be so uncomfortable that I would try to break the cuffs and probably injure myself.

Claypot made a face at me, like this was all a big joke. He stuck out his tongue and rolled his eyes in his socket.

He looked like a clown. I wanted to shake him. Tell him he was messing up big time and would continue to do so until he grew up and took control of his life.

"Call my wife," said Claypot. "Judy will come out for me."

The deputy guided Claypot into the back seat of the car. Claypot looked at home there in a strange way. Like the shelter of the car suited him.

"Where are you taking him?" I asked the deputy.

"County jail."

"I know where that is," whispered Sam.

Then the police car drove out in a crunch of gravel and a billow of dust.

I got Judy's card from out of my pocket and flipped open my cell phone and called the number.

It rang twice. "*Visions*," said Judy.

"Judy," I said. "It's Chris Miller. We talked yesterday."

"Yes? Is Clay okay?"

"Not exactly. He got arrested."

"Oh, shit," she said. "Where?"

"We're in Marysville."

"What the hell are you doing there?"

"He wanted to see Stonehenge. We took him. Anyway, he broke into a church, did some damage."

"They must have taken him to Goldendale."

"Yeah, the county jail. Can you come out here? He asked for you."

"I'll be there."

She hung up. She wanted to get back into Claypot's life. This would be one way to do it.

"That his wife?" said Sam. By now the rest of the

men had disappeared. I didn't know exactly why Sam was still there.

"Ex-wife," I said. "They have a unique relationship."

Sam nodded. "Guy like that, all his relationships must be unique."

"You've got that right," said Gayle.

"He's obviously in some pain," said Sam. "You two know what you're doing with him?"

"Not a clue," I said. "But I'm learning."

"I wish you luck," said Sam. "You going up to the jail?"

"Yes," I said.

"I don't get up to Goldendale much, but if I remember right they're pretty nice people. You shouldn't run into a lot of difficulty."

"Thanks," I said.

"Now I've gotta find someone who'll repair this door," he said, and winked at me like we were co-conspirators in some school kid prank.

I thanked him for his help and Gayle and I got into the car and drove through town. Goldendale was about twelve miles north of Marysville. We got on 14 and headed in that direction.

"I wish we never brought him here," said Gayle.

"Me too," I said. "How soon before Judy gets here, you think?"

"At least a couple of hours."

"Do you think she'll have bail money?"

"She better. We've already spent a thousand on him, we're not going to spend anymore."

I nodded. "You think we should tell them about the

vandalism at the ranger station?"

"Oh, I'm sure they already know all about that," said Gayle.

"Probably right," I said.

The road rose up from the gorge through cut rocks and exposed strata. The fields beyond the cuts were yellow and brown, dried grass blown by wind. In a couple of miles we had risen about two thousand feet. The road abruptly leveled out. The gorge gave way to a flat land of wheat fields. In the distance a couple of mountains tented the horizon line with striations of snow and rock. The town of Goldendale popped into view: a compact collection of houses and other squat buildings, like the eye of the beast that was the sprawling farmland arrayed around it.

We got into town and drove toward its center. The sheriff's station occupied an old storefront across from the grocery store. Nothing much to it at all. We parked the car on the street and went inside. A deputy, not the one who arrested Claypot, sat at a desk behind a glass panel.

"Yes?" he said.

"We're inquiring about Claypot Dreamstance," I said.

"You his lawyer?"

"No," said Gayle. "We're friends."

"He's being processed. You can wait here for word." He indicated a couple of chairs on the other side of the room. I wanted to ask him more questions, but he didn't seem like the type to welcome inquiries.

We sat down. "Judy will be here soon," said Gayle. "Then it'll be her problem."

"I suppose," I said.

"You aren't thinking of continuing our relationship with him, are you?" she asked.

"Not exactly. But if he's locked up for too long he's not going to do himself any good. He's going to make everyone here so mad at him they'll keep him forever. Or maybe beat him up. I don't know. Something."

"Stop imagining the worst. He can be very charming when he wants to."

"I noticed that."

"He's all act and put on," said Gayle. "I didn't think so before, but now I'm sure of it. No one can run hot and cold like that without it being calculated. At least a little bit."

"I suppose you're right about that."

We sat in silence for a while.

I got up. "The suspense is getting to me," I said. "I'm going to go outside and walk around."

"You want me to come with you?"

"No. Let's take turns on the vigil end of things."

"Fine," she said.

I stepped outside to a café a couple of doors down. I went inside and ordered two coffees to go. The clerk asked me how it was going.

"Beg pardon?" I said.

"You're waiting for someone at the jail, right?"

"How'd you know?"

"You have the look. I see a lot of people bailing people out of jail. Friend or family?"

"Friend."

"That's usually easier. When it's family it feels more personal, like you did something wrong raising them, or they brought shame on you because they're your family." She handed me the two coffees. I gave her the money.

"I guess you're right."

"If you want to make things easier, don't bug the cops. They don't like you waiting in the room. Makes them think you're trying to pressure them and they don't like to be pressured."

"I can understand that," I said. "Thanks for the coffees. And the advice."

"Sure," she said. "Don't worry about it. If your friend didn't do anything real bad, it'll be okay for him. He'll do fine."

I went back to the sheriff's office and handed one of the coffees to Gayle. "We need to get out of here," I said in a low voice.

She didn't hesitate. She rose from her chair and walked out with me.

"They don't like us hovering over them," I said.

"Really? How did you know that?"

"A native told me of the local customs."

"Ahh. So now what do we do?"

"Wait for Judy."

"Why?"

"Um, I don't know. Because it seems like the right thing to do."

"We're not going to make any difference."

"We can tell her exactly what happened."

"The only reason she's here is to bail him out. She'll take him home and he'll tell her everything that happened in his own words."

I saw her point. Both of us wanted to wash our hands

of Claypot Dreamstance. I know I did.

"He's going to think we deserted him if he comes out and we're not here."

"We are deserting him, but he deserves no less."

"Wow," I said. "That's kind of harsh."

"There's nothing in this for us," said Gayle. "The only result of spending time with him is chaos. Do you want that chaos in your life?"

I had to admit that she made a lot of sense.

"It still feels wrong," I said. "It still feels like we're letting someone down who is more than a little deserving."

"He's not deserving," said Gayle. "He's had some tragedy in his life. Welcome to the grown-up world. Everyone has tragedy. You don't have to then become a crazy person. You don't have to decide to be a nut."

I wasn't sure Claypot decided anything of the kind, but it was also true he could be coping a lot better than he was.

Judy is on her way, I told myself. Judy will take care of things. She cares about Claypot.

"Okay," I said. "Let's get out of here."

# *Never Use the*
# *Dead Person's Name*

WE WALKED TO the car and got inside. I started the car, put it in reverse, and hooked my arm over the seat to begin backing out of the parking space.

"Wait," said Gayle.

"What?"

"Dammit. I'm feeling like a world class heel right now."

I slipped the car back into park and turned off the engine.

"Me too," I said.

"Dammit dammit. How can he make us feel like this?"

"I don't know. You want to walk around a little?"

She sighed. "Why not? We might be waiting a long time."

We got out of the car and with our coffees in hand

we walked the few blocks of main street.

We found a bench and sat down in waning sunlight. The air held a bit of a chill, evening coolness already beginning to settle in. The hot coffee felt good. We didn't say anything for a few minutes. People ambled up and down the sidewalks. Some of them glanced in our direction and nodded or smiled at us. This town wasn't exactly the cliché of the small American town, but it came close. There was main street, with its shops and businesses, and a lot of friendly people milling around.

"You know," said Gayle. "It's all about Stacey with him."

"Sure," I said.

"It isn't fair of me to criticize him for his loss. He's working through it the best he can."

"This town is so normal," I said. "It's funny that they had some old eccentric that built stonehenge. I always though it was a strange thing to have that structure here where the people are so *not* strange."

"Uh huh," said Gayle.

"And then to have Claypot here doing his crazy stuff. It fit, in an odd way. Like he was born to be here."

"I sense your mind wandering away from the topic at hand," said Gayle.

"There's just something about him being here and doing that trompe l'oeil at Stonehenge. Maybe he should move here. The atmosphere might be right for him."

"Oh, yeah," said Gayle. "It's so conducive to his well-being that he breaks into a church and rants about death to god. While being naked. That's healthy."

I saw her point. But still felt there might be something there.

"He's only going to want to be here," she said, "or any place for that matter, if and only if he thinks he can find Stacey."

"Who's to say he won't find her here?" I said.

"Me," said Gayle. "And you, if you thought about it for about half a second."

"He's a free spirit. Maybe he needs the wide open spaces of a rural setting. Maybe the city is too hard on him. Too many memories."

"The city gives him all kinds of surfaces to do his trompe l'oeil work. He wouldn't have that here."

"I know," I said. "What I'm getting at is that that might be exactly what he needs. The trompe l'oeil is probably unhealthy for him."

We spoke as though we had some control over Claypot's life, and that we had a right to that control. Nothing could be more ludicrous. We could do nothing to make Claypot behave a certain way. And if we could, we probably shouldn't exercise the power.

"Claypot will do his art until he doesn't have to anymore," said Gayle.

"When will that be?"

"When he no longer sees Stacey everywhere he goes."

# *Do Things You Are No Good At*

WE FINISHED OUR coffees and had no wish to leave the bench. It was a good place to be.

Judy came into town a while later. We saw her drive by us. She didn't look our way. We got up from the bench and went back to the police station. By the time we got there Judy had parked the car and was talking to the officer. We walked in and stood beside her.

"Hey, you guys," she said.

"I'm so glad you came," said Gayle.

The officer told us all to go sit on the chairs against the wall. We went and sat.

"He says Clay will be out in a few minutes," said Judy.

"Really?" I said.

"Yeah. I hate this. I hate doing this."

"I know," said Gayle. "No one likes it."

"All he has to do is make bail and they'll let him go."

"He can't pay that," I said.

"I can," said Judy. "I already wrote a check."

"Just like that?" I said.

"Sure," she said.

We heard clattering noises from behind the officer's desk, like things being thrown. Chairs or tables maybe.

"On the other hand," said Gayle.

The officer got up out of his chair and went back to the source of the noise.

"He's going to mess things up," said Judy. "Again."

"I'm getting the idea he's pretty good at that," said Gayle.

"He has many skills," said Judy. "That's only one of them."

The noise of breaking furniture filled the room. We were all three more than a little unnerved.

"He'll calm down soon enough," said Judy. "He gets tired. Then he winds down to an easy quiet."

"Uh huh," I said.

"How did you all get out here with him?" she asked.

"He came to our house. Talked us into going to see the petroglyphs."

"Oh, those petroglyphs. He and Stacey used to go look at them. She was sure kids made them. The simple drawings. Those stick figures. She often did them at home, on the walls. I would stop her. Claypot wanted her to do them. I didn't want to have to clean the walls, but he said I was stifling her creativity. We got into some real shouting matches about it, let me tell you. He was never any good at discipline."

She talked about Stacey like she was someone else's child.

"He must have had something going for him as a father," I said. "He is very devoted to her."

I didn't realize what I was saying until I said it. He was devoted to a dead child. Judy didn't blink or even acknowledge my statement.

"He can be devoted when he sets his mind to it. He just doesn't set his mind to it very often. Like this trompe l'oeil business. It's his whole existence now and you can't pull him away from it to save his life. He just decided to be devoted to it.

The noises from the back had subsided.

"Sounds like they restrained him," said Judy in a matter of fact way, like she was talking about the weather. "They aren't going to want him around, that's for sure."

A few minutes later the officer came back and motioned to Judy. She got up and talked with him for a minute or so. Then she turned around to us.

"They're going to keep him overnight," she said.

"Oh no," said Gayle.

"It's no big deal," said Judy as she headed for the exit. We followed her. "They don't like that he was causing a ruckus. I can understand that. Tomorrow I'll take him home."

"Should we find a lawyer?" said Gayle.

"Not necessary," said Judy. "This is a small thing. They'll probably make him do community service."

"You seem to know a lot about this sort of thing," I said.

"We've been through this before. It's the same everywhere. They don't want to trouble themselves with you anymore than they absolutely have to."

I thought about getting back home. We couldn't wait here overnight. Was Judy going to?

"So," said Judy. "We have some time on our hands. You want to go see Stacey's grave?"

# *Forget the Person Who Died*

I RARELY VISIT graveyards. It isn't that they scare me or give me the creeps or anything like that. It's more that I have been lucky enough not to have had a lot of people I know die, hence have never had much personal business at a cemetery. I am always intrigued by the contradiction they represent. All those headstones, lined up in neat rows, so orderly, as if to say death is not a messy thing at all. Death is dignified, methodical, and well-behaved. When everyone knows it isn't

Gayle and I got into Judy's car. She slipped into the driver's seat and we headed north through town.

"We used to live here, a few years ago," said Judy. "Stacey was born here. I worked at the museum on the river. Clay was trying to do his art. We had a cabin in the woods."

The paved road ended. We continued as it turned

into dust and gravel. We went for a few miles.

"I guess that explains why he wanted to come here today," said Gayle.

"I guess," said Judy. "He doesn't want to admit that she's dead. But he can't stay away from her either."

"It's dusty here," I said.

"It's not too far now," said Judy. "You'll see it coming up on the right."

The trees along the road were coated in dust. Evidently this road had a lot of traffic, or at least enough to turn the trees into ghostly apparitions of themselves.

Judy parked the car. We waited for the dust to settle before we got out.

A chain link fence, waist high, circled the cemetery, holding it in a meshy embrace. The grass was very green, almost dazzling. I caught a view of the river, startling, since I thought we had driven too far north to see it anymore. We all got out of the car and entered the cemetery. A lot of old weathered headstones. Some new ones. Many of the old headstones were for children. The dates were heartbreaking: 1909-1911, for example.

We stood quietly among them. Judy took her time, in no hurry to take us to Stacey's resting place. "I haven't been here in a while," she said.

A slight breeze blew in, carrying some dust with it. We didn't mind. The grit on our faces suited the moment perfectly. A little bit of discomfort was more than appropriate, I thought.

Judy led us across the cemetery to a small white marble marker. It lay on the ground, barely a few inches thick.

"I liked this one," said Judy. "Clay didn't care. Or

maybe it was more that he didn't want to believe it was necessary. Still doesn't believe it."

I felt Gayle's discomfort. I was uncomfortable myself. What made me think it was a good idea to come here?

"You know what all that trompe l'oeil stuff he does is about don't you?" said Judy.

I shook my head.

"Damn," said Judy, interrupting her own thought. "I didn't even bring any flowers. But I didn't know I was going to be coming here."

Gayle walked to the fence and leaned over the other side. California poppies grew along the fence line. She plucked several of them and held them in a bunch. She brought them to Judy, who took them and placed them on the marble slab. They looked stunning, bright orange against the pure white.

I wanted to hear the end of Judy's thought, but didn't want to ask her about it. I already felt like we were intruding on something too private for casual acquaintances, which is what we were. I took Gayle's lead and did not say anything.

Judy stood next to her daughter's headstone. She was with us, but she was also alone. Gayle and I retreated to give her some privacy. We turned from her and looked at the river, blue in the distance.

I pointed to a large rock teetering on the hillside to the left. "That's one of those rocks from the Missoula flood, isn't it?" I said.

Gayle looked in the distance, trying to see what I saw. "Look's like it," she said.

"I thought most of those were in the Valley." I meant

the Willamette Valley, which was south of Portland. Geologists theorized that a massive flood of water, ice, and rock swept through this area thousands of years ago, carving out the Columbia River Gorge. The water was released by the melting of a giant ice dam near what is now Missoula, Montana. Chunks of ice with embedded rocks roared through this area and many of them ended up in the Valley. The ice melted and the rocks remained, still there today, strangely out of place in the middle of fields.

"Looks like at least one of them never made it that far," said Gayle.

"How long you think it's been there?" I said.

"Few thousand years, according to the scientists."

"Makes me think of Claypot."

"Yup," said Gayle. "Completely out of his element. He's like a rock who doesn't belong."

She knew my thoughts exactly.

"He's never going to get better, is he?" I said.

"I wouldn't be that pessimistic about it," she said, "but it does seem like he has a lot of work to do getting past the death of his daughter, work he isn't willing to take on right now."

"It really was a big mistake getting tangled up with him."

"No," said Gayle. "Not a big mistake. More like colossal and all-encompassing cosmic error of epic proportions."

"Oh, good," I said. "At least it's not serious."

"You need to decide if you want to maintain contact with him. He's unstable. You should decide now if you want to be friends, or if you want to let him go. The longer you delay, the crueler it will be if you decide you don't want anything to do with him anymore."

"I don't feel like I can just drop him," I said.

"Are you sure?" said Gayle. "Make up your mind now, but make it for sure. Don't decide you will help, then at some point in the future decide you won't."

"Everyone should have a lost cause in their life," I said. "It makes them nobler. Mine will be Claypot."

"And don't be a smart ass about this, either," said Gayle. "It's too important for that."

I heard sobs. Judy crying over by Stacey's grave. Gayle looked up and over at Judy. I followed her gaze. Judy was on the ground, kneeling before her daughter's headstone.

Gayle went over and kneeled next to Judy. She put her arm around Judy's shoulders. Judy leaned into the embrace. She was still crying, but quieter now.

"I can't see her name without crying," said Gayle through tears. "It breaks my heart every time."

Gayle nodded. "Of course," she said. "It should break. That's how you know you're human."

# *Ignore the Pain of the Loss*

I DON'T KNOW how long we were at the cemetery. I lost track of time. Must have been an hour, at least. Maybe more. Judy was so upset that she couldn't drive. I drove the car for her. That was one thing I could do. We went back to town. Judy took a room in a motel in town. She invited Gayle and me to stay overnight with her, but we had work in the morning. We couldn't blow off another day like this.

"At least stay long enough to have dinner with me," she said.

"Okay," said Gayle. "We'll do that. Did you see anything in town you liked?"

"When we lived here the Big Yellow Grill was always good."

"Big Yellow it is, then," said Gayle.

We walked down main street. By this time it was almost six. We had another two hours drive to get back home, so we were probably going to get in late.

The Big Yellow Grill was only three blocks away. We went inside and took a booth near the back. The air conditioning felt like it had a direct line to the arctic ice cap.

"They always keep it so cold?" I said.

"Tourists like it that way," said Judy. "They can't stand the heat at all."

"It's not even that hot outside," said Gayle.

A waitress came to our table and put down three glasses of water. I sipped mine. It was ice cold. Too cold. I started to shiver.

"Hey, Judy," said the waitress, "it's nice to see you again. What you doing up here?"

"Clay got into some trouble," said Judy.

"They letting him cool off for a while?"

"Yeah," said Judy. "Overnight."

"I always say," said the waitress, "that's the best thing for them, sometimes. Makes them a little more civilized, you know what I mean?"

Judy laughed. "I know *exactly* what you mean, believe me."

The waitress laughed. "My man used to come home from a night in jail sweeter than a honeycomb. I missed it if he didn't go at least once a year."

Gayle laughed.

"You folks want any coffee?" asked the waitress.

We all said yes.

"Be right back," she said, and spun on her heel and disappeared into the kitchen.

"That's Lorraine," said Judy. "Sweet gal. We used to

come here all the time and she always served us."

"I always think I would like to live in a place where the restaurant staff knows you by name. Must feel very cozy."

"It has its points," said Judy, "but it can get tedious, too. Everyone knows your business."

"I would hate it," said Gayle.

"A lot of people do," said Judy. "That's why a lot of towns like this are withering away. Or barely hanging on. Clay loved it here. Taught Stacey to draw here. She was pretty good."

"Stacey do a lot of drawing?" I asked.

Judy nodded. "It wasn't just kid stuff, either. It was competent rendering with perspective and good detail. She wasn't a prodigy or anything, but she had some talent and knew what she was doing on some level. Clay was especially proud of her. They did a lot of landscapes together. The hills around here are particularly inspiring."

The waitress returned to take our orders. We all got hamburgers, the house specialty. She left and a slightly awkward silence ensued. I didn't exactly know where it came from, but it was uncomfortable. Gayle broke it.

"If you loved it here so much," she said to Judy, "why did you leave?"

"Couldn't find work. Or the work we could find was not enough to keep us going. Clay wanted to stay. He would have moved us to a shack just so we could live here. A sod house if that's what it took. A tent, whatever. But I wouldn't hear of it. I applied for jobs in Portland, got one, and that was that. We moved. He still blames me for—well, for everything, really."

The silence returned, as awkward as before. I looked over at the waitress.

"Must be hard on you," I blurted out, "him essentially being a crazy man now."

"He was always a little different. That's what I found attractive about him."

"It's nutty," said Gayle, "that he blames you for anything. It was an accident."

"Yeah," said Judy. "An accident. There is a school of thought that says there are no accidents. I'm sure you've heard of that."

"New Age nonsense," said Gayle.

"Yup," I said. "Not everything happens for a reason. I don't believe that at all. Some things happen because they happen."

More silence. I wondered if I said something wrong. Maybe Judy was a New Ager and I just insulted her. I didn't think so, but it was possible.

"We're waiting," said Gayle.

"Yes," said Judy.

"What?" I said.

"We're waiting for Clay," said Judy. "That's what we're always doing. Without him things are in limbo. We need him to make things interesting. We need him to define things."

Gayle nodded. "That's exactly right. It feels wrong for him to be in jail. He needs to be out here raising hell."

That's why we were all so quiet? I wasn't sure, but there was no doubt in Judy's mind. Or Gayle's.

"You both sure about that?" I said.

"Absolutely," said Judy. "You're the perfect example."

"Me?" I said, "how so?"

"You're still here, waiting for him. Why haven't you left town? Why did you even come here with him in the first place? Why are you interested in my ex-husband?"

"I like his art," I said, but even as I said it I was aware of how inadequate that sounded. I liked a lot of people's art but that didn't mean I pursued them with the intent to make them my friends. Or to find out about their lives.

Judy raised her eyebrows at me. "Really? You really like his art?"

"Sure," I said. "It's amazing work."

Our hamburgers arrived. I was grateful for the distraction as the waitress plunked down the plates and asked us if we wanted ketchup. Gayle said yes. The waitress got a bottle from the table behind her and put it on our table. "Enjoy," she said, and then she was on her way to another table.

We started eating. That felt better. Something for all of us to do besides talk about Claypot.

"He's not going to save your life," said Judy.

"What?"

"Clay. He's just a man with a lot of problems. He isn't some amazing god-like figure who can bring meaning to your existence. You need to get that out of your head right now. For your own good. And his."

"I don't know where you're getting that," I said. "I don't think I need someone to save me from anything."

"I see what you're saying," said Gayle to Judy.

"What?" I said. "You're agreeing with her?"

"Judy has a point," said Gayle. "Who else do you

know like Claypot?"

"No one."

"There's lots of people you could be spending your time with, but you choose Claypot. There must be a reason."

I didn't like where this was going. It was as though I was being psychoanalyzed by my own wife. It wouldn't have been the first time, but I still didn't like it.

"You liked when he defied authority by scratching up that ranger's truck," said Gayle.

"You enjoyed it too," I said, hoping I sounded helpful and not defensive.

"Not like you. You were into it. You liked having Claypot lead you to a mild rebellion."

I was about to protest some more, but I kept my mouth shut and thought about it. Was Claypot my guru of dissent? Did I live vicariously through him?

"Okay," I said. "You might have a point."

Judy raised her eyebrows. "You folded like a house of cards," she said.

"When you're right, you're right."

"Here's the thing," said Gayle. "Claypot is a very compelling person. He has energy and a devil-may-care attitude that is very seductive. But it's all a façade. He is not genuinely like that." She looked to Judy for confirmation, who nodded in agreement.

"Very true," she said. "He was nothing like this when we were married. The very picture of decorum and conformity. Then, after Stacey died—"

She took a breath and let it out slowly.

"He changed?" I said, instantly regretting saying something so transparent and stupid.

"He became an artist," said Judy. "One of the worst things that can happen to anyone. Being artistic makes you strange. You lose touch with your humanity."

"But you said he did art before that," I said.

"Yeah, he did art. But he wasn't an artist."

I didn't know what she meant. "What's the difference?" I said.

"Before the accident he made images for the fun of it. After the accident, he wanted to understand a part of his world through his images. In fact, he wanted to *change* the world. He was an artist. At first I hardly noticed it, but after a while I couldn't miss it. He preferred spending time with his chalk and sidewalks than he did with people. Any people, but especially me. I felt like he was blaming me for what happened to Stacey."

"That must have been hard," said Gayle.

"The worst. Partly because I was already blaming myself, so him chiming in with the blame didn't help."

"You were both in a terrible place," I said.

"I don't want to blame anyone or anything. I still love him. I still want him to be well. I want to live with him again but at the same time I'm not even sure I should be doing this, taking care of him after he vandalizes government property. Maybe I should go and you two can stay. You can have my room. It might be better, seeing as how you—" she nodded at me "—idolize him so much anyway."

Judy looked at me. I wanted to say that Claypot was only an interesting person, not someone I idolized or wanted to idolize, but I couldn't because I wasn't sure it was true. Gayle wasn't helping any. I felt like she was on Judy's side against me. Which was also ridiculous and a further indication that I didn't know what I was talking about.

"I'm sure it would be great for Clay if Chris was here tomorrow, but he doesn't really want Chris. He wants you, Judy."

Judy's face flushed. "Oh," she said. "That's strange. When you said that I felt this chill go through me, like it's true and I'm sorry that it's true. Has that ever happened to you?"

Gayle nodded. "I think it's a very natural reaction," she said.

As the meal wound down and we thought about ordering something for dessert, I saw it was getting dark outside. We still had to drive back home. Spending the night here looked like a more viable option by the minute. Gayle must have had the same idea. "Why *don't* we get a room?" she said. "We can get up early and leave with the rising sun."

I didn't see the advantage. We would still have to get to work in the morning, only we would be tired from driving and getting up early. "We should probably use the next couple of hours to get home," I said.

"I don't want to desert Judy," said Gayle. She glanced at Judy, who didn't say anything.

"I know," I said, "but we'd be deserting her anyway. We'd have to be long gone by the time the jail opens. She'd still be alone here when Claypot gets out."

"Don't worry about me," said Judy. "I used to live here, remember? It's not like this is a strange and dangerous town out on the frontier somewhere."

"I've got an idea," said Gayle.

"Yes?" I said.

"Why don't *you* go? I'll stay the night here with Judy. Work is more important to you anyway."

That was no solution. More like an excuse, although I wasn't quite sure what it would be an excuse for.

"You have a boss, just like me. Isn't he going to be pissed?"

"I'll tell him I'm still sick. Judy and I could have a girl's night. It'll be fun."

Judy nodded. "Sure," she said. "I'd be fine with that."

"There you go," Gayle said to me. "What are you frowning about?"

I was frowning? I had not realized. It wasn't that I begrudged Gayle anything. If she wanted to stay here and meet Claypot when he got out, what was that to me? It was more that she would be spending time with Claypot when I would be back home, alone. It felt like I would miss something big.

"I don't want you two to get into a fight over this," said Judy. "You should both go, like you planned. I can handle Clay on my own."

Of course she could. I knew it and Gayle knew it. That wasn't the point. I wanted to meet Clay when he got his freedom back. I wanted to see him in the morning.

"You know what?" I said. "I think I'll do exactly the same thing. Let's get ourselves a room.

WE SPENT THE evening in Judy's room playing cards, a perfect way to pass the time. I thought mostly of Claypot, and I was pretty sure Judy and Gayle did the same. How could we not? Along about 10 o'clock, after we had played half a dozen hands of Hearts, I mentioned it might be time to retire for the night. Judy got a scared look in her eyes. She asked us to stay.

"Of course," said Gayle. "Let's play more cards."

I took out a package of popcorn from the cupboard and put it into the microwave. It started popping a couple of minutes later. I put the package, now inflated like a paper pillow, on the table for us all to dig into.

"It's not that I'm sacred," said Judy.

"Of course not," said Gayle.

"No," I said. "We know that."

"It's more a case of me not wanting to be alone."

"Right," I said.

"I'm perfectly fine."

"Exactly," said Gayle.

# *Alienate Everyone Around You*

WE WOKE UP the next morning before dawn. Not because we couldn't sleep anymore, but because we heard noises outside the motel window. I looked at the clock on the night stand: 5 a.m. I pulled back the curtain and looked outside. A van from one of the television stations in Portland was parked in the motel lot and a couple of guys were busy raising the collapsible antenna.

"Huh," I said to Gayle, who stirred in the bed. "Looks like something's going on here."

It didn't occur to me until a few moments later that what was going on probably had something to do with Claypot.

"What?" said Gayle.

"A television crew is here."

"Television crew? They're a long way from Portland."

"I think they smell a story about Claypot."

I heard a knock on the door.

"Don't answer," said Gayle. "Let's get dressed and find Judy."

"I'll call her." I picked up the phone and dialed her room number.

A harder knock on the door. "Hey," came Judy's muffled voice. "Let me in you guys."

"Oh, hell," said Gayle. She opened the door. Judy came inside. The television crew hardly noticed us.

"They're here for Clay," she said. "I didn't even know they were interested in him, but they must have found out about his work around town and now he's a human interest story. I can't believe this. It's crazy."

"It's probably not a big deal," said Gayle.

"I'll talk to them," I said. "I'll tell them to leave us alone. This is a private matter."

They both looked at me.

"What?"

"They won't go away because you tell them to," said Judy. "They've already invested time and money by sending a vehicle and people here. They're going to get a story out of the investment."

I never claimed to be media savvy.

"So what do we do?" I said.

"We have to talk to them on their terms," said Gayle.

"I don't know," said Judy. "I'm afraid of how Clay might react to media attention. You know he does all his work in secret."

"I know what you're saying," said Gayle, "but how secret can it be if he does his drawings on public sidewalks and on the sides of buildings?"

Judy had no answer for that.

"What if we all three went and talked to them," said Gayle. "We'd show that we were supportive of Clay and wanted to make things good for him. That would set the tone for whatever they end up doing. You can't make the media work for you if you don't play their game."

Judy looked skeptical. I was skeptical, too.

"What time is Clay's court appearance?" said Gayle.

"Ten o'clock," said Judy.

"Then let's be at the courthouse at a quarter to. We'll talk to the television people then."

It sounded like a plan, of sorts. I was still trying to understand why they would possibly be interested in Claypot. An unknown artist involved in a stupid vandalism incident. But I suppose he was an exotic personality and television likes exotic.

"You think they've done other reports on him?" I asked.

Judy shrugged. "Maybe."

She seemed completely unsure of herself, like she was so scared she didn't know what to do. Gayle tried to reassure her, but it didn't help much.

"Let's go get some breakfast," I said.

"I don't think I could eat anything right now," said Judy.

Gayle wouldn't hear of it. "You need to eat," she said. "Come on."

We stepped out of the room into the parking lot. The crew looked at us like they wanted to pounce. I avoided eye contact and we hurried through the lot to the restaurant we had been to the day before. The TV people looked like they wanted to stop us, but we kept going and they lost interest. I figured they thought they could get to us later.

"There, that wasn't so bad," I said as we approached the restaurant. A few early morning diners sat in a couple of the booths and on stools at the counter. Locals, I imagined, getting their morning coffee. We entered and took a table near the window, the better to watch for the television people. They looked like they were all set up and ready to go. They stood with cups and donuts in their hands. A waitress, different from the one last night, came and took our orders. I looked through the window again.

"Doesn't it seem strange that they set up in the motel parking lot?" I said. "The courthouse is a couple of blocks from there."

"They probably couldn't find a good place to park there," said Judy.

"Maybe it's about communication lines," said Gayle. "Power outlets. Or something."

"They sure weren't interested in us as we walked by," I said.

Judy and Gayle both looked through the window with me. "What are you saying?" said Gayle.

"They're supposed to be here for a story and they don't seem to be pursuing it very hard."

The waitress came back with our orders. She noticed we were watching the television van.

"Oh there they are again," she said as she put down our plates.

"Again?" said Gayle.

"Whenever we have a fire."

"A fire?" I said.

"Sure, haven't you heard? You can see the smoke, from here." She pointed across the restaurant to another window. Sure enough, a plume of smoke, barely illuminated in the still dim morning lights, rose from the horizon and spread across the sky. How had we not noticed that?

"So the Channel 2 people are here for the fire?" said Judy.

The waitress nodded. "The fire crews are staying at the motel between their shifts. Channel 2 likes to come and interview them. They'll be in here soon for breakfast before going back out to the fire."

"Oh," said Gayle. She looked chagrined. The waitress left us to our breakfasts.

"Well," said Judy.

"I guess we were full of ourselves," I said.

"That does look like a big fire," said Gayle.

"Amazing that we thought the Portland media would follow Clay all the way out here," said Judy. "Are we so wrapped up in him that we can't see the rest of the world?"

We finished our breakfasts and took a walk around town. The smoke from the fire had spread out over the sky, turning it from blue to a chalky hazy.

"Thank you both for staying over," said Judy. "It helped knowing you were right next door."

"No problem," said Gayle.

Judy still seemed very nervous. I wasn't sure why. Didn't she want to get Claypot out of jail?

We passed by the television crew. They were talking

to some of the people that were on their way to fight the fire.

We wandered around town a little more, like we didn't want to go find Claypot at all. We ended up at the door a full fifteen minutes before it opened. We waited.

A deputy unlocked the door. We went inside. Judy pulled out her credit card and presented it to the clerk.

"I want to post bail for Mr. Dreamstance," she said.

The clerk took the card. "Dreamstance, did you say?"

"Yes, that's right."

"Let me look."

Judy turned around and half smiled at us. "They always think it's a fake name, but it isn't."

I nodded.

"Okay," said the clerk. "Sign here." He pushed a form through the hole in the lucite window. Judy signed her name and pushed it back. The clerk looked at it, then ran Judy's credit card through her little machine. "He'll be out in a few minutes. You can have a seat if you want." She indicated the chairs across the waiting room. We all sat.

"It's always the same," said Judy.

"What's the same?" said Gayle.

"These kinds of places all feel the same. The depressing little waiting rooms. The fake friendly people that work here. They're all numbed by the tasks they have to do all day."

I didn't say anything. Truth is, by that time I was tired of it all. Waiting can be more fatiguing than hard work.

We heard a noise. Doors opening and closing loudly. The clerk looked down the hall. Her eyes registered something. I felt tense. I stood up. Gayle looked at me like she wondered what I was up to. I sat down again. Then Judy stood. "What is it with you two?" said Gayle.

"Don't know," said Judy. "I'm just nervous."

Claypot appeared from around a corner. A deputy stood beside him.

Claypot looked at us and I tensed, expecting an expletive laden comment. None came.

Judy went over and took his arm. Claypot looked beaten down. He accepted Judy's touch without comment. The deputy glanced at me and Gayle, then addressed Claypot. "Let's not have you back here again, Mr. Dreamstance. Like we talked about, remember?"

Claypot nodded.

We left the office and stepped into the morning air. It felt good to be outside. It felt good to think that maybe Claypot had learned his lesson and was going to be on the straight and narrow now. I had never seen him so polite. It felt like a relief, but also oddly disheartening.

We got a couple of blocks down the road and Claypot stopped. "Now what the *fuck* are all of you freaks doing here? You think I needed you to help me out? Is that it? You think I'm helpless without you bleeding heart assholes here to make my life better?"

"Clay," said Judy. "They stayed to keep me company."

"You don't need them anymore. You've got me to keep you company." He raised his hand and made little up and down motions with the tips of his fingers. "Bye bye now," he said in a child like voice. Then he turned back to Judy. "Where's the car?" he said. "I have to get away from these assholes. They got me into fucking jail for fuck sakes."

What? *We* got him into jail?

He saw my surprise.

"Yeah, fucknuts. You got me into jail following me to that church. I was minding my own fucking business having a talk with god and you drag the law into it."

"We didn't call the sheriff," I said.

"Bullshit," said Claypot.

"It's true," said Gayle. "We didn't. Some guys in town heard you."

Claypot glared at us. "I don't have time to argue with you," he said. "Judy, let's go home. Where the fuck is the car?"

Judy pointed to the motel and Claypot began walking that way. Judy looked at us both. "I'm sorry," she said, then followed Claypot.

Gayle and I stood on the sidewalk in mildly stunned silence. "Go try and help people," she said.

# *Avoid All Do-it-Yourself Projects*

I ASSUMED THAT Judy and Claypot got back together after that. I lost touch with both of them. He obviously wasn't interested in remaining friends with me or Gayle. After an initial disappointment I let it stand at that. I was tired of the drama and happy to get back to my own sane, humdrum life.

Funny thing, he did end up on Channel 2 after all. I caught a segment they did on local eccentrics. They didn't call it that, but that's what it was. They opened with shots of some of his trompe l'oeil. The voice over asked who was the extraordinary artist who had done the work. Then they cut to Claypot, standing next to a building with a smooth concrete surface, chalk poised in his hand. He looked directly into the camera and turned on the charm like it was his natural way of being. A TV reporter stood next to him with a microphone. She asked him why he did public art. He told her he was working on one big picture. It was to be a giant trompe l'oeil, the biggest he had ever done, maybe the biggest anyone has ever done. He had it all planned out in his mind and only had to find a suitable building to place it.

"Will it be here in the city?" she asked Claypot.

He looked at her like she was an infant. "Yeah," said Claypot. "This is where I live. Yeah, here in the city."

The reporter was completely unfazed.

"That's wonderful," she said. "I only hope the owners don't put you in jail!"

And again, a restrained response from Claypot. "I hope so too," he said, "but you know, most people like my pictures so I'm not too worried about it."

"I have to ask," said the reporter, "why you have chosen to live homelessly."

Yes, she said "homelessly." The image flickered and jumped, like they edited out part of the tape, then Claypot looked real thoughtful. He stared into his chalk like he wanted it to smile at him.

"There's no such thing as being homeless," he said. "Wherever you live, that's your home. I'm houseless, but that's not the same thing. I think of the world as my home."

"But even artists need a place to do their art," she said. "They need a studio. They need someplace to store their work."

"I don't have that problem," said Claypot. "I do my work outdoors."

"So then that means you live outdoors as well. Sounds like a perfect solution! Thank you Mr. Dreamstance."

Then she signed off and they went on to another artist.

I could hardly imagine a more painful experience for Claypot than to stand and talk with such a vacuous person. Seeing him on television did bring a smile to my lips. I found him completely endearing, especially his hesitancy in the face of questions he clearly did not want to answer. I wondered what made him agree to the interview in the first place. The talk of homelessness also made me realize he was probably not with Judy after all. That made me sad, something I did not expect. I had hoped they had found a way to get back together.

But why was that important to me? It certainly wouldn't have been a good thing for Judy. Claypot was much too difficult a person to live with on a permanent basis. Judy had already realized that long ago. It was what pulled them apart in the first place. Until he came to terms with Stacey's death, that wouldn't change.

Not that I had any idea what coming to terms with something like that meant.

I'm not even sure it would have been a good thing for Claypot. Living with Judy might not have made him a better person, which, I realized as I thought about it, was the reason I thought they might be good together in the first place.

But their lives were their lives. Nothing I wanted or did not want in relation to them had any bearing on anything.

So I chalked up the television appearance to serendipity and assumed that was the end of that.

Something about Claypot stuck in my head, though. As I went to work that morning I saw opportunities for trompe l'oeil pictures everywhere. On traffic signs, walls, pedestrian overpasses, even people. I imagined tattoos on a person's back that depicted the bones and organs underneath. A strange sensation. I looked at the world with Claypot's eyes and Claypot's attitude.

At work my cubicle wall became a canvas for looking through. I had half a mind to go down to the art supply store and get some paints and draw what I saw on the other side of the wall. It wouldn't have been the next desk over, either. It would have been something more exotic. A landscape of some magnificent island.

Oh boy.

This was not like me, not at all. I needed to shake Claypot's influence. He had a dangerous mind, always unsatisfied with the way things were. Could there be a more efficient way to make your life miserable? I didn't need to have a miserable life.

Here's something else I noticed: People didn't want to be around me. Not that I was ever gregarious. But lately, it was as though me and others had a mutual agreement to stay away from each other. It was the oddest thing. No one looked me in the eye and I was glad for that. I was turning in on myself.

Gayle asked me what was going on. I said nothing. She didn't pursue it, but I could tell she was worried.

All I wanted to do was be friends with Claypot.

I came to that realization, even though it was the last thing I wanted to happen to me. How could I *want* to hang around with such a volatile and unstable person? Who was more crazy, him or me?

After work I went to Forest Park, a large expanse of green space in the middle of the city. Portlanders are proud of it and defend it fiercely, defeating all attempts to develop it that have come down over the years. Many trails snake through it and you only have to go down one of the trails for five minutes before you have left streets and buildings behind and you find yourself surrounded by trees and silence.

I had this idea that I would find Claypot's place of residence. A silly notion, but I thought if I held my nose out I'd smell where it was. Ridiculous, how we fool ourselves into nutty ideas sometimes. I walked about a mile down the trail, noting plenty of secondary trails branching off from the main one. Was Claypot's tent—or whatever he lived in—down one of these? Maybe. How would I ever know? It must have been very well hidden, otherwise the city would surely have kicked him out by now. The park was not meant for camping of any kind, much less any overnight stay.

I stopped. I still wore my work clothes. Stupid. The trail was groomed, but there were a few muddy spots and now my shoes were getting more or less ruined with the wet slop.

I loosened my tie and kept walking. My quest, if that's what it was, had become a mini obsession. I tried to think the way a tracker might. What clues should I look for to help me find Claypot Dreamstance?

I don't know how long I was on the trail. It felt like half an hour or so, but it could have been longer or shorter. In any case my cell phone rang.

I thought Gayle must be worrying about me. I had left a message that I was going to be late, but maybe she didn't get it.

I looked at the phone and it wasn't Gayle. I didn't

recognize the number in the display.

I flipped the phone open. "Hello?"

"You keep wandering around like that and you're going to get hurt." Claypot's voice.

"How do you know where I am?" I said.

"Me and the park are as one. Or something. Go back about two hundred feet. You'll see a garbage can. Go into the woods there and keep going. You'll think I'm a crazy motherfucker for sending you into such thick brush, but eventually you'll find me. Just persevere. Think you can do that?"

"Sure," I said. He hung up without a goodbye.

Typical Claypot. I did as he instructed. The vegetation at the garbage can was indeed much thicker than I would have thought would allow a path. But I plunged in, ignored the scratches on my arms and legs from the branches, and pushed away foliage as I went. It seemed like I went through some pretty thick growth for quite a while, then it thinned out a little and I found I was on the bank of a creek. The trail went upstream a short distance where I saw a flicker of motion in the trees. I stopped and looked carefully. Claypot waved at me. I waved back and kept walking. I reached him a couple of minutes later. He stood next to a small tent. He had a crooked smile and a relaxed demeanor.

"You've hidden yourself pretty good," I said.

"All the better to keep the world away," he said. "You want some coffee?"

"Coffee would be nice."

He motioned for me to go around to the other side of the tent. He had a kerosene stove set up on a milk crate. Also some dishes and assorted eating utensils in a tray. He took a pot from the stove and poured me a cup of coffee. I took it and sipped. It was not bad. I looked around.

"You're pretty secluded here."

"That's the way I like it. It's illegal to be living here, but they haven't found me yet."

I nodded. Now that I had found him, I had no idea what I wanted to talk to him about.

"You're using a cell phone?"

"Yeah. I found it a couple of days ago."

"How'd you get my number?"

"From Judy. From when you were stalking me."

I nodded. "Not afraid of cancer?" I said.

"I smoke, remember?"

He poured some coffee himself and pulled up a stump and sat down. I looked around behind me and found another stump and dragged it over next to him. We sat holding our cups. The sun was sinking in the sky.

"It's getting colder every night," he said.

"You going to stay out here all winter?" I said.

"I did last winter. It wasn't so bad. On the really cold nights I went into town and stayed at one of the shelters. It was ugly, let me tell you. They herd you around like you're livestock. Lot of stinky people stay at those shelters. It's hard on a person, the smells."

"I saw you on TV."

"So what?"

There was the Claypot I remembered. "You looked real good."

"The reporter was a fucking asshole."

I nodded and smiled. "No doubt," I said.

"Seriously. She didn't know fuck about what I was doing. A complete fucking idiot."

"What happened to you and Judy?"

"Me and Judy? What the fuck are you talking about, 'you and Judy?'"

"Last time I saw the two of you, it seemed like you were together again."

"Jesus fucking Christ," said Claypot. "You're more of a moron than the reporter. Judy bailed me out. That's it. End of story."

I tried to remember why I wanted to find him.

"You think," said Claypot, "that someone bails you out of jail, then you and that someone are bosom buddies? Have you always been this stupid, or did you have to work at it?"

"Christ, Clay," I said. "Do you always have to be such a fucking jerk?"

Claypot Dreamstance looked at me and smiled. Then he clapped a hand on my back and pulled me towards him. "I'm so proud of you," he said. "You actually said 'fucking.' I tell you, it brings tears to my goddam eyes."

He was annoying me more than I had ever been annoyed by anyone else. Ever. I shrugged him off. He leaned back and held up his hands so his palms faced me.

"Oops," he said. "Sorr*eeee*. Didn't mean to fucking *offend*."

I don't know how to explain what I said next, except that I somehow dipped into a reservoir of anger I hardly knew I possessed. Claypot brought it out in me, though I had no excuse for the cruelty in what I said.

"You know, mother*fucker*," I said, "your daughter is never fucking coming back because she's fucking *dead*."

More fucks than I had ever said in one sentence in my life.

Claypot smiled at me, but it was a smile from somewhere else, like he had taken it from another person's face and put it on his own.

"You enjoy saying that?" he asked in a completely calm and sedate voice, which gave me chills up my arms and across my back. My ears felt hot. Sweat popped out on my face.

"I asked you a question, fuckhead," he said.

I had never seen red before, but I was seeing it then. I stood up and backed away from him. I wanted to hit him and didn't know exactly why. He was obviously in pain, his life was filled with pain. Who was I to add to it?

But I still wanted to hit him.

Which would have been a mistake on many levels, maybe not the least of them that he was bigger than me and would probably have had no hesitation in pummeling me to a bloody mess. If I had anger in me, he must have ten times as much, at least.

I backed up and caught my foot on a stump. I fell over backward. I was so filled with adrenaline that I hardly felt the fall. I could have broken both legs and an arm and I don't think I would have felt it.

He stepped close to me, loomed over me, still holding his cup of coffee. For a moment I thought he might pour it on my face.

Instead, he carefully set the cup down and extended

his hand and held it in front of me, waiting.

I grabbed it and he pulled me up off the ground until I was standing again.

"You don't know how to do this," he said. "You shouldn't try."

I had a sour taste in my mouth. I thought about looking for a place to throw up. I sat down on the stump.

"Do what?" I said.

"The anger thing," said Claypot. "You don't know how. It takes some skill."

I swayed like a tree in the wind.

"I wasn't always like this," he said. "It took work. And by the way, don't ever mention Stacey again. Ever."

"Okay," I said.

"And as for Judy, she's the finest person on the planet. She doesn't deserve to be burdened with me."

"I think she wants to be burdened with you."

Claypot shook his head. "That's her sense of duty speaking. I know better. If I ever get back to who I was, then maybe I would be worthy of her. But not before."

I saw his point, but I still thought he was going about his life backwards. Or upside down. Something.

He was also right about me. I didn't know how to do anger. It scared me.

"Enough of this shit," said Claypot. "Let's go scouting."

I looked up at him from my seated position. "Scouting?"

He grabbed my cup and tossed its contents to the ground. Then he took my hand and pulled me up. I reluctantly allowed myself to stand.

"I'm looking for a place to do my last big picture."

"What?"

"Follow me."

He turned and went back the way I had come, through the thick brush. We ended up on the trail pretty quickly—he plowed through the bushes with no effort at all. I followed along in his wake. We got out on the trail and began walking back toward the city.

"What are you talking about, last big picture?" I said.

"I'm about done with trompe l'oeil," he said. "I've got to the point where I feel like there's nothing left to accomplish."

"Okay," I said.

"So I need to do one more big picture, my farewell to the medium."

"So you want me to help you?"

He laughed like I was too funny for words. "Yeah," he said. "You nailed it exactly. I need you to help me."

I wasn't insulted, which is what might have happened before. Instead, I was flattered that he was willing to tease me about my insecurities.

"See," he said, "the thing is, I need a large flat surface. You know of one?"

I didn't answer right away.

"You think about it," he said, "and get back to me, okay?"

"Okay."

"In the meantime, what the fuck are you doing looking for me? I thought I disgusted you so much that you couldn't stand me. Weak stomach and all."

"That's funny," I said, "because I thought you were

done with me."

He laughed uproariously. "You are such a dumb shit. You don't even know how insignificant you are. I never had enough to do with you in the first place that I would now be 'done with' you."

I wasn't sure I knew what he meant by that, but I did know it was not an attempt to flatter me.

"Don't get me wrong," he said. "It's not like I think I'm any better. Everyone is insignificant, get it? We're all minor players in the drama of life. That's what makes us heroic. We make our own destinies."

"I'm not heroic," I said.

"That's because you don't think you're heroic. It's all in the attitude."

"Okay," I said, now completely confused by him.

"You know I have to do community service in Goldendale."

"No," I said. "I didn't know that."

"A hundred hours. For scratching a church door. Now isn't that crazy? God doesn't care if his door looks a little used."

There was more to it than a little scratch, but I didn't challenge Claypot on the issue.

"Are you going to do it?"

"Hell no," said Claypot. "They want me, they're going to have to come get me."

"They know where you are," I said.

"Why, did you tell them about my little hideout in the park?"

"No, but you were on TV. Everyone knows you can be found on the street."

We were in the heart of downtown. He slowed his

pace. "Now keep your eye peeled," he said. "I've looked at all these buildings for so long I don't have an objective eye anymore. But you can probably see things I don't. A large flat space. Someplace to make a *big* trompe l'oeil. My last big hurrah. My swan song. My farewell to the world—"

He looked at me. I thought he was finished. I thought he was telling me he wanted to kill himself. I felt immediately like I needed to save him. I was sad and filled with adrenaline all at the same time. Then he dropped the end of the sentence on me.

"—of art."

Of art?

"Had you going there for a second, didn't I?" he said.

"Kind of," I said.

"Suicide is for losers," he said. "You think I'm a loser?"

"No."

"So why'd you think I might kill myself?"

"You orchestrated your sentence in such a way to make me think that." I was aware I sounded like a stuffy professor.

"Orchestrated. That's good. I like that."

"I'm glad," I said.

"Any ideas yet?"

"About what?"

"My surface, you putz. My last hurrah, remember? You're supposed to be looking for a big flat surface." He knocked on the top of his head several times. "Hello?" he said. "Anyone home."

I looked around. I stopped. Claypot stopped with

me. His breath puffed against my ear. I had the urge to step away from him, but didn't. I thought it would be insulting to him and I didn't want to make him feel like he was disgusting. I looked across the intersection to an empty lot. On the other side of the lot stood an old building, all brick façade. The bricks had been painted a long time ago. Parts of an old advertisement extolling the virtues of a long defunct hardware store covered one corner with fading color. I thought that if he could paint over some of those words, this wall, this edifice of brick, would be a perfect place for a large trompe l'oeil.

"Right there," I said.

Claypot looked at it. "It would take some work to make it suitable."

"I know," I said.

"But you think this is the place?"

"I could help you with the preparation."

Claypot stepped back. He studied the wall for a minute or so. "It's got good visibility here," he said.

"Yup."

"Okay."

"Okay?"

"Yeah. You convinced me. I'll start tomorrow. Be here at dusk. We've got a lot of work to do."

I should have said no. I should have told him he was on his own. I should have stepped away, rapidly.

"I'll be here," I said.

*Never Make a
Space Just for Yourself*

GAYLE CAME WITH me the next day. We arrived soon after work. The sky threatened rain, but that didn't bother us. Claypot wasn't there yet.

"This is the wall you're talking about?" said Gayle.

"Yeah," I said. "Let's go look at it while we're waiting."

We walked across the empty lot. It was mostly sand, a few weeds, some broken glass. We avoided the glass. I kicked through some of the weeds. I had on jeans and running shoes this time. Gayle wore some old clothes too. She stood at the wall. It towered over her. Claypot would need a lot of chalk to cover this wall, if that's what he had in mind.

Gayle put her hand on the wall, molding her palm to the bricks. "Does the owner know he wants to do this?" she said.

"I doubt it," I said. "That's not the way he works."

"He can't just swoop in and finish this thing in a couple of hours then swoop away. It's going to take a week, at least. Maybe more. He's going to have to be in good graces with whoever owns this wall."

She had a point. "Maybe he's going to look it over tonight, then approach the owner for permission."

"Where is he, anyway? It's not like him to miss an appointment."

"I know," I said. "I'm getting a little worried. Maybe I should call him."

"Call him? He has a phone?"

"Yeah, he called me yesterday when I was looking for him. He had a cell phone."

"He said cell phones were cancer machines."

"Try to figure Claypot," I said. "It's impossible." I flipped my phone open and called Claypot's number. I got a recording.

"This is Claypot Dreamstance. I found this fucking phone, but it's mine now until the brain dead fucknuts who lost it figures it out and turns off the cocksucking service. Leave a goddam message if you fucking have to, otherwise leave me the fuck alone."

Charming, as always. "Clay," I said. "It's Chris. Where are you? We're waiting."

I flipped the phone closed and turned to Gayle. Judy came walking across the lot.

"Hey you two," she said. She hugged us in turn.

"Nice to see you," I said.

"How are you?" said Gayle.

"Can't complain. Where's Clay?"

"I was going to ask you," I said.

"He called me this morning. Told me he wanted me here when he started his masterpiece."

"I'm getting worried," I said.

Judy went to the wall. "I can see why he likes this so much," she said. "It's rough. It'll be challenge for him. He'll also have to put up some scaffolding. Or at the least use a ladder. That isn't usually his way. He's always been a minimalist as far as equipment goes. Some chalk and that's it."

Gayle wrapped her jacket more tightly around her shoulders. "It's getting cold," she said. "I'm going to go wait in the car until he gets here." She began walking back to the street where we had parked.

"I'll go with you," said Judy. "Come on," she said to me.

"What about Clay?" I said.

"We'll see him when he comes."

Judy and Gayle were already halfway across the lot. I wanted to stay with the wall. I had this feeling I should understand the wall, get to know it, the better to assist Claypot on his project. But I didn't want to be there alone.

I hurried to catch up to Gayle and Judy.

They got to the car and went inside, Gayle in the driver's seat, Judy in the passenger side. I got into the back. We shivered with cold. Our breaths filled the car quickly.

"I thought you and Clay were leading separate lives now," I said.

"We are. He lives in his park, I live at home. He doesn't want to contaminate me. His words."

"Chris says he's got a nice set up at the park," said

Gayle.

"I haven't been. I've wanted to visit, bring him food. But he won't tell me where it is."

"I'll take you there," I said.

"Oh, that would be nice."

"Why isn't he here yet?"

"Maybe he's playing some game," I said. "Maybe we're the art. Some kind of weird performance piece where he gets us all together."

"That's not his style," said Judy.

"No," said Gayle. "That's right."

"Then what?" I said. "It's not like he has a full appointment book. He was very interested in doing this. He told me last night. He was very clear about me being here to help him."

Judy shrugged. "I don't know," she said.

"What happened after Goldendale?" said Gayle.

"I took him home," said Judy. "I wanted us to be a couple again. I wanted him in my house. I had this crazy idea that being in jail, even for as short a time as he was, would make him see that he belonged with me. Ha! That was a joke. He kept going on about how decadent I was, how I was cluttering up my life with a lot of shit. Yeah, shit like furniture, cooking utensils, clothing, etcetera. It's not like I'm extravagant or rich. Sometimes he gets on my nerves, you know."

Gayle and I both nodded.

"Anyway, it was clear he still had incredible issues. He kept saying Stacey wouldn't need any of this. All she needed was love. Our love."

"Wow," said Gayle.

"Yeah. It's not fair of him to bring up Stacey. She has

nothing to do with how we have to live our lives now."

"So how long did he stay?"

"Not even the night. He slept on the couch in the living room. I got up in the middle of night to pee and I went in and checked on him. He was gone. Slipped out like a creature of the night."

"Without even a note or anything?" said Gayle.

"Nothing. I wasn't worried about him. I knew he didn't get kidnapped or anything, of course. It was just Clay being Clay. Later he left a message on the phone. Said thanks for my hospitality. Apologized for criticizing me. Said it was his problem, that he couldn't stand having luxuries when Stacey was still struggling. It was weird. But at least I knew he was okay."

I wondered what it took for someone to finally break bonds with someone who was no good for them. When would Judy finally release Claypot to the wild? She couldn't keep trying to reconnect with him indefinitely, could she? On the other hand, I was no better.

"Where is he now?" I asked.

"Maybe he decided this wasn't the venue he thought it was going to be," said Judy.

Gayle looked up at the wall. "Oh no," she said and pointed to the roof.

I looked up. Claypot stood on the edge of the roof. He waved at us. We got out of the car and approached the wall. "Your lives are still so pathetic," he shouted, "that you have to come watch some homeless guy deface a brick wall?"

"Clay," said Judy. "What are you doing? How did you get up there?"

"Defied gravity," said Claypot. "You should try it.

You should all come up here. It's quite a view."

I was game. "How?" I said.

"Through the building. Climb the stairs. At the top there's a door to the roof."

"Did the owner let you up?" said Judy.

"No way," said Claypot. "I had to break it open."

"Jesus," said Judy. "Is there something wrong with you?"

"Not something. A lot of things. Haven't you noticed?"

"What should we do?" said Gayle to Judy, quietly so Claypot couldn't hear.

"Stop whispering about me," said Claypot in as cheerful a voice as I had ever heard him use.

"We're not whispering," said Judy.

"Sure you are," said Claypot. "Hey, just so you know, I set off an alarm when I went through the door. Some people are so paranoid. Guess the owner will be here soon. Or the police. If you want to get a look at the view, you better come up soon."

We heard the sound of a siren approach from blocks away.

"Oh no," said Judy.

I cupped my hands over my mouth and shouted up to Claypot. "Run!"

Claypot put his hands up to his ears and leaned toward the sound of the sirens. "Oh, that," he said. "They don't bother me."

"You won't be able to finish your picture," I said. "Or even start it."

"I've got it all right here," he said, and pulled out a pice of paper from his pocket. He unfolded it and held it up in the air. I saw there was a drawing on it, in pencil, but I couldn't tell what it was. A plan for the wall? But Claypot never made plans like that. At least I never saw any and he never mentioned any.

"Come down," I said. "The police are going to arrest you."

"Let 'em try," he said. "They'll never take me alive."

"Is he serious?" Gayle asked Judy.

"I've never seen him like this," said Judy.

The sirens were getting very close. Obviously he had no time to get away. He balled up the drawing and threw it down to us. He had a grin as wide as a bridge. The drawing rolled across the lot and came to a stop at our feet. I uncrumpled it and smoothed it out as best I could.

The image was so blurred and wrinkled that at first I couldn't quite see what it was. Judy and Gayle both looked over my shoulder at it. Judy gasped. I looked more carefully and discerned a face. A young girl's face, lost in a sea of waves, floating.

"Stacey," said Judy.

"He wanted to show her coming out of the wall," said Gayle.

"My last picture," shouted Claypot. "What do you think of it?"

"It's fantastic," I said. "Now come down off the roof so you can paint it."

"Okay," said Claypot.

Claypot stood only a step from the edge of the roof. He took two steps forward.

All my life I've heard people say they couldn't believe their eyes about something or other. As I watched Claypot fall from the roof, I finally understood what that meant. He started three stories up and it took him a long time, something on the order of days, to reach the ground. During that time Judy brought her hand to her mouth and screamed. Gayle shook her head and turned from Claypot and looked at me, as if saying "I knew he would do something like this eventually."

I knew it too, I suppose, but tried to convince myself that he was not self-destructive. He was only eccentric in perfectly harmless ways. I dropped the pencil drawing to the sand and ran towards the wall. I wanted to be there at the bottom when he arrived. But even though he descended slower than lava oozing down a mountain, he landed while I was still running. I heard a thump. He landed on his legs and somehow had the presence of mind and the agility—completely unexpected—to roll. To actually do something to help himself. When I got to his side he groaned.

"Don't move," I said. "What the fuck did you do that for?" I don't know what I was thinking asking him a question at that moment. But he answered me.

"When I'm on the roof I'm just a vandal. Down here, like this, I'm an injured man. They have to take care of me. I'll get my own warm room where they will look after my every need. Isn't that cool?"

Was this Claypot logic?

The police car stopped at the curb. Two officers got out and ran toward me.

"An ambulance!" I shouted.

Claypot grinned. Then laughed. "This fucking hurts like you wouldn't fucking believe," he said.

I stood up. "The man needs an ambulance," I shouted. "An ambulance."

# *Never Replace Any of Your Old and Shabby Belongings*

AS IT TURNED out, Claypot did not need hospitalization. At the emergency room they treated him for sprained ankles and a broken rib and some cuts. He was lucky he landed in some dirt, not pavement. He needed to spend a few days off his feet and went to stay at Judy's place for his recovery. I went to visit him. He was not pleased to see me. Told me to go fuck myself. Judy asked me to get him some new clothes, so later that day Gayle and I were at the Goodwill store looking for clothes for Claypot.

"How's this?" I said, holding up a Hawaiian shirt.

"Not his style," said Gayle.

"He has a style?"

"Of course. Everyone has a style."

"I always thought his style was that he would take anything he found or someone gave him or he scrounged for himself. Also, anything that he had already owned for at least two decades. That was his style. Ultra grunge. He makes grunge look chic. He makes squalor look inviting."

"Are you done?" she said.

"Um. Yeah. I think so."

"Claypot would never wear anything with such loud colors. You're his best friend. You should know that."

"I'm his best friend?" I said. The proposition sounded ludicrous. Claypot didn't have any friends, let alone a best friend. He had people he used and abused. He had people he mooched off of. He even had people who had made an emotional attachment to *him*, but he certainly didn't have any friends. Did he?

"Of course you're his best friend. Didn't you run up to him and try to help him after his fall?"

"A lot of good I did."

"I'm not saying you're his savior. I'm saying you're his friend. You care about him."

I did care about him. I had no idea why. Maybe it was because I liked artists. Or at least this artist. This crazy nut of a chalker. So maybe I was the sick one, trying to understand him and establish some kind of meaningful relationship with him. That had to be the dumbest and sickest of all impulses. The closer I got to him the more likely I was to become like him.

Gayle pulled out a button down shirt, grey with black pinstripes. "This is much better," she said.

I checked the front of the shirt. "It looks okay," I said, "but there's no pocket. Where will he drop his ashes?"

"He doesn't need to carry around an ashtray with him. What he needs is to stop smoking."

"Yeah," I said, "good luck getting that to happen."

The sound of glass breaking erupted from the back of the store, where they kept all the household items. Then some very loud crying. More clattering and some shouting. A couple of store employees in blue uniforms hurried to the source of the sounds.

"I hope no one's hurt," said Gayle.

More clattering. More breaking things. It sounded like someone was deliberately destroying things. I was mildly interested, but not enough to investigate.

"Let's get out of here," I said.

She didn't agree, but she didn't disagree either. She hesitated, like she wanted to stay and see what was going on. Maybe the slight risk of danger attracted her? If so, it would be unlike her. Gayle was not one to take any unnecessary risks. Life was dangerous enough. Maybe Claypot's wild abandon was rubbing off on her?

"Let's go take a look," she said.

What would Claypot do?

"Okay," I said. We dropped the shirts and headed briskly to the back of the store where several customers had gathered around an aisle where two men, each looking to be about fifty, had squared off in front of each other, bent over, hands outstretched, each holding a broken glass in their hands. They glared at each other. I could hardly fathom what I was seeing. They were fighting with broken glass? Here in the Goodwill?

"Oh my," said Gayle. "This is awful."

"It's also dangerous. We should get out of here."

One of the men lunged forward with his glass shard held out in front of him. The other man stepped back and slapped the first man's wrist with his free hand. The first man yelped, then stepped back, and they both resumed their defensive crouches.

One of the employees, a small woman who looked barely ninety pounds, stepped out from the rest of the gathered audience. "Both of you stop this now," she said. Her voice had a lot more power to it than I would have expected. It made me pay attention. She did not have the same effect on the gladiators, however. They ignored her and kept their concentrated gazes on each other. I felt jazzed, like some of their toxic energy had leaked through the air and into my lungs and blood.

"Did you hear me?" screamed the woman.

"Lady," said the first man, "this is none of your business. You don't want to get hurt."

The second man chose that moment to make a lunge of his own. He leaned back on one foot, testing the spring of his tendons, then leaped forward. He let out a yell as he did so, going airborne for a split second, then he crashed against the first man, who did not know how to deflect such a frontal assault, and only managed to raise his hands to protect his face and chest. They both fell to the floor in a heap. Somewhere along the way they had both lost their weapons, which clattered to the floor. The men wrapped their arms around each other in grunting bear hugs and struggled, rolling in the aisle and slamming against the shelving. They knocked appliances to the floor. Some of the onlookers stepped back gingerly, not wanting to get bits and pieces of plastic and glass on them.

After half a minute or so of struggle, one of the men, the first one who lunged, managed to pin the second man onto the floor and held him by the wrists against the tiles.

The first man looked up at us all with a giant grin on his face.

Suddenly, from the other end of the aisle a large woman brandishing a cushion from one of the couches for sale at another corner of the store came running at the men from behind and swung the cushion full force at the head of the man on top. He looked more startled than beaten, but she swung the cushion again, nailed him square on the head again, and he fell over to the side and hit his head on the edge of a shelf.

"Get your hands off my husband," said the woman. Her voice dripped venom and she repeatedly hit the man with her cushion.

The pinned man scampered out from under the cushion-assaulted man and stood up. I thought he was going to attack the man now on the floor, but he did not. The man on the floor held his hand over his head. Blood seeped from between his fingers. It looked like the impact with the shelf caused more damage than I thought. He had a nasty cut on his head.

The woman and her husband backed away. He had his arms wrapped around her. Her eyes were wild with fear or rage, I couldn't tell exactly which. She had dropped the cushion. I didn't have the presence of mind to step forward and look after the injured man, but one of the store employees did.

"Call 911," she said as she bent down next to the man. No one moved. She looked up and pointed directly at me. "You sir. Call 911 now. Go." She pointed at someone else. "You, ma'am, go to the back of the store and get me the first aid kit. This man is bleeding."

Still no one moved. Including me. The woman shouted. "Go! Both of you, go NOW."

I pulled out my phone and fumbled with opening it. Gayle took it from my hand and placed the call.

"Yes," she said, "there's an injured man at the Goodwill on Burnside. Please send an ambulance. He is bleeding from his head."

As Gayle made the call I watched the couple. They stepped back quietly, then went around the corner of the aisle and moved toward the entrance. Before they could make it, two police officers had entered the store. The couple stopped cold and looked panicked. One of the officers went over to the couple and began to question them. The other officer went to the injured man.

I suddenly relaxed. The sight of police officers on the scene made everything okay again, despite the shambles the store had become.

A customer arrived with the first aid kit. The store employee opened it and pulled out bandages and began dressing the injured man's wound. The officer stood up and looked around at the gathered customers. "You sir," he said and pointed at me. "What happened here?" He flipped open a notebook and retrieved a pencil from inside his jacket. He held the pencil over the notebook. I glanced wildly at the couple. They too were being interviewed. I felt like I was in trouble, which was absurd. I didn't do anything. All I did was witness a fight. Or part of it.

I thought of Claypot, at home with Judy. He would have liked to have seen this fight. He should have been here. The drama of real life, wasn't that something he adored? Or so he had told me. What could be more dramatic than watching a domestic quarrel escalate into a broken bottle brawl in the Goodwill?

"I came in the middle of it," I said, "but what I saw was two guys fighting, then that woman—" I pointed to the cushion lady across the store "—came up and put a stop to it. The fight, I mean."

"How'd she do that?"

"She started a pillow fight."

The officer twirled his pencil in his fingers. "Is that right?" he asked Gayle.

"Yes," said Gayle. "That's exactly what happened."

"Wait here," said the officer.

"Okay," I said.

He went over to the other officer and the couple. An ambulance drove up to the entrance and two paramedics came into the store with a stretcher. They quickly arrived at the injured man. The Goodwill employee had the wound dressed with white bandages, but a red stain bloomed there, like a flower unfurling in slow motion. A coat covered the man, who was stretched out on the floor. He started shivering. The Goodwill employee stepped aside as the paramedics bent over the man and checked his pulse.

I turned and looked at the couple talking to the officers.

Most of the people who had watched the fight had dispersed by now. Some of them went back to shopping. Others had left the store. Gayle and I waited, like we had been told to do.

Employees began to put merchandise back on the shelves. They swept up the broken items that had scattered across the floor. I heard the electronic beeps of a cash register ringing up sales at the front of the store. Life goes on. People need to buy things. They need to spend their money on stuff.

"I think we need to do something about Claypot," I said. "Besides buying him clothes. He doesn't need clothes."

"Then what does he need?" asked Gayle.

The woman with the cushion had handcuffs around her wrists. Her man, too. The officer ushered them to the front of the store. They walked in a depressed shuffle.

"He needs something to make himself feel normal," I said as the officer who had talked to us earlier came over for more information.

# *Be Suspicious of a Multitude of Feelings*

TURNS OUT THE officer didn't have much to say to us. He thanked us for our time and then he left the store. I felt bad for the cushion lady. Sure, she caused the one guy an injury, but she was only trying to help her man.

We left the Goodwill without buying anything. We suddenly didn't have the will to spend money and we were both very hungry.

"Let's get some takeout and bring it to Clay and Judy," said Gayle.

"Great idea," I said. We went down the street a few blocks to a promising-looking Thai restaurant and went in and ordered some takeout dishes. While we waited I told Gayle that even though the incident at the Goodwill was stupid and ridiculous I enjoyed being a part of it.

"That's because you're a sick puppy," she said.

"No, really. It was fun seeing all that."

"I know. I thought so too. But I'm a sick puppy myself, so don't think that makes it all okay or anything."

"I don't exactly think I'm sick, but I do think there's something to be said for taking a healthy interest in the dark side of life."

She looked at me like I was nuts. I felt a little nuts myself. "So," she said, "does that mean you want to get down and dirty in an alley fight with some low life?"

"Not exactly."

"What, then?"

"I guess I want to get to know people like Claypot. Dangerous people."

"Claypot is not dangerous. He's confused. And depressed."

"He's in grief," I said.

"Depression and grief are almost the same thing. In any case, he does not have a core that takes risks or walks on any dark side. He's completely conventional. I'm surprised you don't see that."

"Conventional? I don't think so."

"Why? Because he lives in a tent and does pictures on public walls?"

"He gets people to do things for him. He's a rebel. He does things in his own way."

Gayle picked up the bag of takeout that the man at the counter brought for us. She pulled out some money from her wallet and gave it to the man. We walked out the door and into the city again.

"He's a classic moocher," said Gayle. "He gets people to do things for him, sure, but that doesn't make him dangerous. Or dark or anything like that."

"He's an independent thinker."

"Don't kid yourself," said Gayle. "He's not independent at all. He needs the approval and attention of others. He craves it. Lives for it."

I felt like she was talking about someone I didn't even know. Claypot craved the approval of others?

We got to our car, parked a couple of blocks away. Gayle got in the passenger seat. I sat behind the wheel. I started the engine and got into traffic. The smell of the food quickly permeated the interior of the car. We sat in the aroma for a few miles, not saying anything. I wanted to find some way to tell Gayle how much Claypot meant to me. Not as a friend, but as a symbol of something other than myself. He was different, she had to admit that. He lived by some other code. Maybe on some other planet, and only visited here.

"You know," said Gayle while we were stopped at a red light, "if you want to quit your job and become a painter that's okay with me."

"What? No. That's not what this is about."

"Or a musician. You used to say you'd like to play the guitar. You could do that at the train station. Put out a hat. Do you know any songs?"

"What? No, I never learned any. I never learned the guitar."

"I'm sure it's not that hard. I've seen all kinds of idiots playing guitars." She put up her hand. "Not that I'm saying you're an idiot or anything. That's not what I meant."

"I know what you meant, but I'm not about to quit my job for anything as chancy as art or music."

"Why not?"

"Because it's crazy."

"But that's what we were talking about. Crazy stuff. Doing crazy things. Are you saying you don't want to be edgy yourself? You just want to hang around other people who you perceive as edgy?"

"I guess so," I said. Was she encouraging me to chuck my responsibilities and become an irresponsible artsy type?

"I'm only saying that if you are going through a mid-life crisis—"

"Mid-life crisis! Where'd you get that idea?"

"It's obvious, isn't it?"

"Not to me."

"This irrational attraction to irresponsibility? The adoration of an unstable person? That doesn't say anything to you?"

I wanted to object to her characterizations, but I couldn't produce any counter arguments. Could she be right? I saw the events of the last couple of days with Claypot in an entirely different light. Probably I was interested in Claypot because I was afraid to do some of the things he did as a matter of course. I could live vicariously through him. Did that mean I wanted to leave my wife? My stomach tightened at the thought. No, I did not. In any case, Claypot didn't leave his wife, either. He was back living with her, wasn't he? It took a stupid fall—if it was a fall—to do it, but he did get back to her. And I fully recognized the self-destructive aspect of some of Claypot's actions. I saw that. I understood it. I thought. It didn't mean I wanted to be self-destructive too. Did it?

My face felt hot.

"It's okay to have these impulses," said Gayle.

"I don't think I have any impulses," I said.

"It's healthy to fantasize about things sometimes. But you have to be clear on what it is you think you're tapping into."

We had gone several miles and were now a couple of blocks from Judy's house. I had no recollection of traveling those miles. My head felt like it was spinning. For a moment I wanted to stop the car, step outside, and run across a field. Or through a stranger's house. Or dive into a lake. Fall on the ground and look up at the sky while the dirt held me.

Nutty thoughts. My hands tingled. I felt as though Claypot Dreamstance no longer existed.

Or never existed. I made him up. It wasn't my fault. I didn't want to, but there was a need in me to create a fantasy character made from someone with a lot more talent than I ever had.

We drove along looking at the view outside the window. I thought of the windshield as a trompe l'oeil template, letting in the outside. All of car culture lets you do that. You don't see the world for what it is, but for what it might be in comparison to your own car. I liked that Claypot didn't have a car.

Not that he didn't use them. He mooched off of others when he needed one. Like Gayle said, he could make people do things. I knew that too. He made me buy him cigarettes and he didn't even have to do much convincing.

The world outside blurred past us, then slowed, and stopped. We were at Judy's driveway. I looked at the trees in her yard. She had several of them. They reminded me of toothpicks topped with pompoms.

We grabbed the takeout and went to Judy's front door. She opened it before we could knock.

"Clay ran off," she said. "I have no idea where he is."

# *Do Not Talk Out Loud to the Person Who Died*

WE WENT INTO Gayle's house.

"How could he run off?" I said.

"I went to the pharmacy to get his prescription filled," she said. "I made sure he was asleep. When I got back, he was gone. He isn't in the house."

"Should we call someone?" said Gayle.

"Who would we call? He's not a minor. He can be on his own."

"Except he's still recovering from an injury," I said.

Judy handed me a note. I put the takeout down on the table and read the note. It was from Claypot, mostly an illegible scrawl, but I did make out Stacey's name and it was definitely Claypot's handwriting. Its loopy, meandering line made me feel like Claypot was still there.

"I can't read it," I said. "What does it say?"

"Mostly it says don't bother looking for him. He will

find Stacey and bring her back."

Gayle sighed. "We have to find him," she said.

"Let's go to his tent," I said.

"Should one of us stay here?" said Judy. "In case he comes back?"

"I'll stay," said Gayle.

"Thanks," said Judy.

"You sure?" I said to Gayle.

"Go," she said. "Both of you get out of here."

Judy and I got into the car and this time I didn't have any weird thoughts about trompe l'oeil windshields. We were united in a wish to find a slightly disturbed individual. And not only because it was the right thing to do. We both cared about him as well.

We got on the road. I pushed the speed limit. "Maybe we should swing by that building first," she said.

"The one he was going to put his big picture on?"

"Yes. I have a feeling."

"Okay," I said. I turned onto the road that would take us there and we were at the corner in a few minutes. Even if he wasn't there, it was a good place to start.

I parked the car on the corner and we got out and walked over to the wall. I saw footprints in the sand. Big feet. Claypot feet.

"He was here," I said. "Amazing."

"Nothing amazing about it," said Judy. "He really wanted something to happen here."

I stepped away from Judy and walked along the wall. The big footprints went all the way to the corner of the building, then disappeared where the sand gave way to a concrete sidewalk. "Looks like he didn't stay here long," I said.

"Long enough," said Judy. "Look."

I walked back to where she was crouched down by the wall. A tiny chalk drawing clung to one of the bricks. It showed a miniature view of the river, the river that swallowed up Stacey. A hint of the rail was also there in the scratched black marking.

"This is his," I said. His style was unmistakable.

"Yes, but it's not trompe l'oeil."

She was right. Claypot always always did trompe l'oeil. Why did he change now?

"We need to go to the river," said Judy.

The place where Stacey fell into the river was only a few blocks away. "Should we drive?"

"There's probably no parking. Let's go on foot."

We went around the corner where Claypot's footprints faded out and hurried down the sidewalk. Neither of us was in good shape. We soon slowed to a trot. I had thoughts that Claypot had already gotten to the rail and had jumped into the river. Was that irrational? I didn't know. I really wasn't sure what he could be up to. I thought he was probably capable of killing himself, but I didn't know for sure.

As we hurried along, Judy began to chant Stacey's name, repeating it over and over for no reason that I could see. Maybe she wanted the comfort of it right then. I imagined that Claypot may have done the same thing.

I saw the rail down the road, past a couple more blocks and across an expanse of greenery where the park cut across the city.

I bumped into someone. I saw that I could go faster than Judy. "I'm going to go ahead," I said.

She nodded. "Find her," she said. "Find Stacey."

She was obviously confused. Stacey was not Claypot, but maybe in her mind they were one and the same, people she loved who she had lost.

I quickened my pace.

And then I saw him.

He looked out at me from inside a coffee shop where he sat on a stool at the window. He registered recognition as I went by. I stopped and turned around. He looked through the window and grinned at me. He held up a cup of coffee, as if toasting me.

Judy caught up to me. She stopped.

Claypot grinned through the window at her and at me.

We went inside.

Judy ran to him and hit him repeatedly on the back like a crazed drummer.

Claypot didn't flinch or move. It looked like he welcomed her blows. I thought of the two guys at Goodwill.

"Stacey Stacey Stacey," said Judy.

"I know," said Claypot.

"What the hell were you doing leaving a note like that?"

"I'm sorry," said Claypot. "I didn't mean to upset you. I had to get out."

"To find Stacey."

"Yes."

"To get her back."

"Yes."

"Are you insane? Are you a fucking crazy man?"

People in the coffee shop looked at us.

"Judy!" said Claypot. "I didn't know you had it in you to express yourself so well. I'm proud of you."

"Never mind that. Tell me what you meant. Bringing Stacey back. You think I don't want her back? You think I'm happy she's dead?"

I have to admit, I was sure at that point that this scene was going to escalate into something truly ugly, with Claypot committing violence on Judy or perhaps on me or even himself. Maybe all three of us. I don't know where I got that idea. Claypot had not threatened physical harm to anyone as long as I had known him. But the anger in the room was palpable. The entire coffee shop was frozen. Nobody dared move. I could feel the guy at the counter wanted to do something. Maybe call the police? I wasn't sure. Maybe he thought it was his responsibility to take care of the situation. But he couldn't handle Claypot. Nobody could. Except maybe Judy, and I'm not sure she thought she could either. Funny thing, I didn't feel like I was in any position to do anything either. This was a drama they had to finish on their own.

"She talks to me," said Claypot.

"She talks to me too," said Judy.

"In my dreams."

"Yeah, my dreams, too. Also when I'm awake."

"I can't discount that," said Claypot.

"There's nothing to discount. We love her so much we can't let her go. She's in our own minds."

"I think it's more than that."

The guy at the counter picked up the phone. I glanced up at him and shook my head. He hesitated, then replaced the phone on its cradle. Quietly.

"How can it be more, Clay?" said Judy. "How can it? She's gone."

"No no," said Claypot. "Here, I'll show you." He pulled out a sheet of paper and smoothed it on the counter. "See," he said, "I had it all wrong. I shouldn't have done the picture on that building. I had to do it at the railing. That's where she would come back."

He turned the paper on the counter so Judy could see it. I looked over her shoulder. Claypot had drawn a pipe. The end of it was front and center on the page. The rest of it snaked away to infinity.

"I'll do this one at the railing," he said. "I'll put up a big canvas and make the drawing. She'll come through it. Back to our world."

"Stacey?" said Judy.

Claypot grinned. "Yup."

"You're on pain meds," she said. "That's why you're behaving in this demented manner."

"It's not demented," he said. "It's hopeful." His voice had grown so soft I could barely hear him. Some of the other patrons leaned over towards him.

"Honey," said Judy, "there's nothing to be hopeful about. Why can't you accept that Stacey's gone?"

"I need to buy a big canvas. Will you give me money for that?"

Judy didn't say anything.

Claypot looked at me. "How about you?" he said.

If Judy hadn't been there, I might have said yes. But she was there and this felt like something they had to figure out between them. It was none of my business. "I don't think so," I said.

"Oh," said Claypot. "You're more afraid of her than

you are of me. That's too bad. Well, I'll find a way."

He stood up and walked toward the door. He had a slight limp from his injury, but it didn't look like anything serious. Claypot was a resilient man.

The guy at the counter looked relieved that Claypot was leaving. I understood completely. Judy and I followed Claypot out onto the sidewalk. He stopped. I got the impression he wasn't sure of which way he wanted to go.

"I'll take you to your camp," I said.

"No use," he said. "It'll be raided by now. Nothing left probably. You can't leave an encampment alone for more than half a day."

"Oh," I said.

"I'll go back to Judy's later, if that's okay with you, Judy. Judy?"

She had already walked away from us. I told Claypot to stay where he was, then I ran after Judy. I caught up with her quickly and grabbed her arm. I shouldn't have done that. It was too much physical contact for her right at that moment. She shook me off and kept walking. I grabbed her again and spun her around. She glared at me.

"What are you doing?" she said.

"He needs help," I said.

"He's needed help for a long time. He won't accept it."

"Help him do this one picture."

She breathed hard and still glared at me. Then she looked down at my hand, wrapped around her upper arm. I was suddenly conscious that I might have bruised her. Me. I felt awful, like I was the worst piece of shit in the world. An over reaction, perhaps, but it didn't feel like it right then. I felt like I had done something that could not be fixed.

"Okay," she said. "I'll help him. But this is the last time. I can't be reliving Stacey's death over and over."

I nodded. "I'm sorry," I said.

"You should be." She pushed me. I stepped back. I looked up the sidewalk for Claypot. He stood with his hands on his hips, evaluating us, or so it appeared to me.

"I'm really starting to hate him," said Judy.

"Me too," I said.

# *Conflate the Meanings of Grief and Mourning*

I CALLED GAYLE and told her we were going to Claypot's hideout to help him with a big project.

"He's okay?" she said.

"He's fine. Judy and I will make sure he gets done what he needs to do."

"And what is that?"

"I don't know," I said. "I don't think he knows either. He thinks he does, but I think he's wrong."

"Keep me apprised."

"I will."

I hung up and followed Judy as she walked back to Claypot, who was still standing on the sidewalk, waiting for us.

"What's with all the shenanigans?" he said. "We have work to do. You going to drive me to my place?"

"I thought you said it was all gone by now."

"Mostly it will be. But there's a few places around there where I hid stuff."

Of course. The ever resourceful Claypot. "Fine," I said. "My car's up this way."

We walked toward the car. Judy didn't have much to say. But then, neither did Claypot or I. We all got into the car and I drove to the park entrance. Claypot and I got out. Judy stayed inside. I leaned back in. "You coming?" I said.

She shook her head. "I'll wait here."

She was so dismissive and curt that I didn't try to coax her out. "Okay," I said.

Claypot, however, was not so accepting. "Come on, Judy," he said. "You've been cooped up in that house looking after me. You could use the fresh air." He opened the passenger door. Judy slid to the other side. Claypot laughed. "You're not getting away that easy," he said. He leaned into the back of the car, putting his big arms across the seat and reached for her. Judy had already been grabbed once today, by me, so I knew she was in no mood for further coercion of a physical nature. Claypot should have known that too.

"Back off," I said to Claypot.

He either ignored me or did not hear me. I suspected the former. Judy was curled up against the opposite door of the car. Claypot had one knee on the back seat and had his hands close to Judy's arms. She hit him.

"What's the matter with you?" said Claypot. "Walk with me. Come on. Please."

She hit his arm again, several times. I shouted at him. "Leave her alone," I said. I grabbed the bottom of his shirt. He kicked back at me.

"What the fuck is going on here?" he said. "I just want my wife to take a walk with me."

"I'm not your wife anymore," said Judy.

Claypot stopped. I heard him sigh and he dropped his head. Judy curled up again.

"I want to do something for Stacey," said Claypot. "I want to make things right."

Judy turned toward the window and looked out at something in the distance. "Things will never be right again," said Judy. "And it's your fault. You let her die."

What a thing to say. I felt the hairs on my neck stand up.

Claypot made no move.

After a few seconds he withdrew from the car. I, standing right behind him, tried to move out of his way, but he bumped into me and we stood awkwardly for an instant, trying to find our respective places in relation to each other. We had nothing to say. He was obviously hurt, maybe angry, and I wasn't in the mood for any retaliation directed at me. I stepped back to allow him room. He turned down the path and started walking. I watched him go, then leaned into the car, but not far. I tried to stay back.

Judy was still curled up tightly. "You okay?" I said.

"He doesn't understand," she said.

"I know."

"You don't understand either."

Oh.

"He thinks he's mourning her, but he isn't. He isn't even in grief. Not yet. I've gotten over the grief, and I've gone back to it a dozen times. He still thinks he can get her back."

"He's not in a conversation with reality," I said, repeating a phrase Gayle had used in relation to Claypot.

"Something like that," said Judy.

"Are you really okay here?"

"Go and be with him. I'd rather be alone right now anyway. Make sure he doesn't hurt anyone. That's what you're afraid of, isn't it?"

That's what I was always afraid of with Claypot. I thought he would hurt me if it suited his whim. Sometimes I was sure it would. I thought that, even though I had never seen him hurt anyone.

"As long as you're sure you're fine," I said.

"You want me to use some Claypot language?" she said.

"Okay," I said. "We'll be back soon." I closed the door and went after Claypot. He was already a long way down the trail. I hurried my pace to a trot and caught up to him.

"Hey," I said.

He kept walking in silence.

"What you got hidden up here?" I asked.

More silence.

"Are you mad at me?" I said.

"That's a woman's question," said Claypot. "You a woman?"

"Just wondering what's going on with you," I said.

"The love of my fucking life tells me to fuck off and you think I'm mad at you. Fucking beautiful. Could you be more of a cocksucking narcissist if you tried?"

Sounded like he was feeling better.

"I'd say you're the narcissist," I said.

"Is that your professional opinion, Doctor?"

"I'm only saying that you maybe need to see beyond yourself."

"Maybe you should shut the fuck up before you say something that might be considered intelligent because then I would have to take you seriously and, quite frankly, I don't want to do that because you're a fucking idiot who should keep his mouth shut."

And so on. He was in fine form, I had to admit. We walked in silence for a few minutes. The ground was slicker than the last time I had been on the path. I had to be careful not to slip. Claypot had no problem. He lumbered over the muddy areas like a tank going through a swamp. Nothing stopped him, nothing slowed him down.

We got to the spot where earlier I had left the path to go to his encampment. He disappeared into the brush. I followed. We got to where his tent used to be. It was exactly as he had predicted. The tent was gone. A few remnants, some rags and broken bottles, a few plastic containers, all lay strewn on the ground.

"Assholes," said Claypot.

I was with him on that assessment. It didn't take any time at all for the scavengers to swoop down on his home and clean it out.

He stood where the entrance flap to his tent would have been. I offered to help clean up the grounds.

"Fuck it," he said. "I'm not here to cry about my lost house."

He walked to a point several yards away from the tent site, under a large oak tree. He turned ninety degrees then took precisely seven steps in that direction. Turned another ninety degrees and took seven more steps. This put him back in the bushes, just outside the edge of the clearing. I followed until I stood beside him. We both looked down. I saw only a woodsy matting of leaves, dirt, lichen, and moss. Claypot bent down and put his hand into the leaves. He found a short length of rope and pulled it up.

The debris slid away as a board rose up. Claypot heaved the board aside where it flopped over onto the adjoining forest litter. I looked into the opening made by the missing board. I'm not sure what I expected to see, but I know I was surprised by what I did see: several dolls. That was it? Claypot had thought to keep some of Stacey's dolls and saved them here?

He bent down on one knee and reached between the dolls. He pushed them aside like they were garbage, and pulled out a metal box from the bottom of the hole. He held the box out for me to see.

"This is it," he said.

"What?"

"Stacey's chalk."

Oh.

"Did Judy tell you she was a great artist?"

"No."

"She was. Her preferred medium was chalk on sidewalks."

"That explains a lot," I said.

"What?" he said sharply. "What the fuck does it explain? That Stacey inherited her artistic preference from me? Is that what this fucking *explains?*"

Was I getting tired of his belligerence? Yes. Was I going to do anything about it? No.

"I meant more along the lines of why you chose your

particular medium."

I expected another round of cursing, but instead he got very quiet. "You may have a point," he said. "Stacey drew on the sidewalks all the time, then the rain came and washed away her drawings. She liked that. Said it was cool how she could now do another picture in the same place. She never mourned the loss. So strange for me to see. She taught me a lot. She's still teaching me things. She's a remarkable girl. She said she learned to draw from me."

"No kidding?" I said.

Claypot nodded. "It seemed strange, because I didn't think she ever watched me draw. But she said I was always drawing in the air. Moving my finger around, making shapes. I never realized that, but she was right. She said she watched me tracing things in the air then went on the sidewalk and tried to copy what I had done. She used these chalks."

The box held at least three or four dozen chalks. Some of them quite large, some worn down to a nub. They had a luminous quality to them, as though filled with a soft light. I had to believe that was only my imagination. They couldn't have been glowing.

"You're going to use these for the big picture you're talking about?"

"Yeah. I had to get them before the motherfucking scavengers got to them."

"It'll be good," I said.

"What'll be good?"

"To use her chalk for your last picture."

"My last picture. What the fuck are you talking about, last picture?"

I was confused. I was sure I had heard Claypot say something about this being his last picture. Or did I make that up in my own mind?

"I thought," I said.

"You thought you thought. Stop fucking thinking, okay?"

"Sure," I said.

"I'm a goddam artist, okay? That's what I do. I make drawings for her."

"I know that."

"She's going to come back and make pictures of her own, okay?"

"Fine," I said. "I didn't mean anything. I thought I heard you say."

"Now what did I just tell you about thinking?"

I heard a rustle of branches behind me. Claypot heard it too. He lifted his eyes, then bolted and started running. I turned around in time to see a couple of men run into the bushes.

"Where are you going?" I shouted to Claypot.

Claypot, still carrying the box under his arm, was in full pursuit, running at top speed. "Those guys stole my stuff," he said, then plunged into the brush without slowing his pace, although he did push a branch or two out of his way as he went.

I followed, but I went much slower. How did he know those guys were the thieves?

I stopped at the edge of the clearing. I didn't want to run into the bushes.

As I stood there, listening to the sounds of the three of them snapping branches and slapping at leaves, Judy came up and stood beside me.

"He'll never catch up to them," she said. "He wants them to get away."

"Why's that?" I said.

"He envies their freedom."

# *Denigrate the Idea of Ceremony*

"I THOUGHT YOU were going to wait in the car," I said to Judy.

"I got over my pout," she said.

"What are we going to do now?"

"He'll tire out soon. He doesn't really want to be chasing those guys. And he shouldn't be, on those ankles."

"If you say so."

I heard bellows from the bushes. Claypot cursed the men as he pursued them. The men, younger than Claypot, laughed at him. "Hey old man," one of them said. "Don't have a heart attack."

This prompted even more curses from Claypot. I suspected this sort of thing had happened before. These men, or others like them, must have been through here in the past, picked at Claypot's possessions, and caused him no end of grief. I imagined the toll it took on him, similar to the toll the ritual now took on the flora of the area, what with the sound of breaking branches prevalent in the air.

Finally the men broke out of the brush and onto the path. I heard their feet pound the ground as they ran by us in the direction of the parking lot at the head of the trail. They sounded like horses in full gallop. A few seconds later another set of feet came down the trail, much slower and without the manic energy of the first two.

"Let's go help him," said Judy.

She began walking back to the trail. I followed. We pushed brush aside and kept walking until we found Claypot on the trail, bent over with his hands on his knees, gulping air. He looked up as we approached. His face was stained so red I thought he might pass out.

"I'm too fucking old for this," he said around gasps for air.

"I could have told you that," said Judy.

"I'm tired of those punk ass fuckheads, too, let me tell you. They come around here all the time. I knew if I ever left camp those assholes would raid it. That's why I buried Stacey's chalks."

I suddenly noticed he didn't have the box with him.

"Did you drop them?" I asked.

He stood up straight. "Oh shit," he said.

"We'll go look for them," said Judy. "They have to be right near here."

Claypot spit a huge gob onto the ground. "I don't think I can go," he said. "I need some rest or I'll collapse."

"I'll go," said Judy. "Chris, you stay here with Clay."

She retreated back into the brush before I could say anything.

"You put the scare into those guys," I said.

He laughed. "Not exactly. They were laughing at me the whole time."

"They were also *running* the whole time."

He shrugged. "I don't want to lose those chalks."

"Judy will find them."

"You know," he said, "this is not easy for me. It's like saying goodbye to my home."

"It doesn't have to be. Get another tent. Another stove. Set up your homestead again. A nice squat."

"Maybe."

His face had softened by now. I began to see in him something besides an angry man. He was wistful and a little vulnerable, like he wanted me to see him as something new. Was this what some called a state of grace? I would not have thought it possible, not after what I had seen of him. He so much wanted Stacey back. The impulse was so strong in him that he even refused to believe she was gone in the first place. Was that his fault? Maybe to a certain extent. But sometimes life is too much for people. Sometimes you have to understand more than you can take in. Maybe that just happened to Claypot, and with the loss of his home, the full extent of his efforts to resurrect his daughter humbled him. I was about to offer some words of comfort and encouragement when he broke out of his little oasis of true feeling and suddenly noticed a rip in his pants. I had seen it and thought he knew about it too, but apparently not.

He must have torn it in the woods. He took the rip in his hands, bunched it up to close it, and looked like he was about to tear the material off.

Judy came back with the box under her arm. "Found it," she said. "Piece of cake."

"Give it to me," said Claypot.

"Sure," said Judy. She held it out to him.

He wanted to snatch it from her. I could see the urge in his eyes, now ablaze with irritation and anger. Judy remained cool and collected. So different from how she was in the car a few minutes ago. This Judy was not afraid of Claypot. This Judy only wanted to make him happy, which was more than he deserved from anyone.

Claypot did not snatch the box. Instead, he took a step closer to Judy and put out his hands as gently as he could and accepted the box from her with a measure of grace and humility I knew he had in him, but which I also knew he kept hidden for purposes all his own.

"Thank you," he said.

"You're welcome," said Judy. "Are you ready to go home now?"

"Your home?"

"Yes," said Judy. "My home. Your home. Whatever you want to call it."

I was sure this scene, or scenes like it, had happened before. It was the aftermath scene, what occurred when the fireworks were spent, the hurt feelings had subsided, and both parties realized life was destined to go on as before. I understood it not as a participant, but as an observer, and therefore did not understand it all.

Claypot took a long breath.

"You know I'm not going to stop," he said.

"I know."

Now I felt completely superfluous. They turned to walk back to the car. I wanted to let them go on their own, but it happened to be *my* car, so I couldn't do that.

I followed behind them. They walked very close to each other. It felt like they had been through this many times before, and this was the end they always labored toward. The happy ending. Or at least the somewhat cordial ending, which might be enough for them.

Judy looked back at me. "Don't worry about us getting a ride," she said. "We'll find our way back."

"Oh," I said. "Take the bus or something?"

"Something."

She was gracious and dismissive all at the same time. Like she wanted to be polite, but also wanted to make sure I knew that she and Claypot were done with me for the time being. I wanted to ask her why she did it. Why did she keep making up with him? It couldn't do her any good at all. Not in the long term, or even the short term.

But you can't choose who you fall in love with. Isn't that what people say?

I stayed back to let them get ahead of me.

I had my own unhealthy relationship with Claypot, after all. Why didn't *I* leave him alone?

I pulled out my phone and called Gayle.

"Did you find him?" she said.

"He was at a coffee shop, hatching out a new plan. He and Judy made up. Or something. I can't figure those two out. They're on their way home. Probably going to have a nice afternoon together. I'll come pick you up."

"I'll be waiting for you," she said.

I walked back along the trail. People passed by me. Some walked leisurely. Some ran. Some had dogs. Some didn't. I smiled and nodded at each one in turn. Most smiled back. It was nice. Cozy in an odd way.

I got to the park entrance, where my car was parked, and saw a crowd of people around it.

Claypot stood in the center of the crowd. He looked like an old wise man holding court. Judy stood next to him. The people around them looked at Claypot adoringly, like they wanted to kiss him.

Claypot held up his hands.

"People, people," he said. "I don't want you to think I'm a messiah. I have no short cut to the divine. I'm just a guy with some chalk."

"He's a graffiti artist," said Judy. "A *good* graffiti artist, sure, but that's all."

A general buzz of denials arose from the group. "No," said someone, "you see to the other side."

"Yeah," said someone else, "you're like a divine spirit."

Did I hear all this correctly? Claypot had disciples?

"Now, now," said Claypot. "You need to stop this reverential treatment of someone as humble as me. I don't have any special capabilities."

As I got closer I discerned more clearly the members of the group. They were a varied bunch: about two dozen total. Some well-dressed, others in street garb: rags and dirty old jackets. Some teenagers and a few elderly. Male and female about evenly divided. They all had one thing in common: an unhealthy devotion to Claypot Dreamstance. I could tell them a little about that. Best to break the habit as quickly as possible.

"But you can bring people back to life," said one young woman.

"Who the fuck told you that bullshit?" said Claypot.

The woman looked stunned. "I've heard it around," she said.

"Get this straight," said Claypot, "all of you. I do my pictures for my daughter Stacey, but they don't bring her back to life because *she's still alive*."

That brought everything to an abrupt silence.

I approached the group with an air of what I hoped looked like authority and a measure of menace.

"All right," I said. "Everyone get away from my car."

Some, who had been leaning on the sides and bumpers of my car stepped back. Others didn't move. They defied me in a kind of mini rebellion, no doubt bolstered by belief in their messiah, Claypot.

Claypot whipped around at the sound of my voice. He looked glad to see me.

"This is *your* car?" said a kid with a skateboard under his arm.

"You don't think *he* can afford a car, do you?" I asked with a broad smile on my face as I hooked a thumb in Claypot's direction.

"We heard he had a shrine here in the park."

A shrine? That was a good one.

"More like a latrine than a shrine," I said.

More shocked looks.

"Who are you?" said the woman who Claypot had startled a couple of minutes ago.

"I'm Mr. Dreamstance's manager."

Judy, who up to now had been quietly taking everything in, put her hand up to her mouth and laughed. Even Claypot smiled.

"Manager?" said the woman.

"Yes, and Mr. Dreamstance needs his rest. He's gearing up for an important piece. He appreciates his fan base, of course, but asks you to please respect his need for privacy and the time it takes to prepare for his work. Look for it soon. You won't be disappointed."

I stood to one side and spread my arms wide, as if to indicate the vast open universe beyond the little orbit of my car.

The crowd got the hint and began to shuffle away.

Before long they had dispersed, some went in the direction of town, others wandered down the path into the park.

"Thanks," said Claypot.

"You'd be a fine manager," said Judy.

"You really want to be my manager?" said Claypot.

"I'd be honored," I said. "I think."

"Okay, manager," said Claypot. "Drive me home."

"I thought you were going to find your own way back."

"That was before. It's a whole new world now."

He stood at the passenger door with his hand on the door handle. "Come on, come on," he said. "Let me in."

I got into the driver's side and unlocked the door for him. He roared in, all muscle and attitude. Judy climbed into the back seat. I could see she was barely able to suppress a grin.

"This is nice," said Claypot. "Home, Jeeves, and

make it snappy. I want to make love to my woman."

I sighed, turned on the engine, and drove to Judy's house.

# *Forget Anniversaries*

AND JUST LIKE that, without any fuss or muss, I became Claypot Dreamstance's manager.

Was such an eventuality inevitable? Maybe. One could argue the whole problem was my own infatuation with the icon that was Claypot, even though I had vowed to release myself from his grip. Gayle had her doubts about the enterprise, but agreed that it might be good for me to do something different for a while. Shake up my life a bit and see what tumbled out. I might find it refreshing. Gayle might even find it refreshing.

"You've been looking for something like this for a while," she said. "It's coming up on your fiftieth birthday. Usually time for some reflection and reassessment. At least to most people."

"You're right," I said. "I'd forgotten."

"Any idea what you're actually going to do as his

manager?"

"Mostly hold his hand and try to keep him from getting into too much trouble."

"Good luck."

"Yeah."

So what exactly *does* a manager do?

I put it to Claypot the day after his encounter with the mob that thought he had a link to God, or whatever it was they thought.

"Ha!" he said. "Fucked if I know. I just liked the sound of it yesterday."

We were walking along the waterfront, scouting the location of his big project.

"May I make a suggestion?" I said.

"Shoot," he said.

"I think it might do you some good to refrain from mentioning that Stacey is still alive."

I felt him tense up beside me.

"Is that right?"

"Yes," I said. "It makes you seem a little over the edge."

"I thought edgy was good. Don't managers want their artists to be edgy?"

"Edgy is good," I said, "but it is only good up to a point. You can get as close to the edge as possible, but you should never cross the edge. You follow?"

"But the edgiest artists *do* cross, don't they? Like the ones who pound spikes through their wrists. Or how about that one guy who sat in a gallery for a few weeks with a loaded gun on a table beside him. As people went by he handed them business cards with instructions on how to shoot him. How about that? That went over the edge, didn't it?"

I wasn't sure if he was making that up or if it actually happened. I decided to ask Gayle about it later that evening. In the meantime I tried to dodge the question.

"Such performance art is not what you are doing anyway," I said. "I think that too much emphasis on Stacey will dilute your message."

Claypot laughed. I think it was more or less a friendly laugh, but something about it unnerved me. It was like he was mocking me.

"And what exactly is my message?" he asked.

"An excellent question," I said. "We need to formulate that. Let's work on it, shall we?"

"Hey, I have a manager so I don't have to work so hard."

"I'll write up a mission statement and then you can look at it and tell me what you think."

"Fuck no," said Claypot. "Sounds like work."

"Then have Judy look at it. She can approve it for you."

He thought about that and must have concluded it was a good idea.

"Okay," he said. "But then what are you for? Wouldn't Judy be acting as my manager then?"

I felt lost already.

"I know," said Claypot. "You can be my manager, and Judy can be my agent. That would work, wouldn't it?"

It sounded good to me.

"Perfect," I said. "I'll get a mission statement over to her as soon as I can. You won't have to be involved at all."

"Oh joy," said Claypot. "That fills me up with a goddam fucking warm feeling, you know?"

"Yeah," I said. "Me too."

"When you write the mission statement?"

"Yes?"

"Make sure you include a lot about Stacey."

"Stacey?"

"Yeah, Stacey."

"Claypot," I said. "We just discussed that. We were going to minimize mention of her."

"Wrong, motherfucker," said Claypot. "*You* were going to fucking de-emphasize Stacey. *I'm* not going to do any such fucking thing. Okay?"

There it was. My grand plan to move Claypot away from the fringe toward some semblance of normal life was in tatters before it began.

"I was trying to find another path for you that wouldn't lead to so much—"

"So much what, motherfucker?" he said.

"I was going to *say*. I was hoping you could leave some of the turmoil of your life behind. That's all. Move beyond the pain."

Claypot stopped at the rail where the central event of his life had occurred. It felt like he had steered us there.

"Okay Mister manager," he said. "Here we are. Where Stacey decided to take her little leave."

I had completely lost my good feelings by then. I was so unnerved that I said nothing. Couldn't make myself utter a word.

"Did you know this is the anniversary?"

"What?"

"Yup. Three years ago today Stacey slipped through

the bars here."

I saw where the city had closed up the spaces between the rails with lucite panels. No one could slip through them now.

"I was standing right here." He took a few steps to the right and planted his feet with emphatic clomps. "She was next to me. Come this way." He motioned for me to move over a few steps. I felt like I weighed tons as I moved. I shuffled my feet a couple of yards over. "Stop!" he said. "That's the place. You know, Judy has forgotten this day. She doesn't remember the anniversary. I don't blame her or anything. It's just interesting, you know?"

I nodded.

"I think I know enough about the art to make it happen now. I'll put the picture up right here and she'll find it and come back."

All my bravado had slipped away. Could he be serious? Or was his whole life a performance piece?

"You are strangely silent, Mister manager," he said.

I cleared my throat. "Do you intend to have an audience?" I said.

"Ah, a good thought. We should sell tickets, yes?"

"Something like that. I hadn't thought about tickets, but something along those lines would be good."

"It will have to be good. The absolute best. She often criticized my drawing. She said it wasn't real. Did you know that?"

No, I didn't know that. How could I know that? "Stacey was an art critic?" I said.

"Yeah," said Claypot. "Funny, isn't it? She used to say that if I applied myself I could get good enough for people to believe in what I was doing."

An offhand remark by a young girl makes a man change his life completely. Did that make sense on any level? Could she make him think he could bring her back?

Claypot leaned over the top rail and looked down at the river far below. It must have had real earthen banks at some point. Maybe not even a hundred years ago. Now a sheer wall of concrete marked the edge of the river. It also marked the place where Stacey fell into the river.

"These seem like odd things for a little girl to be saying."

"My daughter," said Claypot, "is not odd. Motherfucker." He used his signature language, but more as an afterthought with no energy behind it.

"You okay?" I said.

"Yeah," said Claypot. "What do you mean?"

"You don't seem to be yourself. You're subdued. That's not the Claypot I know."

I expected, even hoped for, a string of profanity taking my name, opinions, intelligence, family, country, hair, taste, and job in vain. Instead, he shrugged.

I was trying to think of something that would cheer him up when I noticed a young girl, no more than six years old, approach us from the park. She held a drawing in her hand. She stopped a short distance from Claypot and offered him the drawing.

He noticed her too, and turned around from the river to face her.

Here's the thing that then made me reassess everything I thought I knew about Claypot Dreamstance.

He didn't accept the picture.

From a little girl, who had obviously drawn the picture herself and wanted him to see it. One of the most basic and pure things in the universe, if you ask me, even if I am going over the top a little. You don't say no to a picture drawn by a child and offered to you, no matter who you are. No matter what pain you're in, you don't say no.

But Claypot did.

He wasn't unkind or mean about it. I'll give him that.

"Thanks for the picture," he said, "but I don't think I can take it. I don't think I can hold onto it. I might lose it and I don't want to do that."

The little girl looked a little puzzled, but she didn't seem all that upset. I was a lot more upset than she was.

"Okay," she said, then she turned around and ran back to her parents, or people I assumed were her parents. They stood a short distance away. Claypot noticed them, I saw it in his eyes, but he did not acknowledge them. The parents took the drawing from the little girl's hand. They looked deeply puzzled, even though they assured the little girl that it was fine. She shouldn't worry about it. I imagined them taking the picture home and taping it to their fridge.

"You enjoy dashing the artistic aspirations of little girls?" I asked Claypot.

"Don't start with me," he said.

"I was just wondering," I said. "I was wondering why maybe you didn't pick on people your own size."

"There aren't that many people my size, motherfucker," he said.

He stared down at the water. The river.

"She drew that for you," I said.

"Bullshit. She doesn't even know me."

"Her parents do."

"No, they do not. They think they know me because they've liked some of my pictures. Or something. Seen me on TV. I don't know the fuck what. But they don't know me and I don't want to know them."

"Try to be nice. Here they come."

"What?" He turned around from the river. The parents, along with the girl, approached us.

"Jesus fucking Christ," said Claypot. Under his breath, but still.

The parents came within a few feet of us and stopped.

"Hi," said the mother.

"Hi," I said.

Claypot didn't say anything.

"You're Mr. Dreamstance, aren't you?" said the father.

"Yeah," said Claypot.

"We saw you on television. My daughter really liked you. She drew a picture after she saw some of your drawings."

"My trompe l'oeil," said Claypot.

"Yes," said the man. "Trompe l'oeil. But that's a drawing, isn't it?"

"Sometimes," said Claypot. Tersely.

"Anyway, we were wondering why you didn't look at Evelyn's picture. She was very proud of it."

You could see it in their faces how hurt they were.

They thought Claypot was some famous artist and he could offer legitimacy to their daughter's work merely by looking at it. I think. At least, that was my assessment of their motives. I noticed a certain tension between the man and Claypot. It was like the man wanted something from Claypot and Claypot didn't want to give anything. It wasn't that he didn't know what the man wanted. He did. He knew exactly, and the man knew that he knew. It was simply that Claypot was not capable. And I'm not sure the man knew that.

"Mr. Dreamstance is deep into preparations for a new work," I said. "He regrets that when he is in such a state, he needs to minimize distractions, however charming they may be."

"Huh," said the man. "He doesn't look like he's preparing for anything. He looks like he's loafing around looking at the river."

"The artistic process is a complicated endeavor," I said.

"Fine," said the man. "All I'm saying is that he could have spared ten seconds to say thank you. Would that have killed him?"

"No one wanted to disappoint your daughter. We think it is wonderful that your daughter has artistic impulses. It is simply that at this point Mr. Dreamstance can't offer any support. He has to concentrate on his own work."

I don't know where I found that particular way of speaking. Apparently it had been in me, waiting for an opportunity to be used.

"Then why did he go on TV like he was king of the world?"

The man looked at Claypot, even though his question was directed at me. His wife put her hand around his arm and tried to pull him away from us. The little girl looked up at her father. She wanted him to leave too.

Claypot did not rise to the bait. He took a breath, and then turned from the man and put his attention on the water again. He didn't say anything about Stacey. He did not tell the man to fuck off. He simply adopted this air of serenity, like he was letting the man and the world know he had better things to do at this time.

"I heard your daughter died in the river," said the man. "Is that what turned you into a fuck? Or were you one already?"

I was ready to jump between them. I flexed my leg. The woman looked at me with pleading eyes, as though I could do something. Hell, he was *her* man. Why didn't *she* do something?

"Daddy," said the girl, "I don't like it here. Let's go."

The man still had this attitude about him. He still wanted to confront Claypot in some way. I was mystified by his motives. Was he just a crazy man? I thought Claypot had that role covered.

Evelyn's words softened the man's attitude. He untensed, looked down at his daughter, and mumbled something I couldn't quite make out.

Then they all three of them turned and walked away.

I watched them disappear down the sidewalk.

"Fucking town is going to the dogs," said Claypot. "A man can't walk in the park anymore without being accosted by some weirdo."

"Be that as it may," I said, "have you made any decisions regarding your magnum opus?"

"You in a hurry or something?"

"I'm only thinking it would be a good idea to get going on this," I said.

Claypot sighed again. I noticed he had recently grown fond of sighing. I didn't know if that was a good sign or not.

"I used to think," he said, "that we all had a purpose in life. You ever think about that?"

"Not exactly," I said.

"You should."

"Okay."

"We're not here just to play with our dicks and eat junk food."

"You need to focus," I said.

I was aware of how inane that sounded. Why did he need to focus? No reason. I just didn't know what else to say.

"You're so full of shit," said Claypot, "that you're beginning to smell like an outhouse. Or maybe a sewage treatment plant." He studied the river, *something* in the surface of the water fascinated him.

"You're right," I said. "I don't know what I'm talking about."

"Damn fucking straight, I'm right." He looked up at Mount Hood, visible in the distance. I gazed right along with him. It had a good layer of snow on it. I wondered if he saw things in the mountain I didn't see, simply because he had an artist's eye.

"You ever been there?" said Claypot.

"You mean Mount Hood?"

"Yeah, Mount Hood. You ever climb it? Skied on it? Anything?"

"I've driven up to the lodge there. Gayle and I spent a weekend."

"Did you like it?"

"It was fine. Neither of us do any skiing so it was not all that exciting."

"Why didn't you ski?"

"I don't know. Never learned. Didn't want to buy all the equipment." I shrugged.

"I'm the same way. Don't want to do things that require a lot of stuff. Some sidewalk and some chalk. That makes me happy."

What was all this talk about Mount Hood suddenly?

"Stacey liked the mountain."

Oh.

"I think she would have lived there if she could. She said she wanted to. Loved the snow up there. Even in the middle of August, she liked that you could go up there and find snow. I guess that is a good thing."

"So why don't you go up there?" I said. "Why not go see what the mountain has to tell you. Maybe Stacey would want you to do that."

He still stared at the water. He didn't move a muscle, didn't say a word. I was going to ask if he heard me when he finally spoke up.

"Stacey won't be there," he said.

"I know that. I wasn't saying she would be."

"You don't understand me."

"No one understands anyone else," I said. "We're all

mysteries."

"You can't be my agent." He looked up. Looked me in the eye.

"Okay," I said. "I don't need to be."

"You also don't need to be my friend or whatever the fuck you think you've been to me."

"Clay," I said, "what's eating you?"

"You're eating me. That fucking shithead father is eating me. His daughter. Everything. I just need to be left the fuck alone. Think you can manage that task? Think your motherfucking skull can encompass such a complex concept?"

He turned and walked away. I wanted to follow him, but didn't see the point. He'd be back. When he needed something from me he'd come back. I was sure of it.

# *Sleep Late*

ONLY I WAS wrong. Claypot didn't come find me.

Judy did, though.

She arrived at the house a few days after Claypot had politely expressed his need for solitude to me.

"We need to go to the park," she told me.

"The park?" I said.

"Claypot is losing it."

"What do you mean, losing it?"

"He thinks he's found Stacey."

Gayle approached from behind. "Who's at the door?" she said.

"Judy."

"Well invite her in, dim wit." She brushed past me and embraced Judy, who started crying. Gayle guided her to the living room couch where they sat holding hands while, between sobs, Judy told her what she just told me.

"We need to go to the park and see what's happening," said Gayle.

Judy couldn't stop sobbing. As Gayle comforted her, Judy sobbed louder and shook more.

I appreciated the pain she must be going through. I think. I wasn't exactly sure why she still had anything to do with Claypot, especially since I had decided I would have nothing to do with him anymore. That was the most sane course of action, surely. Anyone could see that.

Only it was not so simple for Judy, obviously. She still had feelings for him and therefore she was upset when he was in trouble.

The only problem with that was that Claypot was always in trouble. It was his default mode. So if his being in trouble tended to upset you, then you would be upset a lot of the time. A simple equation that I had parsed in my mind any number of times.

Gayle went to the closet and got my jacket and threw it at me. I grabbed it out of the air.

"We're going?" I said.

"Of course we're going," she said. "Judy is very upset, can't you tell?"

Sure I could tell. She was upset by a toxic personality. The cure for that was no more proximity to the toxin. Wasn't it?

I reluctantly put on my jacket. Gayle was already zipped up and she had her shoes on. She waited by the door. Judy got to her feet, still sniffling, and held a ragged tissue to her nose.

We must have looked like quite a motley trio, Gayle

leading the way with confidence, even defiance, me and Judy taking up the rear with various shades of reluctance and dispirit between us.

"Should we all go in one car," I said, "or separate?"

"I'll drive with Judy," said Gayle. "You meet us there."

I let Judy pull out of the driveway first, then got into my car and followed them through the city. The whole way to the park I thought this was the worst thing we could be doing. I wasn't even sure why, since despite his difficult personality, Claypot was still someone who needed a friend. Everyone did. I just didn't want to be that friend. Not anymore.

Which made me feel like a first class piece of shit. Which did not put me in the best frame of mind when I arrived at the parking lot of Forest Park. Gayle and Judy, already there, stood beside Judy's car and looked around.

I pulled up beside them.

"Let's go find Clay," said Gayle as I got out of the car.

We began to walk briskly down the path.

"What are we going to do when we find him?" I asked.

"What do you mean 'do?'" said Gayle.

"Just that. How are we supposed to help him? Does he even want our help?"

"We're his friends," said Gayle. "We help our friends."

"Yeah," said Judy.

"I'm not disputing that," I said. "I'm only asking what are we supposed to do for him?"

"I don't know exactly," said Gayle. I noted a definite irritation in her voice, like she didn't want to be hearing this from me. Like she wanted me to get on board with the program even though I didn't know what the program was and neither did she.

Judy was transformed. "We'll make it all better for him," she said in a carefree voice I would have thought impossible coming from her only a few minutes before. "He likes you, Chris. He respects you a lot."

I laughed. I couldn't help it, even though it was absolutely the wrong thing to do at that particular moment.

"What's so funny?" said Gayle.

"It's strange to think of Claypot respecting *anyone*, let alone me. He only respects my credit card."

"That's not true," said Judy. "He's told me that he thinks you are quite a human being. He said to me the other day, 'Chris is repelled by my very presence, and yet he tries to be a loyal friend to me.'"

That did not sound like Claypot at all.

"There," said Gayle, "you see."

"I think you have the wrong idea about Clay," said Judy. "He's not a harsh man. He's in grief. He wants to sleep all day. He doesn't know how to cope with his pain."

To myself I thought: so instead he spreads his pain to others. To Judy I said: "It might be time for him to grow up."

Gayle turned to me. "What a thing to say, Chris."

"It's true," I said. "Neither of you can deny it."

We walked without talking for a few seconds, maybe even a minute. The trail was muddy. The noise of our shoes slapping on the slick trail got louder. There was that feeling in the air of people going over what someone—me, in this case—had said and trying to decide if it was true and important, or true and trivial, or completely untrue.

"That's not something we can make him do," said Gayle.

"Maybe not," I said, "but we don't have to indulge his every delusion and whim. Can't we find a way to support him without reinforcing his more ridiculous and counter-productive tendencies?"

More silence.

"What would you suggest?" said Judy after a long pause.

"Therapy."

"Claypot would never go to a therapist. Also, how could he possibly afford it?"

"I don't know. I'm not saying I have all the answers. I know that what he's doing now isn't working. On any level."

"Not exactly," said Gayle. "He is still wielding power. Over us. He got us to come out here."

Now it was my turn to be silent. Gayle had a point. It was ridiculous how one man could manipulate others so easily.

"Here we are," said Judy.

We stopped. This spot looked familiar. "This is where I cut into the brush when I came to his camp," I said.

"Yup," said Judy. "Right through here." She indicated the greenery with her pointed index finger.

Gayle did not hesitate. She pushed aside branches of small trees and waded into the weedy overgrowth. I noted the path was still mostly ill defined, more of a bending of the grass that looked temporary than an actual footpath. Judy hurried to keep up with Gayle and I followed after them both.

The route had this eerie familiarity, as though I had trodden the same ground for decades, even though I had done so only once.

I stayed back from Judy, wary of the branches swinging back that would slap my face if I followed too closely. Presently we got to Claypot's clearing where we found a much smaller tent than his original. I've seen bigger doghouses than that tent. Claypot sat next to it, legs crossed, arms crossed, looking rather like a bedraggled yogi deep into a meditation session. Judy called to him. He didn't acknowledge her. She increased her pace and advanced toward Claypot and the small tent.

I'm not sure how I knew something bad was about to happen. I couldn't point to any overt sign and say for sure it meant things were going to get hairy. But sometimes those gut feelings are there and no way to explain any of it.

I had one of those then. Fear gripped my belly. The back of my neck prickled.

I ran toward Gayle.

Claypot looked up at that moment. I saw a rage fill his face. He rose from his seated position with a fluid motion and stared down at Gayle.

I called to her. "Gayle, stay back."

I think she saw the danger then, just as I had seen it. She slowed her pace, but Claypot did not appreciate her reticence. He saw only a threat. In Gayle he saw a threat. *Gayle.* Insanity.

He raised his hand in a fist. I ran as fast as I could.

"Stay the fuck away from her," said Claypot.

He meant Stacey. He wanted everyone to stay away from his dead daughter.

Which was fine with me. I didn't want anything to do with Stacey. I only wanted Claypot to stay away from Gayle.

For a big man, he moved quickly. He came close to Gayle and swung at her wildly. He aimed for her jaw, but Gayle ducked down from his swing and instead of her face, he caught only air. I was relieved, but then Gayle stumbled backwards and her arms went up and she raised her head in an instinctive attempt to right herself just as Claypot brought his fist around, retracing its path backwards until he caught Gayle's neck right where it met her shoulder. Gayle fell back on the ground with her arms extended on either side.

I saw her, on the ground like that, and something in me changed. I was no longer willing to give Claypot Dreamstance the benefit of the doubt. Instead I wanted to break his bones.

I ran as fast as I could and I was on him, my arms wrapped around his neck from behind. I pulled on his weight. I wanted him to fall on me. He barely budged, he was so big. I felt his beard under my hands. I smelled his putrid unwashed skin.

"Your fucking daughter's dead, you stupid fuck," I said.

He roared. The sound of it filled the woods. It unnerved me, but I did not let go. I was not about to give him freedom to assault my wife again.

We remained in that position for what seemed like forever. Claypot was tired. I felt his strength wane. I saw

Gayle get up off the ground. She seemed fine. "Chris," she said. "Let him go."

No way. All I had to do was hold on to Claypot for a while and he would succumb. I didn't need to strike a blow or break any of his bones or do anything that would cause permanent injury, even though that's exactly what I wanted to do to him for his attack on Gayle. We both breathed hard. We both knew how this would end, it was only a matter of time. I was surprised at how strong I was. Holding Claypot, a bag of bones and raggedy flesh, a massive *yearning* for something I could barely understand, I felt a little too confident.

"Are you ready to give up?" I whispered into his ear.

He didn't say anything. Just his puffy breaths raking the air. He didn't give up. Didn't want to, I guess. Couldn't, maybe.

I glanced over at Gayle. Her jaw was slightly bruised. Or was that dirt? I wasn't sure. I had this wild idea that I was defending her from evil. That felt good, like I was my true primal self.

"Don't hurt him," she said. At first I wasn't sure if she meant I shouldn't hurt Claypot or Claypot shouldn't hurt me. It could have gone both ways. While I was trying to sort it out, a new wrinkle in our little drama caught me by complete surprise. Judy beating on my upper arms and shoulders with her fist.

"Let go of him!" she said several times, all the while hitting me repeatedly.

Even though I was taken off guard, I managed to keep a grip on Claypot, at least for a few seconds, but that couldn't last.

"All of you," said Gayle. "Stop this right now. I'm okay. Claypot didn't hurt me."

That hardly mattered anymore. Claypot, Judy, and I were caught in some struggle now bigger than any of us. I wanted to hurt them both. It was an urge I did not think I could hold in check if I released my grip on Claypot. So I did not release my grip.

At least not intentionally. But Judy did not let up for an instant. Her fists rained down on me incessantly. She had a lot of strength in her, no doubt amped up with adrenaline.

Claypot fell to his knees, a significant development. It meant I could rearrange my knees on the ground to greater stabilizing effect. I hunkered down on Claypot's neck and tried to keep him from moving any further. I wanted him to get completely down on the ground. If he was prone on the grass, I felt sure he would be no more danger to anyone.

Judy began to weaken. Her blows were softer and spaced further apart. She sobbed and Gayle had come over. To comfort her, I supposed, but I was not sure. Maybe she just wanted to get her off me. I hoped so. She was not helping me subdue Claypot. She was no help at all.

Now, here is where I lose track of what happened. I felt Judy finally pull away from me. Claypot had weakened to the point of offering almost no resistance to me at all. All to the good. Or so I thought. I loosened my grip on him very slightly, enough to let him know I was going to release him if he behaved himself. I sensed no body language in return, so I thought the meaning between us was ultra clear. Gayle and Judy had pulled away to some distance I could not quite register, although I knew they were no longer in close proximity to me.

"Are you going to behave yourself?" I said to Claypot.

"Yeah," he said.

"You sure? Can I count on that?"

"I said I will, didn't I motherfucker?"

"Okay, then," I said and pulled my arm away from his neck and sat back on the ground, with my hands for support. I felt completely beat and wrung out, and all I had been doing was holding onto Claypot for about three or four minutes. Maybe not even that long.

He moved awkwardly, but move he did. He scrambled on all fours to the tent. Gayle came to me and put her hand on my shoulder.

"I was fine," she said. "There was no reason for that."

"I don't know what came over me," I said.

"Jesus fuck!" said Claypot.

"What is it?" said Judy.

"Stacey's gone."

I rolled my eyes. Gayle looked concerned. Judy went to the tent and looked inside.

"Of course she's gone," she said to Claypot.

"Of course she's gone!" said Claypot to the sky. "Of course she's gone? That's what you have to say? This cocksucking motherfucking piece of shit holds me down long enough for Stacey to wake up and walk away and that's what you have to say?" He glared at Judy, but he pointed at me.

I gave him the finger.

"Your daughter's dead, asshole," I said. "Get over

it."

I had seen Claypot angry many times in the short duration of our acquaintance. It was more or less his natural mode of operation. But that comment from me turned him redder than a polluted sunset. He darkened. His eyes grew smaller and seemed to sink deep into his sockets, like they were lost in his skull.

I laughed at him. I didn't want to. Hardly knew where it came from, but I stared at his ridiculous beard and awful hair and stupid raggedy clothes and could not stop myself from laughing as hard as I could.

He took in great deep breaths, like a dragon pulling in air for a push to the pinnacle of some mountain. We watched him, the three of us. I with a mixture of amusement and some small faint dread. Nothing big, but there, a little. Judy I could not read. I thought she might be afraid of him, but I couldn't tell for sure. It might merely have been fascination, which wouldn't be out of line. The crazy fuck was interesting in his demented way.

While Claypot breathed in and out like a bellows, I went to Gayle and put my arm around her shoulder. She resisted me at first. I held back, a little, to let her know I noticed. Then she leaned against me with a gratitude I recognized. She wanted me close right then, especially then. Which was fine with me, I wanted to be close to her, too.

Judy finally hit Claypot on the shoulder. Not hard. Just enough to wake him up.

"He's right," she said. "Stacey's dead. Stop doing this to yourself. To us."

Claypot lifted his head to the sky. "My daughter is not dead," he said loudly.

The sky did not answer.

He lowered his head and looked at all of us in turn. Glared at us. "She was right here. In the tent. She was asleep until you assholes showed up and screwed everything up."

Judy sighed. I felt bad for her. She had been putting up with the guy for a long time. She must have been dog tired.

"Come on," she said to me and Gayle. "Let's leave him to his delusions."

She walked toward us. Claypot called to her. "She's your daughter too," he said. Only his voice was soft, like he wanted to be quiet. He was the tender Claypot for just a second. But he would turn soon. Always did. You could not count on his soft side for long. If you did, you would get smacked, but good.

Judy wanted to turn to him, I could see it in her face and in the way she hesitated with her next step. But she didn't turn around. Instead she looked at us. It was as though she wanted me and Gayle to help her. Help her do what, I wasn't sure. But something.

"Make him stop," she whispered. "It's time to stop. For everyone."

"I don't know how," I said.

She nodded. She knew what I knew: there was no explanation for Claypot's behavior. He was a damaged man. A genius tormented by his own demons. Or demons we could not ever understand.

When do you abandon someone?

It was a question I had been asking myself for a while. When was it okay to, in effect, tell someone that they were no longer needed in your life? Especially when that person was not able to fend for himself in any meaningful and productive way?

I think, somehow, in that moment, we all decided that the time had come.

Gayle kept moving, like a sleepwalker. Claypot looked at us. He was not exactly pleading, but he still wanted something. Redemption, maybe? Or a sign. From who? Surely not us. From God, maybe. Or the cosmos in general.

"I'll keep looking for her," he said. "I found her once. I was going to bring her to you, after she had her nap. Remember she liked her afternoon naps. Such an amazing child, and you turn your back on her. Judy! Judy!"

She didn't look back.

# *Ignore Personal Grooming*

ABOUT THAT TIME, maybe a few days later, I saw a change in Gayle. She had wistful memories of Claypot. She talked about him as full of life and not afraid to confront the reality of his existence.

"Are you serious?" I said. "Claypot is the most out of touch with reality person I've ever known. He has no concept of himself as not knowing what is real and what isn't."

"But he revels in that," she said.

"I'm not following."

Gayle looked at me the way someone looks at a child who does not understand but must be made to for the safety of all involved.

"Think about it," she said. "He is perfectly capable of making a home for himself in the woods. He has no problem using the infrastructure around him to get what he needs. Like when he got you to buy things for him. He is very adept at manipulating the media, and he can pull sympathy for his situation from a rock. He's not incapable of distinguishing fantasy from reality. On the contrary he's very adept at putting fantasy into reality for his own benefit."

Sometimes you need someone else to explain the obvious to you. "So we haven't seen the last of him," I said.

"Nope."

"He's playing us."

"Yup."

"What about Judy?"

"What about her?"

"She still loves him. I think." I needed another woman's perspective on that.

"It isn't exactly that she loves him. It's more that she feels sorry for him. Also, I think she needs for him to move on from Stacey's death so she can move on as well. It's like he's a piece of her and he's not willing to understand that. It's hurting them both."

I wasn't sure I understood what she meant by that. "I think she's moved on from Stacey's death," I said. "I think she's found a way to continue her life without Claypot."

"Not exactly. I think deep down she's holding onto a little bit of Stacey because Claypot is holding onto a big piece of Stacey. She can't quite make herself let go because Claypot hasn't let go. On any level."

It may sound like all we ever talked about was Claypot and his travails. That wasn't exactly true, but it wasn't exactly false, either. We had found that we could not let Claypot and his life go. We wanted to constantly know exactly how he was. His welfare plagued our lives. Or his lack of it, I suppose. It was like having a dog and losing it. You may not know where it is, but you hope it is still alive and thriving somewhere. That's what Claypot was: a stray dog. A mutt that everyone tolerated and loved in spite of their better judgment.

The days went on. I wanted to go to the park and see if Claypot was there. Winter would soon be on us and I worried about him outside with only a thin tent for protection. We don't get the most severe weather in the world, but Portland can be cold, freezing even. We do get one or two good snowy spells every winter. I didn't want my stray dog to succumb to the weather.

But I didn't go. I left him to his own devices.

Then one Sunday morning, while Gayle and I lingered over breakfast and the morning paper, the doorbell rang. We looked at each other: me in T-shirt and underwear. Gayle in a raggedy old robe.

"I'll go see who it is," she said.

"I'll go upstairs and put some pants on," I said.

I scooted up to the bedroom and pulled on a pair of trousers. I heard muted female voices coming from downstairs.

I went back down the stairs.

"Hi Chris," said Judy. "Hope I didn't wake you guys up on your day off."

"Not at all," I said. "Just getting decent. How are you?"

She looked terrible. She had obviously not washed or brushed her hair in days. She looked like she had been wearing the same clothes for at least as long. I flashed on an image of Claypot, the unkempt artist. Had Judy taken up his way of being in the world? I hoped not. It didn't do him any good and I didn't think it could possibly help Judy either.

"I'm okay," she said. "I was telling Gayle that I've figured it out."

Gayle looked at me sideways, like she wanted to tell me a secret without anyone else in the room knowing. She put her hand on Judy's back and eased her into the living room. Judy seemed grateful and relieved, like she thought we were about to throw her out of the house and suddenly changed our minds. She sat down on the couch. She looked hungry.

"Do you want some breakfast?" said Gayle. "I can whip up some toast and eggs."

"No," said Judy. "Some coffee would be nice, though. I haven't had an appetite in days."

"Coffee coming up." Gayle went into the kitchen.

"So what's all this?" I said.

Judy took a deep breath and let it out. "I've been a wreck ever since that last time with Clay, but I think I know what to do now. Finally."

I raised my eyebrows. "Uh huh?"

"I've been practicing." She held out her arm and turned it so her palm faced up. I saw a tattoo of a brick wall on her forearm. I think my eyebrows went up even higher.

"What's this?"

"I got some tattooing equipment from a shop that was going out of business. I've been learning how to use it. What do you think?"

The image was certainly competent. I was no expert

on tattooing, but it looked fine to me, as good as anything I had seen on anyone.

Gayle came back into the living room with a cup of coffee in her hand. She put it down on the end table next to Judy.

"Wow," she said, noticing Judy's arm. "Can I take a closer look?"

Judy swung around so her arm was directly under Gayle's gaze. Gayle exuded frank admiration. "That is amazing," she said. "You got the texture of the bricks and the mortar. I'm impressed."

"Thanks," said Judy. "It's going to save Claypot."

"How so?" I said. Gayle sat down on the couch. Judy looked wildly around. She reminded me of some of those people you see on the street sometimes. The ones who fly a sign and look as though they aren't a part of the known world. Where did Judy disappear to? Claypot Planet?

"Here's the thing," she said. "Claypot thinks Stacey will come through one of his trompe l'oeil things. It's crazy, but that's what he believes. I think Stacey is still in him. In his heart. And it hurts too much. He needs to let her go."

I thought all of that was obvious, but I didn't say anything to Judy. I wanted her to say whatever it was she had to say. For her own sake.

"Here's my idea. I tattoo a wall and a trompe l'oeil hole in the wall. Right over his chest. Then Stacey can come through the hole and he'll be much better. We all will be."

I wanted to say it was a great idea, to boost her up a bit, but I did not feel that way at all. It sounded like a terrible idea.

"Judy, honey," said Gayle. "How are you going to get Claypot to let you put a tattoo on him?"

Judy's face brightened up like someone had installed a 250 watt bulb behind her eyes. "That's where you guys come in," she said.

Oh no.

"He respects you both. I know he does. He likes your strength and determination, Chris."

Strength and determination? That didn't sound right.

"And Gayle," said Judy. "He thinks the world of you. He thinks you are a spiritual force for good."

"I don't know about any of that," said Gayle.

"I know it sounds nutty," said Judy, "but he told me. He said you both are amazing people."

"Okay," I said. "Let's leave that for the moment. It sounds crazy to me, but maybe it's true. But even if it is. How on Earth are we ever going to get him to sit still for a tattoo? I think I remember him saying something about how tattoos are an abomination."

"Oh, he just says things," said Judy.

"I think Chris is right," said Gayle. "Even if he loved tattoos, which I don't think he does, he wouldn't want you to tattoo him."

"That's what I'm saying. All we need is for you two to talk to him and he'll go along with my plan."

What is it about love that makes people think the world works differently than it does?

"I don't know," said Gayle. "I don't see that we would have any influence on Claypot at all."

"I'm with my wife on this one," I said. "Also, we

have no idea where he is."

"I do," said Judy. "He's on Mount Hood."

"He's living on Mount Hood?"

She pulled out a post card from her purse. It showed a picture of Timberline Lodge, the big ski lodge on the mountain. She handed it to me. I flipped it over. The back bore a short message, written in a child-like script of block letters. "Dear Gayle. I've followed Stacey to here. I will find her on the mountain. Do not despair. All is forgiven. Clay." I noted the lack of an endearment above his signature. This was a pretty flimsy pice of evidence to base a life plan on. I handed it to Gayle, who scanned it quickly, then looked up at Judy.

"When did you get this?" I said.

"Two days ago."

"Have you talked to him?"

"No. What does that matter? Let's go up there and find him."

"You don't even know if he's on the mountain. He could have sent this postcard from anywhere."

"Look at the post mark," said Gayle.

She gave me the card and I saw the cancellation over the stamp: "Government Camp." That was a small town at the base of Mount Hood.

"Okay," I said. "So he mailed something from the mountain. That doesn't mean he's living there. How could he? It's cold there. He'd freeze to death."

"He's survived winters outside before," said Gayle.

"In the city," I said. "There's a lot of heat in cities, even in winter. You have buildings to shelter you from wind. Timberline is six thousand feet up. It gets cold there."

"Look," said Judy, "if you don't want to help me, then say so."

She looked lost and helpless. I wondered if that was genuine or calculated, then reproached myself silently for thinking such thoughts. She wanted to help the man she loved. And she wanted our help to do it.

"We could go up there," said Gayle. "Why not? It would be a nice Sunday drive, if nothing else."

I had been just about to tell Judy her husband was not worth the effort. Even reveled in the anticipatory joy of saying that out loud. But when I saw Judy's look of relief mixed with astonishment, I changed my mind. I never was a tough guy. No use trying to start to be one now.

"Sure," I said. "Why not. No big loss, right? Even if we don't find him?"

# *Be Suspicious of Scents*

JUDY WANTED TO take her car, but I wanted to be in control of the situation, so I made it clear it was our vehicle or no one's. Judy readily agreed. Gayle threw together a quick lunch while Judy and I moved her tattoo equipment from her trunk to mine. "You think he'll let you ink him right there when we find him?" I said.

"Probably not, but who knows? I want to be prepared."

The ink had an oily odor to it. It wafted up from the needles and canisters.

"Where'd you learn to tattoo?" I asked as I closed the trunk. We leaned against the car, me relaxed, she very nervous. I knew this was going to be just an ordinary drive. No way were we going to find Claypot on Mount Hood. I think she was nervous because she more or less believed the same thing, but did not want to. She still had some crazy idea that she could find the motherfucker. For myself, I didn't know why she still wanted to.

We felt the sun on our faces. It was one of those nice fall days: brilliant light, but not too much heat. Comfortable. "From books," she finally said. "I learned it all on my own. It's not that hard."

"I've often thought that there is a lot of responsibility in tattooing," I said.

"Oh yeah? You think about tattooing?"

"Just that if you make a mistake, it's always there on the person's skin. You can't decide to get rid of a picture if you don't like it or think it doesn't suit you anymore. I'd be nervous as hell putting ink into a person."

She shrugged. "It's not that big a deal. People are very forgiving of errors, I've found."

"You know none of this will help," I said. "You know that, right?"

She didn't look at me. She kept her gaze on the sky, as though she could find an answer there, a soothing something. I didn't know. In a way, I didn't want to know: it was all futile. She must have known it too, on some level.

"Let's go in and help Gayle," I said.

She jumped away from the car and we both went inside.

"Got the equipment all stowed away," I said to Gayle, who was wrapping up sandwiches and putting them into a small cooler.

"Good for you. We want to take anything else besides some sandwiches?"

"Fruit would be nice," said Judy.

"I've got apples and bananas."

"Perfect."

"What does Claypot like?" I said.

They both looked at me.

"When we find him," I said, "I suspect he's going to be hungry."

"Good point," said Gayle.

"He's always been partial to pears. Loves the crunch of unripe ones."

"We don't have any," said Gayle.

"We'll stop at the store on the way out of town."

We weren't in any hurry. I think we all assumed Claypot would keep. Whatever place he had sunk to, he probably wasn't about to leave it on his own, so we did not necessarily have a tremendously pressing reason to get to the mountain quickly. For myself, I think I would have been perfectly happy to leave him to his own devices for the rest of his life. But that would have been unkind, and I had never seen myself as an unkind person. Oblivious at times, yes, but generally not purposely cruel or negligent. Claypot was a human being in trouble. I didn't see how I could help him get out of trouble, but trying to do so was a kindness to Judy that I was more than willing to extend.

We got into the car, me driving, Gayle in the back seat, Judy in the passenger seat. She seemed very tense.

We stopped at a supermarket on the way out of town. I went inside and bought a few pears. They were hard as rocks. If Judy knew her man, Claypot would like them.

When I came out to the car, Judy and Gayle were both in the back seat.

I got behind the wheel.

"To the lodge, Jeeves," said Gayle.

Judy laughed.

"When did I become a chauffeur?" I said.

"We just promoted you."

"So I get a raise."

"In this economy?" said Judy. "Don't be ridiculous. You should be happy we provide you with a roof over your head and gainful employment."

"We?"

"Yes, Gayle and I have started a new business. We're going to save husbands from their lame selves."

"Oh," I said. "And that would include me?"

"Of course it would include you. You're a lame husband just like all of them."

Ha ha.

"I leave you two alone for five minutes and you've decided to reconfigure civilization?" I said.

"Something like that," said Gayle. "Now get this vehicle moving. We've got a mission to attend to."

Traffic was light through town. I got on the expressway going east and in less than an hour we exited at the town of Hood River, not too far from the peak. We climbed a slightly meandering two lane road for the next hour and a half and passed through the Hood River Valley, lush with orchards on either side of us.

"We should have got some pears from here," said Gayle.

"They'd probably be overpriced," I said.

"Silence!" said Judy. "If we want to hear your opinion, and it is very unlikely that we would, we will ask for it."

Okay. I guess they were having fun with their game. I did not see the charm.

The mountain loomed up before us, draped in pure white. Glaciers covered the slopes up there and a lot of snow had fallen in the last few days. I was sure the skiers were very happy. It occurred to me that perhaps Claypot could scavenge a half decent living from the well-to-do who frequented the ski slopes up there. Maybe he could mooch something from the lodge kitchen, although if he was too belligerent or obnoxious, they would probably chuck him into the snow. Serve him right, too.

As we got closer the mountain seemed to bow down to us. I had the feeling it could scoop us off the road and lift us to the sky. Absurd, but there it was. I have been to Mount Hood a few times and each trip I get the same sensation: that the mountain not only wants to take care of me, but is eager to make me as comfortable as possible. Maybe Claypot saw the same thing. Maybe that's what made him come here.

If he was here.

I glanced at Judy and Gayle in the rear view mirror. They looked out the window in the back. Apparently the mountain gave them something as well.

A few minutes later we were above the tree line. Bare rock streaked with snow and ice surrounded us on all sides. The road had been plowed, but some slushy patches remained here and there, as well as several stretches of compact snow that the sun had not yet melted.

I drove slowly, not wanting to skid on any of the road hazards.

Others were not so careful. I saw a car fishtailing on

the road a quarter mile in front of us. I took my foot off the gas to give the fishtailer all the room he needed.

Judy and Gayle looked away from the window. "What's going on?" said Gayle.

"A guy up ahead is having trouble," I said. "Doesn't know how to drive in this, I guess."

"Slow down."

"I did."

The guy could not get his car under control. His swerving not only continued, but worsened. His back wheels caught the gravel on the side of the road and dug in. The car flipped over, rolled once, touched the rock that lined the roadway as though it was prepared to drive across the cliff face, then rolled back on its roof, where it lay still like felled prey.

I had faded a good distance behind the car by then. I slowed even more and eased onto the shoulder.

"Call 911," I said to no one in particular.

"Already on it," said Gayle, who had her phone flipped open and punched in the number.

Judy and I got out of the car and sprinted over to the wreck. Other cars had also stopped on the other side of the road. Before long a dozen people had gathered around the wreck. I peered into the window. I saw a young man, maybe in his late twenties, suspended by his seat belt. He appeared to be conscious but unable to move. He said something, but I couldn't make out what it was with all the people outside shuffling around and making noise of their own. I pulled on the passenger door but could not budge it. Someone behind me touched my shoulder. I looked back. He looked a lot bigger than me so I stepped aside and let him try to pull the door. He got himself situated and yanked for all he was worth.

No go. The door had been crumpled when it rolled over and now it was jammed up in its own frame.

"We need to get him out," said someone. "The car could catch fire."

I did smell gasoline. The tank must have ruptured. Could this car explode? I didn't know.

Gayle grabbed my arm. "The ambulance is coming," she said. "There's nothing we can do here."

She pulled me away. I let her, reluctantly. The man was very scared. I didn't want to leave him alone. He should be seeing human faces around him. He might die. He shouldn't be alone.

But I also saw Gayle's point. I wanted to do something. Anything. I listened for the sound of the ambulance siren. Nothing. We were up here on the mountain. Where was the ambulance coming from? How far?

Then, in the middle of this chaos, me feeling completely helpless and even useless, a familiar voice.

No, first a familiar smell. Body odor mixed with chalk dust.

I turned around.

"What the fuck is going on here?"

Claypot came lumbering up the road. He brushed past me like he didn't know who I was. He went right up to the wrecked car. "Get the fuck out of my way, motherfuckers," he said. A couple of men, who were still attempting to dislodge the passenger door, parted for Claypot. He wedged his foot against the car's chassis, planted his other foot on the rock next to the car, took a deep breath, and pulled on the door handle.

Metal screeched and scraped. We, the people gathered around the wreck, were all startled by the sound. The door cracked open a short distance, barely wide enough to see a seam of light along its edge. Claypot put his fingers into the seam and peeled back the door so it flopped against the side of the car. Then he reached into the interior where the man had his hands extended toward the open door. Claypot released the seat belt so the man fell from his seat. Then Claypot grasped the man's forearms and pulled him out of the car, carrying him like he was light as a piece of paper. He turned around, looking for someplace to put him down. One of the onlookers had retrieved a blanket from her car and arranged it on the bed of a pickup truck that had parked some short distance away. The woman guided Claypot toward the pickup.

He carried the man the short distance and laid him on the blanket with a gentleness I imagined Claypot had reserved for his daughter. Maybe for Judy, once, a long time ago.

After he put the man down, several people attended to him. One had a first aid kit from her car.

I was stunned into complete silence and stillness by Claypot. Not others, though. They clustered around him and patted him on the back and shoulder. General murmurs of congratulations and adoration floated up from everyone. Claypot took it in stride for the most part, but you could tell he was not comfortable with all the attention. He wanted to get away. He slid to the side, away from the pickup. Several people took pictures of him.

Someone said, "Hey, aren't you that guy from the TV, that artist who does chalk murals."

"No," said Claypot.

"Yeah, yeah, you're the one."

Claypot looked like he was kicked in the stomach. He didn't want to be here anymore.

I heard the siren getting closer. All of us did, including Claypot, who's ears perked up like a dog's. "The professionals are coming now," he said. "They'll know what to do."

I realized Judy and Gayle were no longer next to me. They had gone to the man in the pickup and helped put blankets and jackets on him to keep him warm.

Judy stood beside Claypot. She was so small next to him.

"Are you all right?" she said.

Claypot nodded.

"What were you doing here?"

"I heard the crash. Figured something was wrong. I came down to take a look." He shrugged.

I had finally found a way to move. I walked over to Claypot.

"Good job," I said. "You saved that guy's life."

"Did I?"

"Hell, yeah, you did."

"I think I saved him from a few minutes of discomfort. The ambulance is on its way. He wasn't in danger of dying or anything. He's mostly okay."

"Whatever you did, it was amazing. You took care of business, did what had to be done."

"I think I'm going to go now," he said.

Such a strange manner of speech for Claypot. So tenuous and unsure of himself. I felt shame for him at that moment and then felt ridiculous for feeling it. I had nothing to be ashamed of, and neither did he.

He made a motion to his side, as though he was about to walk away from us. Walk off the mountain.

Judy grabbed his arm. He stopped, a mountain himself, stilled.

"Did you find her?" she said.

He closed his eyes and looked even more lost than before, if that was possible.

Judy put her hand on his chest.

"You can't save everyone," she said.

Claypot nodded.

"Where are you living? How are you getting by?"

"There's people here that help me."

The wail of the ambulance grew louder. We all turned toward the curve in the highway behind us. The lights flashed periodic red bursts across our faces. I left Judy and Claypot and went over to Gayle, still attending to the man from the wreck.

"How is he?" I asked.

"Seems mostly okay. He might have a broken bone or something. Hard to tell. He's conscious."

"That's good, right?"

"Yeah, I'm sure. How's Claypot?"

"Dazed and confused. I'm worried about him."

"He's a hero now," she said.

"He doesn't think he's a hero."

The ambulance stopped next to the wreck. The paramedics got out. People guided them to the injured man. We watched as they bundled him up and put him on a stretcher and got him into the ambulance. By that time a police car had arrived and the officer was interviewing witnesses. The ambulance drove away. I heard the officer say, "Who pulled him out of the car?"

Someone pointed to where Claypot stood not five minutes ago. "He used to be there."

I looked in the same place. Claypot and Judy were gone.

I took a deep breath. The air smelled like metal.

"So where did they go?" said Gayle.

# *Cut Down a Tree*

WE TOLD THE officer what we knew. He asked us what happened to Claypot. We said he probably didn't want any fuss made over him.

"Too bad," said the officer. "He did a good deed. He should get recognized for it."

"Oh," I said, "that's not like him at all. He's a very modest man."

I didn't mention that he had been in trouble with the law over multiple instances of vandalism.

We stayed long enough to watch a tow truck come and haul the wrecked car away, hoping that Claypot and Judy would come back, but by the time our feet began to feel like lumps of ice, we decided they weren't coming back.

We drove up to the lodge, a short distance away.

Timberline Lodge was built in the thirties, part of

the governments plan to get people back to work during the depression years. It is made of local trees and a lot of stonework. When you walk into it you have the feeling of strength and solidity, like nothing will ever wreck this place, not weather, or earthquakes, or even economic upheaval.

Maybe that's why Claypot came here. He needed the safety of an imposing structure.

Several ski lifts snaked away from the back of the lodge and took people a couple of thousand feet up the mountain to the top of the ski runs. Despite it's more or less domestic feel, the mountain is still a wild place. If you venture off the ski trails too far, you can get lost. Hikers do every year. A staple of Portland news shows is the report of people on the mountain waiting to get rescued. Sometimes people die.

"So," said Gayle as we stood in the lobby of the lodge and looked through the wide windows to dots floating down on the powder.

"Yeah," I said. "So where are they? Why'd they leave us at the wreck?"

Gayle went to the clerk at the desk.

"We're looking for a grubby big guy," she said. "Large beard, wild hair. Has he been around here?"

"You mean Mr. Dreamstance?"

Gayle looked startled. "You know his name?"

"Sure. He's been working on the mural."

"Mural?" I said.

The clerk nodded. "Around the back of the lodge."

"Thanks," said Gayle.

We hurried away from the desk and out the front door and walked briskly around the lodge to the back.

The ground swelled up and we had to clamber over patches of snow and rock. The lodge presented a face of hewn wood. As we continued around the corner, both of us slipped on the slick surface and we had to dodge snowboarders whooshing past us at the end of their runs.

"Sorry man," one of them said as he whizzed by.

"It's dangerous here," I said.

"We could use Claypot right about now for protection," said Gayle.

We hurried as best we could until we were uphill from the lodge. Then we turned around to look at the back wall.

I'm not sure what I expected to see, or what I was hoping to see, but what I did see made me stare in silence.

Claypot had recreated the mountain, the mountain we now stood on, but he had populated it with trees. We were at the six thousand foot level here at the lodge. The lodge is named Timberline because trees do not grow higher than about six thousand feet of elevation on Mount Hood. Except they did, at least in Claypot's imagination, and in the picture he created for the lodge. Mount Hood positively bristled with evergreen trees, like they were the pins in a giant pincushion.

A pine cushion.

"Wow," said Gayle.

"Yeah, it's amazing," I said. "What a fantastic picture."

"I'm not wowing about the picture," said Gayle. "I'm wowing because it isn't a trompe l'oeil."

She was right, and I had not noticed that at all. Claypot was always about the trompe l'oeil. Except now.

"There's something else," she said.

"What?"

"Step back a little more. I think you'll see it better."

I was a little puzzled, but nevertheless did as she said. I stepped up the mountain a few yards, then turned and looked at the picture again.

It took a few seconds, maybe half a minute, for me to see what she was talking about. The trees were more than a random collection. They had a second dimension to them, a secondary representation. I did not immediately recognize the image, but knew it was a face. The details of the boughs and the spaces between the trees: Claypot had artfully arranged them so that they formed a portrait.

Of Stacey.

She looked exactly like that snapshot I had seen earlier. I knew it was Stacey as soon as the floating image locked into view.

Gayle clambered up the mountain and stood beside me.

"He did find her," she said.

I wasn't sure that was right. "He at least recreated her," I said.

"Same thing," said Gayle. "At least for him."

"How did he ever get the management to agree to let him do this?" I said.

"Who knows? He can be very persuasive."

I knew Claypot was a good artist with good technical skills. I didn't know he had this in him, the ability to make one picture appear to be two very different kinds of pictures at the same time.

"So where is he?" said Gayle.

A scaffolding clung to one edge of the mural. Evidently Claypot still had some work to do. But not much, by the look of it.

Then I thought of something else. This mural was temporary, like all his work.

"It's chalk, isn't it?" I said to Gayle.

"Appears to be."

"So he's still not ready to make a statement that lasts."

"Maybe that's how he got them to agree to it. The rain will wash this away in a few weeks."

I felt an incredible let down at that moment. I thought Claypot, by the evidence of this mural, had come to some new understanding of the world, or at least some new way to be in the world, a way that allowed him to make something that lasted. I felt so proud of him, as though I myself had something to do with his new found blossoming. Which was absurd. But now, seeing that it wasn't permanent at all, that he still needed to let his creations slip away into nothing, I felt a deep sadness. Like something had seized my bones and wrestled them into twisted bits of metal. I felt nauseous.

"You okay?" said Gayle. "You look white as a ghost."

"I think I need some water," I said.

We gingerly retraced our steps to the front door of the lodge and went inside. Gayle waited by the front desk while I went to the bathroom. The nausea subsided, but I still felt off, as though my head didn't quite fit on my neck properly. It was as though I did not fit properly into my own skin. An odd sensation, and not something I would have expected just from seeing Claypot's mural.

I ran some water in the sink and splashed my face. I was pretty sure I wasn't going to lose my breakfast and once I dried my face with some paper towels I left the restroom to find Gayle. She sat on a bench underneath a wood carving of Mount Hood.

"Better?" she asked.

"Better," I said. "Out there I felt like something was getting pulled out of me."

"Pulled out?"

I nodded. "All of a sudden back there, looking at the trees Claypot drew, it was like I was in the wrong skin and it didn't feel good or right."

"You know," said Gayle, "I think it's long past time that we divorced ourselves from Claypot."

"We keep trying."

"We have to try harder."

"I'm amazed he could get the lodge people to let him mark up their wall like that."

We heard a thump, muffled but definitely there. It didn't exactly shake the building, but it did make it shiver.

"What was that?" I said.

"An earthquake?" said Gayle.

My cell phone rang.

I flipped it open.

"Hello?"

"Where have you been?" Judy's voice.

"We're looking for you," I said. "Where did you go?"

"We're up on the mountain. Claypot wanted to take

the ski lift."

"What for?"

"He said he needed to get away."

"Do you have skis?"

"No."

"Snowboards?"

"No."

"How do you expect to get down?"

"We're walking. It's quite a view up here."

"Judy."

"I know, I know. He's ahead of me right now. Taking giant steps through the snow. He still thinks he can find Stacey."

"What's going on?" said Gayle.

I put my thumb over the phone and whispered to her. "They're higher up on the mountain. Walking down."

"Give me the phone."

I handed it to her and listened while she told Judy she needed to get down the mountain. It wasn't safe.

They talked for a few more seconds. Then Gayle snapped the phone shut. "She says she saw a snowboarder run into the lodge."

"What?"

"From up the mountain. A snowboarder smashed into Claypot's mural."

We ran out the building and went around back to look at the mural. Sure enough, a young man lay sprawled at the bottom of the wall. A snowboard stuck out of the snow next to him and what a lodge employee was busy administering first aid to the snowboarder's arm.

"That must be the shake we felt earlier," said Gayle.

I looked away from the wall and the fallen snowboarder and turned my attention to the mountain. I scanned the snow for Claypot and Judy. I thought I saw them, two slow dots way up the slope, crawling along while the skiing and snowboarding dots whipped by them at alarming speed.

"Judy said Claypot was going crazy that someone was trying to mar his mural," said Gayle.

"That's nuts," I said.

"Of course it is."

"Claypot is a crazy man."

"Yeah."

"Did Judy get to propose her plan to him, the one about the tattoos?"

"She didn't say on the phone."

We both looked at Claypot and Judy. The distance between them lengthened. We both studied the gap for several seconds, each of us unsure what to make of this development.

"That asshole isn't even letting Judy keep up with him," said Gayle.

Claypot fell. He toppled like a tree cut down for timber. He got up immediately.

Gayle shook her head. "I hope Judy doesn't try to run down the hill."

Claypot fell again. Got up. Took a few steps, fell once more.

He tried to rise one more time, but he was a lot slower. He got to his knees and I could see the breath coming out of him. He moved slowly, as if he could not find purchase for his feet.

Judy was getting closer to him.

"Should we go up and help?" said Gayle.

"That probably wouldn't be wise." I said.

"I know. You're right. But look at him."

"He does it to himself," I said.

"I know I know."

The lodge employee who was tending to the fallen snowboarder called to us.

"Hey you guys," he said.

We turned around.

"You know that guy on the mountain?"

"Yeah," I said.

The snowboarder sat up. He had a nasty looking bruise on his face, like he had slammed into the wall on his nose and chalk dust colored his cheek. I wondered how someone could miss the back end of the lodge and run right into it. Must have been distracted by something.

"He's a strange guy."

"We've been told that," said Gayle.

The snowboarder spoke up. "I saw this little girl in the picture."

"What?" I said.

"From up the mountain, at the top of the run, I looked down at the picture. I had seen it before, but I didn't pay much attention. Then I saw that it wasn't trees at all. It was a little girl."

"Stacey," Gayle and I both said at the same time.

"Who's Stacey?" said the snowboarder. By this time he had gotten to his feet. The man attending to him tried to help him along and take a few steps, but the snowboarder brushed him away. "I'm fine," he said.

"Stacey's the artist's daughter."

The snowboarder nodded. "That guy up there has a daughter."

"Had," I said. "Stacey died."

The snowboarder nodded slowly. "Right," he said. "That makes all kinds of sense, because the picture is way sad. Like the saddest thing I've ever seen in my life. The little girl, she should be happy, you know. Like, if you're not happy when you're a kid, then forget it. You're *never* going to be happy, you know? And she is, she's laughing or whatever. But it isn't real. She's sad at the same time that she's laughing. You have to be up at the top of the run to see her. Then she pops out of the wall. It's amazing."

The snowboarder had a definite limp to his walk. He hobbled by us with a goofy grin on his face, like he was a character in a cartoon.

"Huh," said Gayle after he had gone, presumably back to his room at the lodge. Or maybe to sit by the fire in the lobby and tell tales of his encounter with the wall.

"The kid's right," I said.

"I still don't want to go up there," said Gayle.

We looked back up the slope. Claypot was sprawled out on the snow. Judy stood over him. She had her hands on her hips.

Gayle cupped her hands to her ears, aiming her palms up the mountain to try to hear them.

I did the same. Deer ears, Gayle called it. It can bring in sound from far away.

"Hear anything?" I said.

"Shhh," said Gayle.

She took a few steps up the mountain. So his mural

was finished, and Claypot had decided he would spend his days luxuriating in the snow of Mount Hood. If anyone could do it, live in the cold at six thousand feet, Claypot could. He was not civilized in any real sense of the word, but he was resourceful and he knew how to make people do things for him. Or how to allow him to do what he wanted. Like make a portrait of his daughter on the wall at Timberline Lodge.

"I think," said Gayle, "that she's telling him he's full of shit and needs to get his fucking life together and start grieving Stacey's life instead of trying to bring her back to life."

"You think?"

"Her voice is very faint, but that's what I would be saying to the cocksucker right about now."

"You seem very comfortable with Clay speak," I said.

"It grows on you after a while. It's very expressive."

I still heard nothing from the mountain except for stray shouts and snippets of conversation from the snowboarders and skiers cruising down the slope and sending up sprays of snow. As I watched, one of those skiers came to a stop on the slope next to Claypot. Claypot didn't move. He lay on the snow with his legs apart and his arms flung to his sides. He looked like a black X on the white snow. Like someone had typed him on a big sheet of paper, x-ing out his life so now he was just a single character. Nothing but a glyph, not even hoping for redemption anymore, not trying for anything at all.

Other skiers stopped with the first skier.

"He always gets people to feel sorry for him," said

Gayle. "That's quite a gift, you know."

"I suppose so," I said.

Two of the skiers bent down and grabbed Claypot's hands. They tried to pull him up to a seated or standing position, but their efforts came to nothing. Claypot is a big guy. You don't get him to go anyplace he doesn't want to go.

Before long a large group of downhillers clustered around Claypot and Judy. Judy's arms tossed around in the air like she was doing semaphore in fast motion. I think she was telling them all to leave Claypot alone. He had his own way of being in the world. He didn't need them to help.

Or maybe she was telling Claypot to stop being such a stubborn ass and let these nice people help him. It could have gone either way and there was no sure way to tell from where we were.

"You think he's coming down?" I said to Gayle.

"I think we've watched this movie long enough. Let's go get something to eat."

We went back to the car and pulled out the bag of sandwiches and took them to the lobby.

Both of us ate quickly and quietly. As I neared the end of my sandwich, I looked around for a garbage can. I didn't see any. Maybe there was one outside?

Gayle must have had the same idea. She usually ate slowly, but this time she didn't linger over her food.

"How long you think Claypot will stay up that mountain?" I said.

"I think he wants to die there," said Gayle.

"Oh." I hadn't thought of that.

"We can't save him, you know. We all want to do

that, but we can't. Only Stacey could do that, and only if she rose from the dead."

"So then he's not going to be saved, is that what you're saying?"

"No, he won't. Not as long as we keep coddling him and trying to make him see the light. Our light."

"Is that what we've been doing?"

"I think so," she said.

We gathered up our lunch trash and bunched it into a big ball. Then we went outside, looking for a trash can.

"Hey." Judy's voice.

We turned around.

"Why did you and Clay run off like that?" said Gayle. "We were worried about you."

"He wanted to," said Judy. "I couldn't say no."

"We saw you up the slope. Where is he?"

"Still there. He won't move."

I sighed. More dramatics from the drama king.

"What do you mean he won't move?" said Gayle.

"He says he'll stay up there until Stacey comes back."

I checked my watch. It was almost noon. Not too cold yet. The sun was directly on Claypot, so even though he was lying on snow, he shouldn't be in too much danger of getting cold. Nevertheless, soon the temperature would drop. Below freezing, probably. No way could he stay up there all night. Time to arrange another rescue of Claypot Dreamstance. Time to put our lives on hold while we figured out what to do about the great artist and his temperamental ways.

"Did you tell him about the tattoo idea you had?"

said Judy.

"I think maybe that was what made him decide he wanted to live on the mountain."

"What?" I said.

"We went up there to show me the mural from far away. It really rocks when you step waaaaay back."

"So we heard," I said.

"Anyway, I went up there with him. And I saw Stacey in the trees. It was important to him so I told him how wonderful it was to see her again. He liked that."

I looked up at the sky momentarily in a here-we-go-again way. Discreetly, or so I thought, but Judy caught the gesture.

"I know," she said. "I'm a push over for him. I can't help it."

"We all are," said Gayle. "Go on."

"It's crazy, but then he told me there was a spot where he knew Stacey would come back to him. To us. He said the spot was a little bit down the slope from where we were, so we started walking down."

I held my tongue, though I wanted to tell her she needed to be more direct with Claypot. She needed to tell him that his whole Stacey coming back to life fixation was flat out insane.

"Something happens on mountains," said Gayle. "You get this feeling that life is much more grand than you have known. He said she was up here, lost in the snow or the trees. As we started walking down, he made sure I looked at the mural. The snow is so deep and slippery up there. It was not easy coming down. We slid on some parts, fell in up to our knees in other. I wanted to walk more on the groomed parts of the slope, but here were lots of snowboarders going by too fast and it didn't look like they paid much attention to civilians like us, so we stayed off and made our way as best we could."

"We saw you coming down," said Judy.

"I thought that was you looking at us."

"We thought you were both going to come all the way down," I said.

"Oh, hell," said Judy. "So did I. But I made the mistake of saying that I didn't see Stacey in the mural anymore. I just saw the trees."

"Oh, oh," said Gayle.

"Yup," said Judy. "As soon as I said that, he stopped walking and plunked his sorry ass on the snow and he wouldn't move. He said this was the spot he was talking about. When we didn't see Stacey in the picture, that was when we should wait for her to arrive. Out of thin air, I suppose." That last phrase she said with a definite touch of disgust in her voice. I related to her annoyance completely.

"So that was that. He said if I really loved him and Stacey I would stay there with him and wait for her. I tried to get him to stand up and keep walking. A bunch of skiers stopped to see if he was okay. They thought he hurt himself or something. None of them could get him to move either. I was at the end of my rope. I told him we could wait for Stacey in the lodge. She would find us. I thought that made a lot of sense. He told me I was full of shit."

"Bastard," said Gayle.

"Cocksucking asshole," I said.

Judy smiled in spite of herself. "We're all channeling him," she said.

"He lives, though he may die," I said, making it sound like a quote, even though it wasn't.

"He won't die," said Gayle. "He'll come to his senses eventually. He may spend a cold night there but he won't die. He's too tough for that."

"I'm not so sure," said Judy.

"Go on with the story," I said.

"Right. The snowboarders didn't know how to take us. We were like bizarre old people to them. Most of them were kids. They asked if we needed help. I said we needed a lot of help, but Claypot said he wanted them all to leave him alone. He was there to meet his daughter."

"That must have made them think you were extra special crazy," said Gayle.

"With sprinkles on top," said Judy.

She enjoyed telling the story. It was a way to spread out the burden of Claypot's existence. She didn't have to bear the weight of his delusions herself.

"Should we go up there and check on him?" I said.

"Fuck him," said Judy. "Cocksucking motherfucking asshole. May he freeze to death in the snow."

That sounded a little extreme. But Judy grinned the whole time she expressed disgust for Claypot.

"So then what happened?" said Gayle. "After Claypot told the snowboarders about Stacey."

"They wanted to know if she was coming down the slope. I told them no. They didn't know how to take that. 'Is she lost?' they asked. I told them no. 'Because a lot of people get lost on the mountain, you know.' I told them I knew that. 'So where is she, your daughter?' I told them she died three years ago. Clay didn't like that.

He glared at me. I told him it was the truth and it was about time everyone knew the truth. Stacey was gone and she wasn't coming back. I was completely fed up with him. I didn't want any more of his pictures or his delusions. I was so mean to him, but I couldn't help it. The snowboarders saw there was something going on with us, you know, the way people try to back away from couples having an argument in public? Claypot was turning red. He wanted to hit something, I think. Maybe me. I don't know. He would have settled for one of the snowboarders, I'm pretty sure."

"So did he?" asked Gayle.

"No. Instead, he fell back onto the snow. He put his hands and his legs out and didn't move. I asked him what he was doing. He said he was working on a new piece. He was drawing in the snow, using his body. I told him to get up and come down to the lodge. It was getting cold. My feet and hands were cold. He told me to fuck off. Me. Who was trying to help the piece of shit. So I told him about the tattoo I wanted to do on him. I said, sure, wait here if you want to. I'll come back with the equipment and I'll tattoo you right here on the mountain. Right over your heart. A picture of our daughter who you let die."

Judy stopped. She looked at both of us. I didn't know what to say.

"You told him that?" said Gayle.

Judy, who had been full of anger, now looked defeated and miserable, like someone suddenly told her house had been foreclosed on. She nodded. "God help me, I did."

"I'm going to go see what's up with him," I said.

Gayle nodded to me, and then guided Judy to the entrance of the lodge.

I went around the building and saw a cluster of people up the slope where Claypot had decided to make his stand. Many of them leaned over into the center of the cluster, their hands on their knees, their heads craned forward, as though trying to get a better look into an abyss. I thought of that first sidewalk picture of Claypot's that I had seen, how people stood around it, trying to look down into a hole. A hole that wasn't there. A drawing on the sidewalk. Was Claypot nothing but an image in the snow?

I sighed. What good was philosophical rumination now? I couldn't let the poor sap freeze to death up there. I began walking up the slope.

I thought I could get to him fairly quickly, but before long I was breathing hard and my legs felt like weights. I got tired within a short time and it still looked like I had a long way to go before I would get to Claypot. Downhillers still zipped by, though far fewer of them. Most of the skiers and snowboarders had stopped at the group that had formed around Claypot. They needed to see what was going on, I suppose.

I started to sweat and got a little chilled. I kept moving, one foot in front of the other, plod plod plod.

A snowboarder, evidently a beginner, was having trouble on the slope ahead. He wobbled back and forth, obviously going too fast for his skill level. I observed his difficulty with detached interest, until I realized that his erratic path was about to bring him directly into me.

Now here was a dilemma. I had to decide how to dodge the guy. Should I move left or should I go right?

I could see the guy's face. He was wild with fright and indecision. Not knowing what to do, he was barely holding on and hoping not to wipe out. I wanted him to wipe out before he got to me, but that did not appear to be a possibility.

He loomed up very rapidly. I saw pleading in his eyes, like he wanted me to fix it for him. Was this how that other guy slammed into Claypot's mural? I thought I saw the snowboarder veer to my left. I therefore leaped to my right. The guy came by me a split second later, going remarkably fast. I felt the spray of snow from the edge of his board, and heard the icy slide of his board over the snow.

He said something I couldn't quite make out, probably an apology, then he was by me and heading down the mountain. I turned to look. He managed to execute a ragged turn and ended up going off slope and into the trees. The snow there was quite deep, however, and he didn't slam into any trunk that would injure of kill him. Instead, the deep snow slowed him way down and he stopped short of any dangerous object.

"Whew," I said quietly as he lay sprawled on the snow. Then he got up, excitement filling him, and grabbed his board and headed for the lift.

I turned around to go back to climbing toward Claypot, just in time to see a skier fill my field of vision and hit me full on, smack dab in the center of my body. As I fell, I wondered if any limbs had broken.

Mostly, I saw trees, the tops and boughs of them, spiral away from me, careen across the sky, and reach for infinity.

# *Never Go to the Cemetery*

I FULLY EXPECTED to have to go to the hospital. I was completely prepared for a body cast or even a wheelchair, if it came to that. I accepted these possibilities with a certain calm trust in the infrastructure of the medical establishment and the good will of people whose job it is to look after those in trouble, especially those who have been injured by an accident. Or life.

Or, going further, lying there on the snow after the skier had finished with me, seeing the blue sky cupped over me, with patches of darkness here and there as my vision did strange things to me, I was even prepared to accept the possibility that I had severe, inoperable internal injuries, and that I had less than a couple of minutes of consciousness and not too much longer in the way of life. Like a true accepting Buddhist, I was prepared to let go of everything, all attachments and allow the world to be as it was, even in relation to me. What I'm trying to say in my faltering way, was that I was completely prepared to die and I understood Claypot Dreamstance at that precise moment as I had never understood him before.

I'm going to delay the story of Claypot just a little bit more to try to convey to you the enormity of the moment.

I was in considerable discomfort. My chest felt like it had been hit with a sledge hammer. I was sure I had a cut or two on my face: I felt blood trickle down my cheek. The back of my skull, firmly fixed to the ground, felt enormous, like my brain had swelled up and was trying to burst out. I felt a low level panic somewhere at the core of my self, but it was held firmly down by the peace I felt. I did try to move my arms and legs, but they were frozen solid, like if I did move them they would fracture and crumble into a shower of flakes.

All of which is to say that I was in a daze, but a clarifying rather than an obscuring daze.

The main clarification to my mind was that Claypot was right. He knew what life was about and his attempts to confront life's mysteries was a model for anyone grappling with what exactly we all were.

Moans, somewhere northeast of my head and out of my view, interrupted my ruminations.

I gritted my teeth and twisted my neck around to look at the source of the moans. The skier and his skies and poles were amassed in a heaping tangle near me. He looked funny, all twisted up in the snow.

"You okay?" I asked, a little surprised that my own voice remained intact.

"Wha . . . ?"

"Anything broken?" I said. "Anything bleeding?"

My arms raised themselves up. I watched my hands swing around, not quite realizing, for an instant, that they were my hands, but then my brain caught up with my muscles and I slotted into the physical reality of where I was and what I was doing.

The guy who had collided with me pulled out his cell phone and placed it next to his ear, which was still buried down in the snow, just out of my view.

"Yeah," he said. "I had an accident. Send someone up here. I don't know if I can get up on my own."

I raised myself on my elbow. I gulped air in gasps, but I felt like I was not permanently damaged. I had no chest pain as I drew in air, and my limbs felt more or less pain free.

A miracle of sorts, but I was still concerned that my companion in mayhem had not spoken to me.

"Smart," I said. "Getting out your phone like that. I didn't even think of that."

He raised his head and looked at me.

I don't think I've seen anyone quite so angry in a long time. Maybe never. I felt the blood drain from my head. He looked ready to kill me. My previous acceptance of the moment faded away.

"What the fuck were you *doing*?" he said.

"Um," I said. "I didn't mean to run into you."

"No, seriously. What the fuck are you doing on this hill, going *up* when you have no equipment and even less in the way of any kind of motherfucking brains?"

I wanted to ask him if he knew Claypot. "I could ask you why you felt the need to run into *me*."

He let his head flop back on the snow. "I saw some guys grouped together back there. Wondered what was going on."

"Ahhh," I said. "Distracted skier. You should have been watching where you were going."

"I guess so. But still. When I looked forward, there you were, fucking *standing* there like an idiot."

"I was going up to see how my friend was doing."

That satisfied him. He raised himself on one elbow, then managed to sit up. I did the same.

"Next time," he said, "find a better way to help your friend."

"I *guess* there's no permanent damage done," he said.

"Looks that way," I said. I put out my hand. "Name's Chris."

He looked at my hand like it was a bad breakfast. I smiled at him, but my smile soon felt pasted on. Finally he sighed and shook my hand for the briefest of moments. "Stu," he said.

"Hi Stu," I said. "Sorry to mess up your day like this. Do you come skiing here often?"

"Whenever there's a good snow I try to get away."

One of his skis lay in the snow a short distance away. I got up (I got up!) and walked over to it and picked it up off the ground and brought it to Stu.

"Thanks," he said, but I'm not sure he meant it.

I looked back at the place in the snow where I had just been. The impression reminded me of a twisted piece of metal, like the sort of thing I might see at a car wreck. The clumps of snow had coalesced into a meandering snowbank that defined my shape, but also warped it a little: it was me, but a metamorphosed version of me.

In the interior of the snowbank, a hilly snowscape, like a relief map of a mountainous land. It had the look of something deliberate, as though a giant took his index finger and pushed aside mountains to make a three-dimensional map.

"Are you okay?" said Stu.

I shook myself from my musings and realized I must seem like a strange man, staring at snow.

"I was thinking about us hitting each other."

"What about it?"

"You never know where revelation is going to come from. Sometimes it sneaks up and smacks you right in the face."

Stu stood and retrieved his other ski. He laid both skis on the ground and snapped his boots into them, then slid past me at slow motion speed and stopped.

"Your equipment looks like it survived," I said.

"Oh, I'm fine. My stuff is fine. If you're okay, I'll continue my day."

"Sure," I said. Continue his day? Going up the mountain on a lift, going down the mountain on skis. How many times was Stu going to do this today? How many times had he already done it?

"My advice?" said Stu. "Get off this slope. Turn around and walk down. You're a menace to everyone else on it."

I suddenly remembered. I was up here to check on Claypot. Huh. Somehow my rescue mission had slipped from my mind. "Good advice, Stu," I said.

He continued to slide past me and sped down the mountain to the bottom of the slope. I looked up the mountain to where Claypot had been sprawled out. The cluster of snowboarders had dispersed. Presumably, like Stu, they had all gone down the slope and were either at the bottom, or were already on their way back up.

Which meant I should be seeing Claypot.

Only he wasn't there.

I began to walk up the mountain again, completely ignoring Stu's advice. Why should I listen to him? He was just some passing stranger. He didn't know anything about me. Especially about how I had become a seeker after the life of Claypot Dreamstance. How I needed to satisfy myself that Claypot was not only getting by, but thriving. Claypot Dreamstance had become my quest. I needed to know what happened to him. And now, because of my encounter with Stu, I had no idea where he was.

I'll stop and examine my reaction to the situation for a moment. Please bear with me. I understand now, from a certain remove, that it was entirely my fault that Stu and I collided. I obviously had no business on the slope. However, at that first post-collision musing, I was convinced that Stu had ruined my lead on Claypot. If he had not smacked into me, I would have had the opportunity to see where Claypot had disappeared to. By all rights, I should have been angry with Claypot for being such a stubborn ass. Instead, I was angry at Stu for being a regular person, enjoying his day on the mountain. Now how crazy was that? How crazy had my quest for Claypot made me? It had completely warped, at least temporarily, my perception of the world.

I suppose that is what artists are supposed to do. Or at least one of the things they do.

Now here I was, poised on the mountain. Below me, Gayle. The one person in the world I could depend upon to support and love me. I should have gone back to her. But I didn't. Not right then. Above me, up the mountain somewhere, the one person in my life who I could depend on to betray me and let me down. To *disappoint*.

I was aware of my position. It felt like a tipping point, a knife edge of life expectations.

But here's the funny thing: I had no real dilemma or choice. None at all. I had to find Claypot.

I turned my back to the lodge, to the mural of Stacey in the trees, to Gayle, and kept trudging up the mountain. They could all look after themselves. They all had grips on reality. Even Stacey. Poor Stacey.

In what seemed like forever, but must have been something less than fifteen minutes, I got to the spot where Claypot had spread himself out on the snow.

Numerous footprints adorned the snow around his impression. They mingled into a formless mess of scattered snow, but left Claypot's impression untouched. It was as though the snowboarders had decided to keep a respectful distance from Claypot and did not want to intrude on his reverie.

I found myself respecting their respect, even in Claypot's absence. But what I found especially interesting was the shape of Claypot's sprawl. It was not arbitrary. It was not the record of a man who was in a sulk and had decided to plunk himself down with stubborn assertiveness. Instead, it looked to me to be as deliberate and artfully arranged as any of his trompe l'oeil work. In fact, looked at with a certain point of view, it *was* a trompe l'oeil. He had created a window into the snow.

I stared at the work for a few seconds. I made sure I was well off the slope, so no one would run into me. Clouds had moved over the mountain, over me. A chill had begun to hit me: The temperature dropped. The sun edged closer to the horizon, like a gear meshing with the sky and winding everything down.

I remembered one of the first things Claypot had said to me, that first day we met. He asked me if I knew anything about art, about why people did art. I didn't have an answer for him then, beyond the generic and banal reply that art was a way of interacting meaningfully with the world.

But if he asked me the same question now, I think I might have something resembling a coherent answer for him. It came to me while I looked at the form carved into the snow. The snow itself, spread out flat and expansive, reminded me of a canvas. Even though Claypot did not normally work on canvas, I saw no reason why he would not be able to. Since the snow would melt, it would be at least as ephemeral as chalk on concrete, his chosen medium. The snow was his blank slate, his tabula rasa. This shape before me, which was his outline, could only be seen as his proclamation of self. His own tired, worn out self.

And that's when the purpose of art, or at least the purpose of Claypot's art hit me: he was not trying to communicate with the world, except in a peripheral way. What Claypot was doing with his images was trying to plumb the depths of himself. The paradox was that he chose a medium and form that disappeared, so if you wanted to see Claypot in his art you had to be there as he did it or immediately after. He asserted the temporary nature of life, and most especially the temporary nature of his own life.

I looked up from the work before me.

Snow fell from the sky. Fat clumpy wet flakes, so numerous they made their own solidity. As I looked up the mountain, I could not see the peak, usually so prominent and clear against the sky.

I knew that weather patterns could change within seconds on the mountain. This snow could fall for hours, or it could clear up in a couple of minutes. No way to tell for sure. If it fell for very long, it would fill in Claypot's latest work. Indeed, it would fill in my similar attempt at art, further down the slope.

The snow clumped up on my jacket in a layer. I felt the weight of it: not an unpleasant burden. Quite cozy in its way. The snow embraced me. I appreciated the wildness of its unconcern for me, as nature never concerns itself with me. Unlike art, nature is arbitrary and its bounty will fall on all of us or none of us and no way to tell for sure until it happens.

So now Claypot was still wandering around in the woods somewhere. Could I even find him if I tried? I saw his tracks going to the trees, but they were filling up rapidly and I did not think I could track him for long.

More snow fell. I could barely see ten feet in front of me. I looked down the slope to the lodge, now completely obscured. I might as well have been alone on the mountain. I heard the sound of skis and snowboards slicing into snow, somehow magnified in the airborne snowbank that had materialized around me, but the frequency of the runs had diminished.

Then I heard another sound: quiet. I realized, almost

as an afterthought, that the lift had stopped. The steady hum of the wheels of the lift chairs rolling over the cable was gone.

They must have stopped the lift because of the poor visibility. I was sure they were going to start it up again as soon as the snow dissipated a bit, but for now I was as alone in the quiet as I could reasonably expect to be.

Quiet is made for contemplation. Since I had already started thinking about my life and my place in the world, I continued. Claypot was still out there, somewhere in the woods. What did he expect to find there? Stacey? Was he still hoping to get her back? Could anyone, no matter how eccentric, truly believe there was a way to bring back the dead?

And why did he place her portrait in a grouping of trees on the wall of the lodge?

I could not shake the idea that he had put her there because he thought of the forest as a graveyard. Her resting place.

So going into the forest now was visiting her in her grave.

I stepped closer to the trees. They were there, even though I could not see them.

I could keep going. There was nothing to stop me, even though I would be walking blind. That did not matter. I did not have to see the future to move toward it.

I thought of Claypot as a thick manifestation of will. Certainly more solid than anything he or I or anyone else might encounter in the woods, including the woods themselves, the trunks and branches of trees, which were puny splinters compared to Claypot. He was like the ground that supports the woods. He was the earth itself.

But he was no visionary. He was as blind as I was in this snowstorm, seeing only what was directly in front of him and only if it was inches away from him. He knew nothing of the pain or needs of others. He had no way to empathize because he was conscious only of his own pain, a pain, I might add, that was entirely self-centered. It did not acknowledge the possibility that Stacey's other parent experienced loss. It only allowed Claypot's limited perceptions to acknowledge his own failure.

So now here was the question: Did Claypot finally realize the truth, that Stacey was not coming back? Was that why he put himself down in the snow and would not get up?

The three of us, Judy, Gayle, and me, had been amateur psychologists to Claypot for weeks on end. We had gotten nowhere, most likely because we didn't know anything, or at least not enough to help him. In reality, he could probably only help himself. People got lost on this mountain. He was somewhere in the trees. I wanted to go after him, but I didn't want to be stupid about it.

I turned my back to the trees and looked down the slope of the mountain. I could not see the lodge, but I could tell the ground here sloped down. I needed only to follow the slope and I would get back to Gayle.

So I set out on my journey. I was aware that mountains were symbolic images for many people and had been considered so for many centuries. I could see the point. Even when snow covered this mountain, its essential mysterious quality came out. Humans looked to mountains for escape and lofty ideas of what it meant to be human. With mountains around, you always felt like you had something to reach for. Even if you never wanted to climb one, it's blank slate whiteness made you think that if you did, it would be like writing a page in history. Not only would you reach the pinnacle of the earth, thereby getting closer to the sky, but you would be doing it in full view of the world and by putting your footprints in the snow, making sure that others would see the extent of your audacity.

Or insanity.

So Claypot coming up here was no accident. He wanted his revelation, if that is what he found, to be known to the world. He wanted everyone to see what was happening to him. To him to him to him.

I stepped carefully. I did not want to fall. The fresh snow made the slope slick and if I was not careful I would fall on my ass. Which would not be such a terrible thing, but no fun either. I did feel some pain, an ache, where Stu had run into me. I expected I would have bruises on my chest, arms and maybe legs. I wasn't exactly sure, but that is where the aches were located. My record of my encounter with a stranger.

Even though the lift had stopped, people still came down the slope. I heard their skis on the snow, loud and uncomfortably close.

They must have been stragglers. People who waited at the top of the slope for the snow to clear, maybe, then they got tired of waiting and decided to come down anyway. Risking everything as they came. How did they know they would not run into a tree?

Or maybe they were daredevils who wanted to come

down blind. Such people existed, to be sure: crazy fucks, to use a term Claypot might endorse, who wanted to risk their lives for the adrenaline rush.

So I thought of them as stupid and ridiculous, these ghostly swooshes passing by me sporadically as I gingerly put one foot in front of the other, letting gravity draw me down slowly.

While the snow accumulated significantly, I started to wonder if I would actually get to the lodge before my progress was stymied. I had lost all contact with the ski slope. I knew it was there beside me, and I had been trying to hug the border of it, but I was not able to discern my place on the mountain at all. I could have veered off into the ungroomed portion, or I could be smack dab in the middle of the ski area, a sitting duck for any downhiller. On the theory that a moving target was more difficult to hit than a stationary one, I kept going.

Here's the thing: I had come up this mountain in a car, on a road. It was about as civilized and tamed as a mountain could be, and yet it had a wild aspect to it still. It could kill me. It could kill anyone.

So I sat down to consider the position I had put myself in. I sat for some minutes, how long exactly, I could not say. As I sat there, the snow began to thin out. I heard a voice. It was muffled, but familiar.

I looked around me. I looked behind me.

A looming shape, brown and green, I thought, settled in behind me, slipping into the white space of the snow like a blimp landing or a ship easing into port.

Now what could possibly be that big? It was the lodge. I looked back at it dumbly. I could make out the front door and the roof, barely. I had walked past my destination.

I felt a peculiar sense of triumph. I had gone further than I thought.

The snow was dissipating. Which was a pity. I had enjoyed thinking of the lodge as a ship returned from a journey with exotic cargo aboard, perhaps, or passengers with stories to tell.

It occurred to me that I was thinking in an odd way. I had slipped into a fantasy life without any coherent reason for it. Did the whiteout do something to my brain?

Like the blank walls that Claypot looked for and attempted to change with his art, I saw the whiteness of the snow as a blank slate completely receptive to my imagination.

My imagination? I wasn't supposed to *have* an imagination. I was a government worker, doing boring work that brought people electricity. I had a cubicle. I lived in the suburbs. My only claim to an imagination was by piggybacking onto someone with an imagination so strong that it was debilitating to him and to others around him.

"Hey, asshole, come in out of the fucking snow you dick wad."

I looked more closely at the ship in the snow. A familiar figure stood in front of the ship's prow. He held a shape in his hand and lifted it above his head. It looked like a lamp. Was Claypot lighting my way? I stepped forward and began to walk up the mountain toward the lodge.

Claypot stepped down the front steps. As I got closer I saw tattoo equipment in his hands, the equipment Judy had put in our car. He waved the hoses and the arm at me. "Come inside. You look like a goddam ghost."

I felt ghostly. Paper thin. The snow had accumulated on my head like a thick cap. I felt the weight of the world for some reason. No more the airy lightness of being on a mountain. Now it was more like the oppressive heaviness of being under too many blankets. It was warm, but it suffocated.

What happened next was completely unexpected, and yet, given the history of Claypot and me, I should have realized nothing is unexpected when it comes to Claypot Dreamstance. He ran across the distance between us. So quickly that I was struck by the improbability of it: how could someone so big move so rapidly? I stopped walking myself and waited for him to get closer. I felt like a lost soul, and Claypot was going to rescue me.

As it turned out, he did not exactly rescue me, but he did stop right in front of me. Inches from me.

"You look a sight, you cocksucking dipshit," he said.

"Nice to see you too," I said. "I thought you had disappeared into the woods."

"Thought about it," he said. "But I don't want to die."

"Could have fooled me," I said.

Then he stepped forward, grabbed me before I could step back, and wrapped me up in a hug I had thought he was completely incapable of delivering.

"Thanks for looking for me," he said.

I wanted to push him away at first. Then it felt like I was doing him a favor by not.

"You're welcome," I said.

# *Do Not Look at Photo Albums of the Deceased*

CLAYPOT AND I walked up the stairs and into the lobby. Stepping across the threshold was like stepping out of a foggy television set. No flakes descended through the air. Amazing.

Gayle came to me and embraced and kissed me. "I was worried about you," she said. "When Claypot came in I expected you right behind him. He said he saw you, but didn't know what happened to you."

"I was debating whether I should go look for him in the woods," I said.

Claypot laughed. "Ha," he said. "He still thinks I'm suicidal. I'm not."

He delivered that last sentence with an odd hesitation, as though he had not exactly convinced himself of the proposition.

"So you've all been waiting for me here?" I said.

"We were about to ask the authorities to launch a search party for you," said Judy, "when Clay stepped outside to look for you. Luckily you were right there."

"A search party?" I said. "A bit of an over reaction, don't you think?"

Gayle punched me on the shoulder. Lightly, but enough for me to feel the sting.

"People die on this mountain," she said.

I didn't say anything. No one said anything. It was like Gayle had punctured some silent agreement and now we didn't know how to punish her properly.

"I have a room," said Claypot.

Gayle looked at him. I looked at him.

"What?" he said. "I can't have a room?"

"You don't have any money."

"They let me have it while I work on the mural. Come on, I'll show you."

We walked toward the elevator. My hair was thoroughly soaked through and water dripped down my back. I leaned forward and ran my hands over my hair to try to shake off some of the excess water. I dripped rivulets of it onto the floor.

Claypot punched the UP button and turned to me, then looked at the puddle I had created. "Can't fucking take you anywhere," he said.

"Nope," I said. "I'm an embarrassment wherever I go."

Judy had her arm around Claypot, who still held the tattoo hoses in his arm. She looked comfortable with him, like they were old friends, which, I suppose in a way they were.

Claypot put his big hand on my hair and ruffled it

around. A peculiar thing to do, and I didn't like it. It was as though he was behaving like my father. Was that necessary? I felt myself turn red.

I put up my hand in a gesture meant to make him go away. He noticed my annoyance and pulled back immediately, which I appreciated. "Thanks," I said.

"Don't mention it, dipshit," he said.

"Clay," said Judy, "isn't it about time you stopped insulting everyone you know?"

He looked at her for a few seconds. I almost expected him to scream at her. But he didn't. "You may be right," he said. "I will consider it."

As we passed one of the lodge employees in the hall, he nodded to us and said if we wanted to get off the mountain we might think about doing it now. "They're predicting more than three feet of snow," he said. "Unless you have some industrial strength vehicle, you're going to be stuck here for the night."

Was that something I was willing to do?

"What do you say?" I asked Gayle. "Should we get out of here?"

Claypot turned to me, an obvious pleading in his eyes. "Don't go," he said. "You just got here. We all can bunk down in my room. It'll be fun."

All night cooped up with Claypot? Didn't sound like fun to me.

"I think it would be okay," said Gayle.

I sighed. "Okay," I said.

"Oh, that's fantastic," said Claypot. "You'll like it here. I've been all over the lodge. There's all kinds of art on the walls. You'll like the restaurant too. Not great food, but lots of it. Hearty stuff."

"That's great," I said, but my tone must have belied my words.

"Oh don't be such a stick in the mud," said Claypot.

"Okay," I said. I felt miserable and I wasn't even sure why. It wouldn't be so terrible to spend the night here. It *was* a beautiful building. I could do worse.

The elevator was taking a long time. "Why don't we walk?" I said.

"That's a great idea," said Claypot. He began to run down the hall. "This way."

We followed him. We passed a sculpture of a leaping salmon on the wall. Also numerous paintings of northwest scenes: mountains and a panoramic view of the gorge from high up on a cliff. We got to a door, big and wooden, and pulled it open. A stair case led up. We started climbing. Our shoes clattered against the stone steps.

We got to the third floor and pulled open another big wooden door and went down the hall. When we arrived at Claypot's room he fumbled in his pockets for his key, and opened the door. I was hoping for a big expansive room, but expecting the worst. I got the worst. The room was cripplingly tiny. One small bed took up most of the space. A tiny desk occupied one corner and a chair sat in another corner. The less said about the bathroom, the better. It was beyond small.

Gayle caught my eye. We both clearly decided, on the spot, that we had made a mistake. Now it was time to extricate ourselves from the situation.

"The birds come right to the window," said Claypot.

He went over to the window and lifted it up. Pieces of apple on a small plate rested next to the window. Claypot picked up a piece and held it at the open window. Before long a small bird, a species I did not recognize, came to the sill, snatched the apple piece from Claypot's fingers, and flew away into the snow.

"How can they know you're even there?" said Judy. "In this snow I mean."

"Nature is wise and mysterious," said Claypot.

"Let me try," said Gayle.

"Sure," said Claypot.

Gayle took a slice of apple from the plate and put her hand out into the snow. Flakes immediately attached themselves to her palm. She laughed. Two birds swooped toward her hand. One of them veered away at the last minute. The other one touched down on her extended finger, took the apple in its beak, and disappeared into the snow, like Alice going down the rabbit hole.

"That's so amazing," said Gayle.

Judy went to the window too. I watched the three of them gradually deplete the apple supply from the plate. I was as enchanted as they were, despite myself, but did not join in. I wanted to stay aloof from it. I'm not sure why.

"Chris," said Gayle, "you've got to try this. It's so amazing when they land on your hand."

"I'm good," I said.

"There's such trust," said Claypot. "It is truly amazing. How can they know we're safe?"

I wanted to tell him they didn't know. They got lucky with us. We weren't going to kill them, but someone else might. It could happen.

Such morbid thoughts. I wondered if Claypot was going to jump out the window. Mostly I wondered how the four of us could possibly all sleep in this room. Even if we arranged ourselves on the floor, it didn't look possible.

"Any other rooms available?" I asked no one in particular.

Claypot turned from the window and the birds. His eyes looked ablaze. "I told you you could all sleep here," he said.

"I know, but we're bigger than this room."

"Oh for Christ's sake," said Claypot, "it isn't like you're all giants. Fuck."

A silence fell over us, even more quiet than the world outside, where the snow was soaking up all the outside sound like a great white sponge. Claypot put his hand over his face and bent his head. He took in a deep breath and held it, then exhaled slowly. "Sorry," he said. "Sorry, sorry."

A bird swooped down to the windowsill from out of the cloud of snowflakes. No one had any apple piece for it and it strutted a couple of steps along the window sill, then retreated back to where it had come from.

"Aren't there any other rooms in the lodge available?" said Judy.

"No," said Claypot. "When a storm comes up like this, the rooms get taken pretty quick."

I nodded. "Thing is," I said, "We can't get stuck up here on the mountain. We have work tomorrow."

"Work," said Claypot. "Fuck work. You're already stuck on this goddam motherfucking mountain. Don't you get it?"

We all got it. Claypot was no different than he had been. I shouldn't have told myself he was capable of change. That wasn't possible in his case. Never would be. At that moment I did not want to spend another second with him, let alone the night in his closet of a room. I would rather have spent the night in the snow. Or, at the very least, on a bench in the lobby.

"You know," said Gayle, "there's plenty of floor here for all of us."

I wanted to scream.

Instead, I nodded. "I guess you're right," I said.

"We could all go to the restaurant downstairs," said Claypot. "Eat our dinners there, then come up here and tell stories to each other then sleep on the floor. Us men, I mean. There's extra blankets and stuff in the closet. The ladies would get the bed, of course."

Tell stories? Was he serious?

"I could sure use a meal," said Judy. "Then I want us to think about that tattoo, okay Clay?"

"Oh," said Claypot. "Yeah. The tattoo. I'm not sure that's such a hot idea."

"You said you'd think about it," said Judy.

"Okay okay okay," said Claypot. "I'll fu— Um. I'll think about it some more. I'll give it some real serious thought."

"That's all I ask," said Judy.

They looked at each other in the way couples do when they decide to ignore anyone else in the vicinity. Like they were telling each other no one else matters, ever. Certainly not right then in the time and place they have carved out of existence for themselves.

It surprised me, that Clay and Judy could still have something like that between them.

I looked away. First to the door, then I let my gaze scan blankly across the room to a binder that lay on the tiny desk.

I had noticed the binder when I first came in and had briefly wondered what it was, then forgot about it in the horror of trying to consider how to extricate myself from spending the night with Claypot.

Now I reached for it, thinking it was something provided by the lodge. Maybe there was a menu inside and I could distract myself by considering what I would get for dinner.

Claypot saw my motion and came across the room in two steps and dropped his hand on the binder.

"You don't want to look at that," he said.

"Okay," I said. "Just wanted to see what they had in the restaurant."

"You won't find that here," he said. "Look in the drawer." He indicated the bottom of the desk. I saw a handle on a drawer, pulled it open, and found a phone book and a sheaf of menus. Most of them pizza delivery places.

"Pizza?" I said.

"When the roads are open, they can drive up here with the pies."

"I see," I said. "What's that you have your hand on?"

"Nothing," said Claypot. "None of your business."

You will have noticed, if you've been with me all the way up to here, that I rarely contradicted Claypot Dreamstance. Even when I was so fed up with him and his troublemaking that I wanted to hit him or have him arrested, I rarely did anything that could be called open defiance. He called the shots. Which was why I didn't want to be around him anymore.

This time, I didn't let him control the situation. I grabbed the binder out from under his hand, quickly, before he had a chance to notice what I was doing, much less stop me. I took a few steps back, then held the binder tightly in both hands, stepped past Gayle and Judy, both surprised by what I had done, and ended up through the open door and in the hall.

I heard a roar come from Claypot. Judy's sharp rebuke: "Clay, stop it."

Some scuffling. I couldn't quite see into the room from where I stood in the hall, holding the binder. I felt vulnerable, like I had done something irreparable and I was going to pay.

A sense of satisfaction filled my heart. I felt my chest swell. I had put one over on Claypot Dreamstance. It felt good. I embraced the rebel gesture and the sense of being a defiant outlaw. No one ever pulled anything on Claypot and I had gotten his precious binder. I held it in front of me and flipped the cover open.

And then my heart got so small I was ashamed of my own existence.

The binder was a photo album. Mostly of Stacey, with some snapshots of Claypot and Judy, when they were young parents. I saw pictures of Stacey in the backyard, Stacey with her toys, her stuffed animals, her dolls. Stacey in a Halloween costume, a lion. Stacey carrying a cat, dragging it along the floor. Stacey sitting in the sun with a bonnet on her head, looking up and squinting at the camera.

I wondered how long Claypot had had this. I didn't remember it at his encampment.

I didn't have time to wonder for long. Claypot roared out of the room, all wild hair and crazy eyes. He ran toward me. I had time only to put up my hand in a futile gesture (I was trying to protect the photo album). Claypot ran into my hand and bowled me over onto the floor. The album went flying. I fell on my back. Claypot stood over me, staring down and breathing hard.

"What the fuck, asshole?" he said.

I wasn't sure if I had hit my head on the floor or not. I might have. I put my hand behind my skull and felt for blood or a bump. I didn't find any. Claypot reached down, like he was reaching into a hole in the earth, and wrapped his fist around my shirt front and pulled me up on my feet. "You proud of your fucking punk ass self?" he said.

I didn't answer. Didn't want to, and wouldn't have known what to say anyway.

By this time Judy and Gayle had come rushing out of the room and attached themselves to Claypot's arm. They looked comical trying to keep him from punching me out.

Either they succeeded, or Claypot never had any intention of doing so. I was prepared for his blows. I even felt I deserved them at that moment.

Instead he relaxed his arm, let me down on the floor where I scrambled to my feet to get a good purchase, and then he turned around, picked up the album, which was splayed on the floor behind him, scooped up a couple of pictures that had been shaken loose, stuffed them back into the album, in no order that I could discern, and kept walking.

"Chris," said Gayle, "do something."

"What am I supposed to do?"

"He can't go out into the snow," said Judy. "We'll lose him again. Plus, he has my album."

I looked at her. "Your album."

"I brought it with me," she said. "I was going to find one he liked to do the tattoo."

I shook my head. "It didn't occur to you that he would flip out?"

She stared at me. "It didn't occur to me that *you* would do something crazy like try to steal it from him."

"I wasn't stealing it."

Gayle held up her hands. "Stop it," she said. "Who cares about the album? We need to get Claypot."

"You go after him," I said. He was already at the end of the hall. He opened the door and went through it to the stairwell. Which went down to the lobby. What he did after that I didn't care.

"Come on Chris," said Gayle. "Is he your friend or not?"

"Not," I said without thinking. The truth. If I thought about it I might have said something else.

"Fine," said Judy. "I'll go." She went down the hall after Claypot. Gayle looked at me.

"You don't like him either," I said.

"No," she said. "But I care about him."

"Why?"

"He's hurting."

"Lot's of people hurt."

"He's trying to get better," said Gayle.

"I don't see that. He's still the same jerk he's always been."

"Okay," she said. "You're right. But that doesn't mean we shouldn't keep trying. He has a good heart."

She didn't say it was me who brought Claypot into our lives. Which I appreciated. What did that matter now? He *was* in our lives. How he got there was beside the point.

Or was it?

"I'm sorry I ever looked for him," I said. "Even sorrier that I ever found him."

"Stop being sorry and come help keep him inside. He'll die out there overnight."

I sighed, took Gayle's hand, and ran down the hall with her.

# *Never Make a Snow Angel*

DOWN IN THE lobby, Judy stood near the front door of the lodge with the album in her hand.

"Where's Claypot?" I said.

"He must be outside," said Judy. She held up the album. "I found this on the bench."

I looked at it, but did not reach for it. Why did he make such a fuss about the album, then just leave it here? I saw a shirt on the floor. I picked it up. Claypot's.

"Oh no," said Gayle.

We went outside. A pair of pants lay in the snow in front of the door. Claypot's pants. Down the stairs, a pair of shoes and socks, thrown down like they had been torn off, the snow already almost covering them.

"What is he doing?" I said.

"He's like this sometimes," said Judy. "He gets tired of clothes and shucks them aside."

"It's like those people in the desert," I said. "When they get close to dying of thirst and heat exhaustion they think they're getting cold and they start getting rid of their clothes."

"You think Claypot is dying?"

"I think he wants to die," I said.

"Jesus, we have to find him," said Judy.

The snow fell so rapidly and in such volume that any tracks were already covered over.

"He can't be far," I said.

"You don't know Claypot," said Judy. "When he wants to disappear he knows exactly how to do it. He's very good at it."

I didn't doubt that.

"I'll go around back to the mural," said Gayle. "You guys fan out. Quickly. Don't let him gain ground on us."

I walked straight away from the lodge, treating his shoes and socks as pointers away from the front door.

But I was in the middle of the falling snow in no time and I was completely disoriented. My second time lost in the snow in less than an hour. I think it was coming down a lot thicker than before. I couldn't see the dark shape of the lodge anymore. One good thing: Hardly any wind blew and it wasn't that cold. If I was not wearing any clothes, though, it would have been plenty cold enough.

I kept walking. My shoe snagged something on the ground and pushed it along, getting entangled around my ankle. I looked down. A pair of underwear. I thought: oh shit, Claypot's naked. Then: Huh, Claypot wears underwear. Who knew?

It also meant I was going in the right direction so I kept going. If I knew the terrain around the lodge, I would be more confident. I wanted to proceed slowly, but I knew Claypot was probably not doing the same. He was hell bent on something—I didn't know what—and so I picked up my pace to try to catch him.

The world was as white as concrete dust. I swam in its strange enveloping comfort. It *was* a comfort, even though my mission was desperate. How long could a person last exposed to this environment before succumbing? I didn't know, but it couldn't be very long.

I cupped my hands to my mouth and called out. "Claypot, you fucking asshole, come back here. Don't die on me you prick."

I had the feeling my words did not go very far. It was as though the falling snow snatched them from the air and pushed them down into the ground. A strange sensation. I called again, trying to be as loud as I possibly could. Then I put my hands behind my ears and turned my head slowly. I listened for a response. None came. It was eerie, like I was the only person in the world and the world had become a vast white canvas.

I thought of chalk, white chalk. Something pure and clean about white: all the colors mixed into one color, that looked like it was no color. Maybe that's why Claypot liked using it. It had this cipher quality to it, like a blank slate, it had the same blankness: it invited any meaning you wanted to give it.

Only I wasn't in the mood for giving it meaning. I only wanted to find Claypot.

A peculiar melancholy came over me at that point. It was as though I had found a way to make myself sadder than the situation warranted. I stared into the snow, willing it to yield up the vision of Claypot, sky clad, walking out of it like a trompe l'oeil version of himself.

Gayle walked out of the snow and stood beside me. "I heard you calling him," she said.

I nodded. "I found more of his clothes. Underwear."

Gayle wrinkled her nose. "I'm sorry," she said.

"It isn't funny," I said.

"I know, but I can't help laughing about it.

"What are we going to do? I can't see a thing."

"He's a tough old bird," said Gayle. "He'll be fine even if we don't find him."

I couldn't share her optimism.

"What is he trying to do?"

Gayle shrugged. Snow accumulated on her shoulders and the top of her head. I wanted to brush it all away to show her bright face better. She looked awfully pretty here in the snow, grinning like a fool. We were all fools for being here, trying to extract something from the snow.

"Who knows?" said Gayle. "I don't."

"Guess," I said.

She shrugged. "Maybe he thinks by going back to his elemental state he can better understand where Stacey is now. Maybe, like you said, he wants to die. Or maybe he feels like all the world is conspiring against him so he wants to experience what it would be like to leave the world? I don't know. I'm not an expert on the crazy fucks." She grinned again. Wider this time.

"I don't see how this is helping anyone. Especially him."

"Oh, Chris, don't you know? He doesn't want to help himself. He wants to suffer."

She had a point, I suppose. No one could look at what he had done the past few months and not see that he had a self-destructive bent to him.

I don't want to give the impression that we stood around talking as though we had martini glasses in our hands quietly discussing the state of the world in convivial terms to pass the time. It wasn't like that. I've stretched out the time to better understand the events for myself, to try to convey to you what was going on as we looked for Claypot.

Gayle and I decided to stick together. We kept walking in the direction Claypot's underwear indicated.

We walked without saying anything for a couple of minutes.

Then we heard a muffled sound. Something like a bellow. We looked at each other.

"Was that him?" I said.

"Has to be," said Gayle. "Who else?"

"Didn't sound like him."

"That might be a good sign."

I called his name: "Claypot Dreamstance!" I called as loud as I could, trying to cut through the dampening effects of the snow.

More bellows. Like the sound an animal might make. A large animal.

Gayle and I tried to run in the direction of the sound, but it was hard going. The snow on the ground was inches deep now, almost impossible to traverse with any speed. So we slogged through it, pushing snow aside like our boots were snowplows.

I called his name repeatedly. Gayle joined in. The bellows grew louder and the sound of labored breathing groaned behind it. We must have been very close.

But how close was close? I had no way to tell. I called Claypot's name as loud as I could.

I heard an echo. No, not an echo, but another voice, also calling Claypot. It was Judy. She must have gone behind the lodge and come around the other side.

Gayle joined in. Now all three of us called Claypot's name. I don't know if it was helping us find him, but I liked that we were in contact with each other, at least verbally and aurally.

I didn't think Claypot was in serious danger. Nothing like close to death or anything like that. Looking back on it now, it was a failure of imagination, I suppose. I think of the time Claypot asked me about art, about what it meant to do art and why someone would even have the idea to make art in the first place. I didn't have any idea, exactly as Claypot had said. I didn't have the imagination to figure out *why*.

This latest escapade with Claypot, for example. Why did he shed his clothes and go out into a snow storm? I couldn't understand it. It was so completely beyond my imagination that it was as though it could have happened to someone from another planet.

I think I had the idea that he would come to his senses, eventually, and go back to the lodge, warm himself up, get dried off, have some coffee, maybe a cigarette, and curse at us for taking so long to rescue him and then everything would be normal.

That's probably what I hoped. It *is* what I hoped. But it was not a reasonable expectation.

Gayle was suddenly next to me. How did she find me? Probably followed my voice. The three of us were getting hoarse from all our yelling.

"We need help," she said.

"Yes," I said.

"One of us needs to go back to the lodge and find someone who can find him in this."

Back to the lodge. She was right, she was right. But where was the lodge? I looked behind me. Blinding white snow swirled all around. I was suddenly acutely aware of how disoriented I was. It occurred to me that we might need someone to find *us* soon.

"How are we going to find the lodge?" I said.

My feet were cold. My hands were like lumps of ice.

"I think it's this way," she said. She indicated a direction that might as well have been up to the sky.

"Okay," I said. "I'll keep looking for him here."

She walked into the snow.

She looked like one of Claypot's trompe l'oeil paintings, with the snow like one of his backgrounds. Then she disappeared, swallowed up in the cold. I felt my belly sink. True fear grabbed hold of me for the first time. Up to then I had felt like this was more or less a lark, a crazy game Claypot and the rest of us were playing. Suddenly it felt like more than that.

Judy's voice again: "Claypot, you fucking asshole. Get back here. Where are you?"

No answer. No bellows. Nothing. I was already cold, but nevertheless felt a chill go through me right then, like I had been momentarily dipped in ice water.

I was also angry. At Claypot, at his stupid antics, at

myself and everyone else who ever had anything to do with him and wanted to help him. As though he needed help of any kind. Even if he needed it, he certainly didn't want it. Not from me, or Judy, or Gayle. Not from anyone, except Stacey.

I recalled two of the pictures from the album I had looked at not half an hour ago. One of them showed Stacey in the snow making a snow angel. Maybe it was right up here on this mountain. Maybe in Claypot and Judy's backyard. It was impossible to tell, but there was definitely snow. Stacey's arms and legs were splayed out in a star, wild abandon evident on her face. She looked completely happy in the world, pushing snow aside to make her imprint on the ground underneath.

Then another picture. Right next to it. Stacey gone, and the snow angel remaining. It was a trompe l'oeil of impeccable execution. It looked like a painting of the ground had been done on the surface of the snow. An outline of an angel, falling into the snow. I thought of the picture as I tromped around in the snow looking for Claypot. Was he out here trying to make a snow angel? Was he looking for a way to bring Stacey back by doing what she did?

We are born naked and leave the world naked. I remember him saying that once. So was this his way of leaving the world? Is that why he came to the mountain?

In any case, we aren't born naked, not in the spiritual sense. We arrive in the world with a whole host of lives and attitudes attached to us. We're only naked if we refuse them, or make them disappear.

I wanted to find Claypot and tell him all these things.

He wasn't alone in the world just because his daughter was gone. Forget the fact that he couldn't bring his daughter back, that was almost irrelevant. What mattered was that even without his daughter, he still had something of life in him.

I had the idea, though, that he wasn't interested in that aspect of his life. He had other things in mind, things I could barely fathom, much less understand.

I'll tell you the truth, though: Even though I was in this desperate search to find him, I would have been very happy to see him die. Does that sound harsh? I suppose it does, but I'm telling the truth. Isn't that part of art too? Isn't art supposed to be honest?

What was honest about being out here in a place that scared me, under conditions that threatened me, looking for someone I couldn't stand and didn't care about?

I surprised myself with my capacity for thought at such a time. Even if I didn't care about Claypot Dreamstance, wasn't it important for me to do this humanitarian thing and try to save him?

I ran into a tree. It popped out of the white air, a column of rough bark like a wall of rock. At least I didn't bump my nose on it. I hit it with my knee.

So. I was lost in the trees.

Did that mean Claypot was just as lost? Maybe.

Panic began to grip me. I imagined myself then careening from tree to tree, like a pinball, blind, with no place to end up.

But that's not what happened.

The snow storm began to weaken. Or, at least, the amount of snow falling began to thin out. I saw the trees around me, emerging back into the world like ghosts materializing out of thin air.

I stood in a copse of trees, but I saw I had not gone too far into them. All I had to do was step here, go around that tree there, and I would be out in the clearing. I thought I even saw the lodge in the distance, still like a ship at sea, floating, it's bulk like an immense hull in the void.

Figures ran from it. Rescuers? Perhaps. I thought I recognized Gayle's shape and gait but I could not be sure from this distance.

I retraced my meandering steps and came out of the woods.

"Hey asshole." Claypot's voice. Thin and weak. I looked down. He was as red as anything I had ever seen. Which I instantly took to be a good sign. At least he wasn't blue. Or white. Red meant his heart and blood were still going strong. He was spread-eagled on the snow, completely naked. His arms had swept out wings to either side of him. His legs had swept out an angel's skirt.

"I'm the asshole?" I said.

"Don't step on me, man." He sounded defeated. I put my hand down and waited for him to grab it so I could pull him up.

He didn't take it.

"Come on," I said. "You've made your point, whatever it is. Let's get you inside before you freeze to death."

"I don't want to go inside," he said. "I want to die."

"Nope," I said. "You're not that much of a jerk."

"I *am* a jerk," he said.

"Yes you are, but not that much of one."

My hand was still out, spread and waiting for him.

He blinked at me several times. I could see he wanted to close his eyes. I kicked the sole of his foot. Not too hard, but hard enough.

He blinked several more times.

A few minutes ago I wanted him dead. Now all I wanted was for him to come to his senses. Whatever senses he had.

"She's gone," he whispered.

"I know," I said.

I heard voices in the air. Shouts from the figures who had run out of the lodge. I saw them in my peripheral vision, running toward us. My eyes locked on Claypot's. He never took my hand. In a few moments the people from the lodge were upon us with blankets and a stretcher.

They wrapped up Claypot like he was a precious piece of sculpture and rolled him onto the stretcher and took him away.

I watched them carry the artist into the lodge and I walked back, trudging through the deep snow.

I met Gayle on the way.

"He should be fine," she said.

"I hope so," I said as I put my arm around her.

# *Never Reach Out to Anyone Else*

JUDY NEVER DID ink that tattoo on Claypot. She's prepared to this day to do it. She's told Claypot any number of times that it would be a fine idea, a picture of his daughter on his chest. I'm not so sure, but it's none of my business.

It's been ten years since that time on the mountain. I retired from the electricity business. Being a government worker, I got a good pension, so I spend my time loafing around the house, gardening in the summer, carving wood in the winter.

Gayle and I take a couple of long trips each year, seeing different parts of the country. But we always come back to Portland. The rain is in our blood.

As for Claypot Dreamstance, the story of his life isn't over yet. After that snow angel on the mountain, what he still calls his best work because it perfectly mated subject to medium, Claypot Dreamstance was no more. The foul-mouthed, coarse living, anti-social asshole disappeared. In his place, a generous and sweet man. He'll insult you if he thinks it necessary, but he will keep it clean.

He reconciled with Judy. They live in a new house on the other side of town. It's somewhat more modest than their old place, but it suits them.

Judy still works for a gallery and Claypot teaches art at one of the community colleges. Gayle and I go to their house a few times a year. We have dinner and play cards.

We were just there last week.

"I'm back on the street," said Claypot as he dealt out cards for a hand of back alley bridge.

"Really?" I said.

"Don't let him kid you," said Judy. "He's doing caricature portraits of people at the Saturday market."

"Caricatures?" said Gayle. "I never thought you'd do that kind of thing."

"Why not?" said Clay. "It's a lot of fun and people like it."

On the wall behind him hung a portrait of Stacey. It looked newly drawn. Not a trompe l'oeil, it was a simple pen and ink of her smiling. I thought I recognized the setting.

"Is she on the mountain?" I asked, indicating the picture with a nod of my chin.

Clay nodded without looking at the picture. "She liked that mountain. Said when she was on it she felt like she could touch the angels."

"They were her kin," said Gayle.

Clay nodded.

"I think you're right," he said.

## *About the Author*

Mario Milosevic has published poems, short stories, and novels in numerous venues, both print and online. He lives with his wife, fellow writer Kim Antieau, in the Pacific Northwest, where he works at a public library. Learn more about the author and his work at mariowrites.com.